The Fell Walker

For some – a walk in paradise
For others – ....

MICHAEL WOOD

Pen Press

Printed and bound in the UK
Pen Press is an imprint of
Indepenpress Publishing Limited
25 Eastern Place
Brighton
BN2 1GJ

ISBN13: 978-1-905621-02-6

Printed and bound in the UK

A catalogue record of this book is available from
the British Library

MYS
Pbk

Cover design by Jacqueline Abromeit

Love's not Time's fool, though rosy lips and cheeks
Within his bending sickle's compass come;
Love alters not with his brief hours and weeks,
But bears it out ev'n to the edge of doom

W. Shakespeare

Prologue

His first cry took place in a small, dilapidated cottage on the shore of the Kyle of Tongue, on Scotland's north coast. His 40-year-old, inadequate mother died soon after giving birth. His 53-year-old, alcoholic father was not pleased to see him.

When he was five-years-old his father died, leaving him in the care of Uncle Maurice, a mean, church-going bachelor in his late 40s. Maurice lived on a croft on Strathy Point headland, a few miles east of the Kyle. He supplemented his small croft income by working as a night security guard at the nearby Dounreay Nuclear Research Station.

Uncle Maurice did not like the look of his scrawny nephew, and would see that the boy got plenty of discipline so he wouldn't turn out bad like his father.

He was enrolled in the village school at Strathy, three miles from the croft. His withdrawn attitude and skeletal looks soon made him unpopular with the boys. The girls were less cruel, but kept their distance.

Each night, after supper, he was locked in his room while his uncle went to his night shift at Dounreay. He often cried himself to sleep, and woke up with a wet bed. His uncle always beat him for that, and for sneaking out of the window to sleep with the collie in his kennel.

His only friends were the collie and the rabbits and the gulls. He gave them names and fantasised about living with them in the secret cave he had discovered on one of his many lonely wanderings around the desolate headland.

Shortly after his tenth birthday, he found an injured fox at the foot of the cliffs. He carried it to the cave and, over the next few days, attempted to nurse it better.

When it died, he cried a lot, and didn't want to part with it. So he took a knife, and chopped it into pieces, and put it in plastic bags. He dropped the bags into a rock pool inside the cave. Now he had a permanent friend.

Chapter 1

The new state-of-the-art headquarters of Keswick Mountain Rescue Team stands close to the shores of Derwentwater lake. Like most buildings in the Lake District National Park it is made from weathered stone and slate, making it difficult to tell whether it is one or 100-years-old. Upstairs, above the drying and equipment rooms, lies a large meeting room and separate control room. Inside the control room one man sits surrounded by an array of phones, screens and monitors. Today, he has no need to use the three pre-programmed phones that simultaneously activate the pagers of the 38-team members. They are out there already, continuing yesterday's systematic grid reference search of the Skiddaw massif, using their satellite-controlled global positioning systems. The room is full of voices when Ben Foxley walks in.

'Keswick Mobile to Keswick Echo - over.'

'Keswick Echo - go ahead Keswick Mobile.'

'Have the Cockermouth team turned up yet, and have they brought any dogs? If so, please ensure a thorough search of the gullies below Lonscale Fell as discussed - over.'

'Hello Keswick Mobile Leader. We have 12, repeat 12, arrived from Cockermouth team. We are allocating areas to them. They have brought two dogs. Confirm they will be sent to Lonscale Fell gullies - over.'

'Patterdale Leader to Keswick Leader - over.'

'Keswick Leader - go ahead Patterdale.'

'Reporting Longside now complete. Moving on to Barkbethdale - over.'

'Understood Patterdale. Keswick Leader out.'

'Keswick Control. This is Search 131.' The background sound of whirling helicopter blades is unmistakable.

The man in the control room acknowledges: 'Go ahead Search 131.'

'Reporting three, repeat three, more 131's are approaching. Confirm we will all be using channel 73 direct to Keswick Control - over.'

'Understood Search 131. Please let me know their call signs - over.'

Ben had always admired the Controller's calm, methodical, manner.   He listened to the exchanges for a few more minutes, then walked, quietly, to the kitchen. He returned carrying two cups of coffee, and placed one on the desk beside the Controller. There was a lull in the radio chatter.

'Busy morning, Ian,' Ben observed.

'Aye...a bit,' the Controller said, picking up his coffee, while continuing to make notes on the papers in front of him.

Ben knew better than to interrupt or to ask too many questions.

Officially, journalists were not allowed inside the building during an incident, but in the past year they had come to trust Ben, now known as the new local man; a term Ben enjoyed as he approached his 50th birthday. In that time, he had grown to respect their tremendous effort, dedication and professionalism, and he tried to reflect this with succinct, factual reporting in the Tribune.

So far so good, but he knew he was still there on sufferance. He was not supposed to question team members, and they had strict instructions not to talk to the press; only the Team Leader did that.

These unfortunate battle lines had been drawn up due to bad experiences with the national tabloids, particularly when youngsters on school adventure trips went missing, or worse. They hated giving interviews to podgy city journalists who usually sensationalised the incidents, then went on to demand the head of some poor teacher or adventure leader, who had been trying to bring excitement and adventure to equally podgy youngsters.

Apart from the laid down rules, Ben knew, anyway, that he wouldn't get much out of the taciturn Controller who, conscientiously, got on with his job of link man, record keeper and general administrator. Long after an incident was over, he could still be found filling in paperwork, making entries on the computer spread sheets, filing, and finally, taking Leader reports and photographs of the incident to the police station.

'Bit unusual having three search teams and four helicopters,' Ben said conversationally.

'Bloody government minister and his wife,' Ian snapped, handing Ben the Incident sheet. 'There's a full RAF ground team coming as well. Wouldn't happen for you and me.'

Ben glanced at the sheet. 'I wonder what a government minister is doing staying at a caravan site?'

'Who cares,' Ian growled.

Ben had never seen him so animated, but before he could continue the conversation, the voices started again:

'Keswick Dog Mick to Keswick Leader - over.'

'Keswick Leader - go ahead Mick.'

'Stand by. I think we have contact. I have a barking dog. I am approaching the Little Man gully from the south. Stand by. Out.'

Ben envisaged the scene. The dog must have found somebody and returned to its handler, Mick. Here it would bark to announce its find, then return to the find, bark at it, then return to Mick. It would continue doing this until Mick and the find were brought together.

There was a long silence. All radio voices stopped. Instinctively, Ben walked to the window and craned his head to the right. From here, he could just see Skiddaw and the Little Man search area. He imagined the rest, while absent-mindedly sipping his coffee. He barely reg-istered that it had gone cold.

A sudden intrusion into the silence: 'Keswick Dog Mick to Keswick Leader - over.'

'Keswick Leader - go ahead Mick.'

'I have contact. I have contact. I am with two casualties in Little Man gully. Both are Condition Zero. I repeat - both are Condition Zero.'

Chapter 2

The town of Keswick is used to invasion. Ever since the Victorians built the railway, millions have flocked to see it, nestling, idyllically, in a lake blessed vale of unutterable beauty. Its core population of five thousand might agree with Ruskin's claim that it is 'a town almost too beautiful to live in' as they are regularly overwhelmed by walkers, climbers, campers, boaters, fishermen, yachters, caravanners, and ubiquitous tourists sauntering down the narrow streets, carrying their ice creams, like slow motion relay teams. But it has never seen an invasion like this.

Two days after the discovery of the bodies of Secretary of State for Trade and Industry, Jack Fraser, and his wife Elaine, at the foot of Little Man, the world's media have taken over the town. Throughout the market square, down the narrow streets, outside the police station, television, radio, and newspaper journalists are speaking to camera, interviewing locals; pressing for information at the police station. The town's hotels are full.

Before the invasion, Ben Foxley had interviewed the local police. The small police station had become one of his weekly calls, picking up the crime news. Most of the crime involved thefts from tourists' cars, parked in remote places, while the occupants were out walking the fells, the occasional burglary, and a bit of teenage bad behaviour in the town's beautiful parks.

Ben had established a friendly relationship with the small staff at the station, and, eventually, had been invited by station sergeant Bill Unwin to join him in a game of golf. This had become one of Ben's weekly highlights, combining, as it did, a course in a spectacular setting, with occasional insights into a world with which he was not familiar.

From the brief police statements he had been given he wrote a factual few hundred words, which would appear in the weekly Keswick Tribune in three days time. Then he sat back to watch as the big boys moved in to do their thing.

Within hours, the tabloids were running incredible stories of possible ministerial adultery, murder then suicide by the minister, rifts in the marriage, suicide pacts. One tabloid discovered that Jack Fraser's research assistant was glamorous, and carried large photographs of her, with reputedly her quotes: 'Jack Never Made A Pass At Me.'

The serious papers came up with interminable articles about Jack Fraser's life; how he had risen from shipyard worker to minister. *'From Back Yard to Front Bench,'* and *'From Metal Bashing to Tory Bashing'* were typical headlines.

These papers were also theorising about possible causes of death, since the police were treating them as suspicious, even though they looked like an accidental fall. One suggested murder by a disgruntled Sellafield worker anticipating that the minister was about to preside over the closure of the local nuclear plant. Inevitably, terrorist organisations were also touted as possible suspects.

Ben admired the speed with which all this information was compiled for public consumption, but was surprised that no reporter mentioned the minister's wife. It was as if she did not exist. Clearly, they had decided she was not as newsworthy as her VIP husband.

A hard faced professional lot, Ben concluded, while beginning to feel like a very small fish in an appropriated pond. He was glad that his late entry into the word industry probably still qualified him as a softhearted amateur. He knew that his piece for the Tribune paled in comparison to most of the big boy's offerings, but he consoled himself with the fact that he did not have a host of staff and researchers to back him up.

Normally, his natural reticence would have made him stay at home until the media shoals had gone. But he sensed that this was too big to be missed; that something unexpected lay behind these tragic deaths. He knew Little Man intimately. It was not inherently dangerous. It was not a likely place for walkers to fall.

That is why, on the third day of the invasion, as the sun lapsed below the western fells, casting shadows across the recumbent lakes, he was driving to Keswick's largest hotel, where many of the journalists were staying.

The imposing Keswick Hotel had been built by the Victorians right at the station exit, so that the rich gentry didn't have far to walk after their 'arduous' train journey from London, Birmingham or Manchester. Here, Ben planned to spend the evening, rubbing shoulders with his professional peers, hoping they might have some important information to share.

Chapter 3

In the lounge bar of the Keswick Hotel, Ben carried his pint of Cumberland ale to a corner table beside an ornate marble fireplace. Its ostentation was matched by extravagant ceiling mouldings and chandeliers, but not by the green seating which was showing signs of wear.

He was soon able to pick out the journalists from the tourists. The old stereotype had been replaced by young men and women who had taken the trouble to shower, and dress casually smart, before putting themselves on parade.

There was something disturbingly clone-like about them. Many were glued to their mobile phones. Most of their drinks were non-alcoholic. Nobody smoked. The days of cigars, sweat, and whisky were over, apparently. He caught hints of soap, deodorant, and scent. It was all very depressing.

'Poor bastards,' Ben muttered to himself. How miserable their world had become. Efficiency was today's god. 'Thou shall not be old, individual, or unavailable,' was today's first commandment. There was no place left for the idiosyncratic, the eccentric, the comedic.

On each of his visual sweeps of the earnest gathering, he had been brought to a halt by the striking looks of a woman, sitting on her own, nursing what appeared to be a gin and tonic. It was hard to tell whether she was 25 or 45. Her straight black hair framed a pale face in which large sparkling blue eyes supported too much eye shadow, and generous lips, too much dark lipstick. She looked familiar, though he may have been confusing her with a young Elizabeth Taylor.

He was finding it difficult to muscle in on a conversation, though he did overhear that the police were only treating the deaths as suspicious because Jack Fraser was a government minister and all ministers were regarded as possible targets for terrorists. Had they been ordinary members of the public, then it would have been treated as just another unfortunate mountain accident.

But this merely confirmed the information he had already been given by Sergeant Bill Unwin, who had also told him that detectives would be visiting Sellafield nuclear plant to investigate the disgruntled worker theory, and searchers had still not found Mrs Fraser's missing ear.

*

He was draining his second pint, feeling disappointed, and thinking of calling it a night, when Elizabeth Taylor appeared in front of him.

'Can I buy you another,' she offered, in a voice as deep as her eye shadow.

Ben sat up straight, blinked himself alert again. '... Yes...thanks...a pint of Cumberland ale...'

She turned to go to the bar.

'Now there's a turn up,' Ben thought, as he watched a barman rush to serve her. 'I came to pick their brains -

now they come to pick mine. We're like vultures, gathering at the scene of death, picking, probing, devouring. Maybe that's what being a journalist is....'

Elizabeth Taylor sat down opposite him, placing his beer and her gin carefully on the table. She picked up her glass. 'Cheers Ben,' she smiled, studying him intently as she raised the glass to her lips.

'How do you know my....'

'The barman told me.'

Ben glanced over to the barman. 'I don't know him.'

'Journalists tend to be better known than barmen, even in small towns,' she explained. 'My name's Sophie Lund.' She paused, as though expecting a reaction.

It was not surprising. Now he knew why her face was familiar. Years ago she had been the 'enfant terrible' of journalism. At the age of 25, she had established a regular 'must read' column in one of the broadsheets. At the age of 30, she was a tabloid editor, and a celebrity. She appeared on television - on late night political discussions, panel games, and even trendy fashion and pop programmes where she was seen as an icon of anti-establishment youth - her open promotion of drug use no doubt facilitating her reputation. Then she had disappeared, apparently giving it all up to help her French lover grow grapes in the south of France.

Ben held out his hand. 'It's nice to meet you, Sophie,' he said.

'You must be wondering...' she started. 'I could see you were not one of those.' She turned her head indicating the journalists over her shoulder. 'Wrong clothes, wrong drink, aged but innocent,' she observed.

Ben swallowed. 'I take it those are compliments,' he countered.

Sophie smiled enigmatically. 'Do you mind if I ask you some personal questions, Ben?' she asked.

'Go ahead,' Ben said easily, the alcohol providing bravado.

'Okay, here goes,' Sophie announced, as though she was about to jump from a high building. 'When did you last have a bath, are you married, would you like to sleep with me?'

Ben took a long drink of his ale. He was always surprised at how calmly he reacted to unusual situations, when he could be driven to distraction by the minutiae of everyday life. Perhaps it was in his genes. Perhaps he had been pre-programmed to eschew the prosaic, cherish the poetic.

He knew that he was being tested. She was looking into his eyes, waiting. How he answered was obviously very important to her. This was not just a casual pick up.

As a young man, he had promised himself never to forego any experience, providing it didn't endanger his life. He hadn't gone looking for excitement or kicks, but when a new experience was offered, he never turned it down. He decided to match her directness.

'Answers,' he announced confidently. 'Last bath - two weeks ago, but shower every morning, I'm extremely married, I would like to sleep with you.'

'Good,' she said simply, never taking her eyes off him. Her closed hand came out of her pocket and reached across the table to him. She lowered her voice. 'Here's my room key. Please take a bath and help yourself to the mini bar. I'll be up in 30 minutes.'

Ben took the proffered key without question, and rose from the table. This only happened in Hollywood movies, this was exceptional. If she was Elizabeth Taylor, then he must be Cary Grant. This was quite...incredible. Incredible enough to make him leave his Cumberland ale unfinished.

*

In the bath his mind raced. Why had this well-known woman picked him out? Surely not just for sex? What about Helen? He didn't feel as though he was cheating on her. His soul would always belong to her. It was the situation that intrigued him more than the prospect of sex, he told himself. And, he had to be true to his youthful promise. But he knew that Helen would never understand this. She must never be told.

His mind was still preoccupied when he walked, naked, into the bedroom.

'Not bad at all.'

The voice made him jump, automatically cover himself with his hands.

Sophie Lund sat, smiling, in a chair beside the dressing table, now displaying a bottle of gin and two glasses.

'You said 30 minutes,' Ben objected.

'I like to surprise people.'

'You succeeded....'

'Now Ben, be a good man, get dressed, and come and have a drink with me.'

'But...what about?'

'You didn't expect me to sleep with you *now* did you Ben? We hardly know each other.' She spoke with mock coyness. 'Maybe later, when we're good friends eh?'

'You're taking a bit of a risk aren't you,' Ben snapped, feeling angry and ridiculous in equal measure. 'I'm damned annoyed. What if I was...'

'But you are not going to be aggressive are you. Men without trousers are never aggressive, I've found. As for taking risks? Tell me something that isn't risky. Living, I call it.'

'So those questions downstairs?' Ben queried, angrily.

'Just my fun way of sorting the men from the boys, Ben. Believe it or not, most married men run a mile when propositioned like that. They're the timid, unimaginative ones. I like brave, inquisitive, people around me. They call it 'having bottle' these days.'

Ben turned and headed for the bathroom. He was beginning to feel mentally as well as physically naked in front of this supremely confident woman.

*

In the bathroom, while putting his clothes on, he gradually began to see the funny side of things. 'Caught with my pants down,' he smiled to the mirror, as he fastened his tie. The whole embarrassing situation now appealed to his ironic sense of humour. And, somewhat reluctantly, he had to admire the nerve of the woman

He re-entered the bedroom in a calmer mood.

'Feeling aggressive now?' Sophie taunted, sipping her drink.

'No,' Ben smiled. 'In fact I'll probably laugh about this for weeks.'

'Good. I knew you would see the joke. I've poured you a drink.'

She offered a glass to him, and indicated the chair on the other side of the dressing table.

Ben said 'no thanks' to the drink, as he sat down. 'So what's this charade all about?' he asked, evenly.

'I wanted to talk to you...'

'You could have done that downstairs.'

'Privately.'

'What about?'

'Jack Fraser.'

'Why me?'

'Because I need your help. You do work for the local paper?'

'Yes.'

'So you know the local scene, where to go, who to ask, I haven't got time...'

'Whoa!' Ben interrupted. 'Let me stop you there. I've just dropped out of one rat race and I've no desire to enter another.'

'Dropped out?' Sophie queried.

'Yes, dropped out,' Ben confirmed. 'Industrial management; I hated it. I dropped out three years ago when the kids flew the nest. This thing with the Keswick Tribune is just part-time freelancing. Rest of the time I'm painting landscapes to sell to the tourists. I don't make much money, but I love it. In fact, I'm a kept man. My wife, Helen, is the main breadwinner. She manages a leisure centre at Windermere.'

Sophie looked pensive for a moment. Then her eyes searched his face again. Then, apparently, she reached a decision.

'Look, it doesn't really matter how experienced you are as long as I can trust you. And I'm not asking you to join another rat race, just sniff around a bit and let me know what you find. It sounds as though you have plenty of time to do that, and I'll pay you for your time.'

'There's no need for that,' Ben replied. 'I'll be sniffing around anyway.' The prospect of associating with the famous Ms Lund was starting to intrigue him.

'I insist on payment,' Sophie said, adamantly. 'It's the only way to succeed. If I pay you, I can put pressure on you. Pressure gets results. And I need a result on this.'

Ben's interest grew. If she was prepared to pay him for something he intended to do anyway, why not go along with her. 'Tell me more,' he said. 'For a start - why me? You must have lots of contacts?'

Sophie took a gulp of her gin. 'I don't know many people in this neck of the woods, and anyway, I need a complete outsider. I've been out of circulation lately, and I'm not sure who I can trust anymore. I've made a lot of enemies in my time.'

'What are you afraid of?' Ben asked, still puzzled by the whole thing.

'I can't explain.'

'You'd better, if you want my help.'

'Look,' Sophie sighed, as she leaned towards him across the dressing table. 'I'm working on a book. It's about the government's connection with the nuclear industry. I'm here because Jack Fraser was deeply involved with both, and now he's dead. I want to know who killed him. That's all I can tell you.'

'How can you be sure it wasn't an accident?' Ben asked the obvious question.

'Because I knew Jack and Elaine. When I worked at the Mirror, I met them frequently. He was a good man; they were a devoted couple. They were just walkers, they didn't take risks. Apart from that, I know that Jack had some enemies in the Cabinet as well as at Sellafield. I won't tell you who or why, but believe me my sources are impeccable.'

Ben's puzzlement continued. 'Why don't you just wait to see what the police come up with?' he asked, simply.

'You really are an innocent aren't you,' Sophie scoffed.

'You don't trust them?'

'Of course not.'

'Not even in a little town like this? I know them. I play golf with them. They're okay.'

Sophie sighed. 'Of course they're okay when they're doing their routine work. Why shouldn't they be? But look what happened in the miners' strike. Your friendly, golf playing, bobby became a soldier of the state. They did some bad things, quite brutal. Don't forget they are employees of the government. They are a disciplined force trained to take orders without question. If somebody at the top says jump, they say 'how high?' The same thing could happen with this case. I believe the truth could be suppressed by orders from above. Anyway, it isn't your golfing buddies who are handling it. It's the big boys from

County headquarters, and they will be taking orders from a department of the Metropolitan police; it's inevitable when a minister is involved.'

Ben glanced at his watch. It was time to wrap this up, get home to Helen and normality, put this down as one of those unique experiences you tell your best friend about, years later, over a drink.

He had already decided to do a bit of investigating on his own. It couldn't hurt to pass on information to Ms Lund, and he would make a few quid.

'Okay,' he announced, as he stood up to go. 'What exactly do you want me to do; how do I contact you, and how do I get paid?'

Sophie's smile was slightly glazed as she looked up at him. 'Glad to have you on board,' she said, slowly. 'I'm leaving for London tomorrow.' She reached for the hotel stationery pack, tore a page out, and wrote on it. 'Here's my contact number. I'll only be there at 7 p.m, and I'll only pick the phone up after the sixth ring.'

'Sounds a bit cloak and daggerish,' Ben quipped, lightly.

'This is a very serious business, Ben,' Sophie said. 'I want your word that you will tell no one about our meeting or our arrangement.

'You have it,' Ben said, as seriously as he could, anxious to get away. 'Now, tell me exactly what you want me to do.'

'I want you to be my stand-in. Ask all the questions I would ask, based on the assumption that Jack Fraser was murdered, possibly by government agents. Use your local contacts, the police, anybody. Telephone me with *any* information you get, however trivial. Particularly listen out for anything relating to Sellafield.'

'We'll meet in a month's time at a halfway house. You can bring me completely up to date. I'll bring you one thousand pounds cash, and who knows, eventually we might even enjoy ourselves. How tall are you?'

'Six one.'

'And suitably proportioned. Is it a deal?'

'I'm not sure about meeting in a month's time,' Ben said, ignoring the sexual reference, putting it down to the gin. 'I had enough of fixed monthly meetings when I had a proper job. They were usually a waste of time. Why not be more flexible?'

'Alright,' Sophie agreed. 'We'll meet whenever one of us thinks it is necessary. But you'll have to wait for your cash until then. I am not writing cheques.'

'How long is this going to last?' Ben asked, edging towards the door.

'As long as it takes,' Sophie replied, firmly. 'I'll decide when to end it.'

She rose from her chair, and held out her hand to shake his. As they shook hands, her blue eyes probed his.

'I know you'll do your best for me, Ben,' she said, like a general addressing his troops.

*

Ben drove home slowly, aware he was over the limit, but confident that police rarely patrolled the quiet country road leaving Keswick's northern outskirts. As he drove, he tried to come to grips with the evenings' events. It all seemed a bit unreal, a bit dream-like. Was Sophie Lund telling the truth? Maybe she was unbalanced, still on drugs, living in a fantasy world? Why expose herself to a stranger? Could there be danger involved? Was he being set up for something?

If she was completely genuine, it was quite the most fantastic thing. And, the extra money would be… He hit the brakes. A deer and fawn pranced in front of him. They were a familiar sight at night, coming out of the forests to graze in the valley fields. They trotted down the road, herded by his headlights, then jumped left, through a gap in the trees.

They brought him back to reality. They reminded him of the simple, stress-free, pleasant life he was leading.

Soon after, as he opened the cottage door - the door that led to Helen, and peace, and normality - he was still wondering if he had landed himself with one experience too many.

Chapter 4

The only luxury to be found in the space that Leni Gonzalez shares with her friend Vilma is a full-length mirror. It stands on the wooden floor propped at a slight angle against the breezeblock wall, unintentionally affording shade and protection to the cockroaches that shelter in the humid darkness behind it. One of Leni's younger brothers, who works the streets of Manila, stole it for her 21st birthday.

He was proud of his oldest sister who had gone to College, and got a job, and had a room, and was beautiful, and still a virgin. Leni had thanked him and cried, and hugged him, and begged him not to take risks, and not to get into drugs.

Now, in the cold early morning light, Leni, and the rest of the city, rise to earn their living. She rolls up the single blanket and stuffed quilt that turns a steel storage shelf into her bed each night, and jams them into a plastic bag under the shelf. A few paces, and she is outside in the enclosed yard where she lifts an old vegetable oil container onto the steel girders above her head. Quickly, she inverts the container, grabs a small piece of soap hidden on top of the girder, and proceeds with her shower.

In spite of the shock of the cold water, it is her favourite time of day – a time for renewal, for cleaning body and mind, for confirming vows.

After drying with a thin cotton rag, she steps back into the room and ritually examines her body in the full-length mirror. A shaft of morning sunlight highlights her olive skin against the grey concrete.

She knows she has been blessed, or is it cursed, with beauty. Large brown eyes, small nose, generous mouth and lips, perfect breasts, square but delicate shoulders, narrow waist, a hint of muscle tone in long-legged thighs that seem to take up an inordinately large share of her 60 inches.

She stares at her beautiful body, and, suddenly, lapses into sadness. This is what her future depends on - her fate is in its hands. The fact that she has a degree in chemistry, can converse at any level, is an accomplished swimmer, and has many other social qualities, is of little importance in the Philippines.

Just as quickly, her sadness gives way to pride. Not many girls from her background have achieved like her. Most are married with kids, some are abroad doing domestic work for pitiful wages; some are prostitutes.

She was determined to fight against this tide of inevitability. Even her mama, back on the island of Mindoro, to whom she sent money to support her five brothers and sisters, pestered her with adverts from newspapers offering *'Good marriages and homes in America for Filipino women.'*

'Hey, ugly bitch, quit fancying yourself.' Vilma's voice made her jump. Then she felt a playful slap on her bottom, as Vilma rushed past to the shower, shouting, in her American accent: 'We'll be late ugly bitch if you don't stop posing. Get that coffee on.'

By the time Vilma came back from the shower, Leni had their breakfast of coffee – in paper cups stolen from work – and hard-boiled eggs, ready. The eggs were always prepared the night before, to save time, and hard, to save on washing up water and detergent.

Leni watched Vilma, fondly, as she dragged the communal comb through her short, thick hair. Vilma did not have external beauty. She had small eyes, a squat nose, tight lips, poor skin, a short neck and bow legs. But she was beautiful inside.

They had teamed up at College, and been together ever since. Vilma was cleverer than Leni, but not as determined, coming from a gentler background. Sometimes Leni worried whether Vilma had the resilience to withstand the years of struggle that seemed to loom ahead. If Vilma went under, then so would she. They needed each other, desperately.

It was Vilma's uncle who had to let them use his storage shed as their home while they established themselves in Manila. He had come to Manila from his fishing village on the island of Samar after the fish had stopped returning to the dynamited reefs.

Leni and Vilma gulped their breakfasts, grabbed their shabby brief cases, and dashed out into del Pilar Street. They must not be late for their seven o'clock start at the office.

In spite of their qualifications, they had only managed to find jobs as sales representatives with a company that sold construction products. There was no salary, only a small commission on sales. They were expected to work six days a week, ten hours a day, and to provide their own transport. This, inevitably, meant using the jeepney.

Most weeks, they made just enough pesos to cover their food and transport costs. In good weeks a few pesos went back to Mama, and maybe a new pair of knickers went into the shoebox. In bad weeks, they stuffed themselves with rice and held each other's hand.

A 200-yard dash from their suburban street brought Leni and Vilma into chaotic Tugatog Street. The next two miles into the city centre had to be by jeepney.

They watched as one after another growled past, horns beeping, until they saw the driver they wanted. They recognised him by his missing front teeth. They didn't need to wave, he was looking out for them. It was only a matter of time before he would ask them for sex in return for his free rides into the city. Then Leni would have to charm another driver, usually spotted during their lunch breaks in Jollybees or MacDonald's. Frequently it was difficult to persuade them to let Vilma travel free as well, but eventually they all succumbed to Leni's dazzling smile, while mentally calculating how many free rides she was worth before they demanded to ride her.

Up to now, Leni and Vilma had managed to avoid paying their dues. They had developed the knack of reading a driver's eyes and body language, anticipating when the demand might come. So far they had managed to stay one jump ahead, so to speak.

Today the driver had lust flashing in his bloodshot eyes, and broad toothless grin. Quickly, the girls disappeared into the crowd, and went looking for another jeepney, knowing that they would have to pay cash this morning. Not a good start to the day.

'We must be losing our touch,' Vilma joked. 'I figured another week out of that guy didn't you?' Then her voice took on a deadly seriousness, and her head slumped as she stared vacantly at the ground. 'I would hate to lie with a man like that. I don't think I could.'

Leni grabbed her hand and dragged her in front of the next approaching jeepney. 'Come on, jump on, we'll be late.'

There were no seats available, so they hung on to the handrail protruding from the back and, holding hands, joggled their way to work.

*

This morning, as they entered the offices of Wayne Industrial Supply Inc. on Severino Reyes Street, they were half an hour earlier than usual. Their boss, Yul, had asked to see Leni before normal work begins. Vilma was just keeping her company.

They figured that he would be looking for some sort of technical help, as usual. He frequently called on them to explain the technical jargon used by their foreign suppliers. Yul wasn't a bad boss, but he wasn't very bright. He had changed his name from Sung Chen to Yul Wayne because he thought that an American sounding business name in a country dominated by American money and culture would be more successful. And who better to choose than his Hollywood heroes Yul Brynner and John Wayne.

Leni left Vilma in the tiny general staff office and, after knocking, passed into Yul's large air-conditioned office. His immaculate white shirt stood out against the dark buttoned leather chair, in which he reclined confidently and lazily. He smiled at Leni and gestured for her to sit opposite. He, like everyone, was always pleased to see Leni.

'I have an important project for you Leni,' he began.

He was prone to exaggeration, so Leni didn't get excited. 'Yes,' was all she could manage.

'In their wisdom, our wonderful government have agreed to let the Americans build a nuclear waste processing facility on Panay. One of our British suppliers has been in contact - Amtex - you know them?'

Leni nodded.

'They have informed me that they have a unique...' he paused to read off the paper on his desk...' high density concrete product that is used in the British nuclear processing plants. And they doubt if the Americans or anyone else have yet developed anything similar. They reckon there would be a very large requirement on this new facility at Panay, and since all supplies have to go through a Philippine company, there could be lots of business for both of us.'

'Great.' Leni tried to sound enthusiastic, but knew that little, if any, of the money made would be coming her way.

'However, there is a lot of ground work to be done before we can count our chickens,' Yul grinned, always glad when he could show off his grasp of western phrases. 'As you know, we will have to submit a product like this to government agencies for approval. And we will all need technical training in how to sell it and use it on site.'

Leni noted the 'we' with amusement. Yul always left the technical stuff to them.

He paused while he searched through other papers on his desk, then went on. 'Now, Amtex are proposing to send out their sales manager and somebody from a company called British Nuclear Fuels who invented this product. They are going to train us about this product, and explain how it works to the government agencies. 'They will be here in two months time, and will stay for as long as it takes. I will be setting up meetings with the agencies, and informing our staff about when and where our training will take place. What I want you to do, Leni,' and here a knowing smile crossed his face, 'is to take these men under your wing'…the smile widened at another western phrase…'and look after them. I want you to be their escort, their entertainment guide; their friend. I will provide you with a car and a driver. I've already booked them into the Sheraton. I want you to see that they have a good time in Manila, no expense spared. But most of all I want you to pick their brains about this product. It sounds like very profitable business, so we must get it right. General training sessions are okay for some products, but this sounds complicated, and I need at least one of my staff to know everything about it.'

'He may not be very bright,' Leni thought, 'but he is astute at business.'

He rose from his chair to signify the meeting was over, a ploy he often used to avoid questions about payment.

Obediently, Leni left the office. Although she was concerned about how she was going to be paid, she was quite looking forward to some time off the sales grind, even if it did mean entertaining westerners who were invariably large, loud, arrogant and pathetic in their attempts to seduce her.

Chapter 5

Three weeks after the deaths of Jack and Elaine Fraser, Keswick was almost back to normal. The hotels resumed playing host to walking boots and backpacks instead of laptops and cameras. The massive police presence had dissipated, and the Incident Room had been closed, though, according to a police press release, a team was still assigned to the case at County HQ.

Like a student trying to please his teacher, Ben had dashed about asking questions, searching for something to give to Sophie Lund. He had pushed his friendship with Sergeant Bill Unwin to the limit, questioning him surreptitiously during their golf sessions to see if he had any variance on the official statements of the detective chief superintendent handling the case.

Apart from an insight into some political infighting about what should and should not be released via the police press office, he had nothing significant to contribute. The police had found nothing to link the deaths with terrorists or disgruntled Sellafield workers, but 'their investigations were continuing'.

Bill's small uniformed team had spent the weeks searching Little Man gully, looking for Mrs Fraser's ear, or remnants of it, without success. Apparently, the pathologist had some doubts about the head wounds and needed the ear to clarify his conclusions.

Ben had even retraced Jack and Elaine Fraser's last day. Mrs Telford's caravan site, where the Frasers had been reliving their honeymoon, was part of one of his daily walks. He often called into her little shop for an ice cream nearing the end of a regular eight miler.

Mrs Telford had confirmed that the Fraser's called into the shop to let her know they were going up Skiddaw. 'Such a lovely couple...so considerate...they always held hands...I still can't believe it.' Her lips had quivered and a handkerchief had appeared from underneath her flowered apron, to dab her eyes.

From the caravan site, Ben took what he considered to be the easiest route up Skiddaw; not the picturesque Ullock Pike route taken by most tourists, and probably the Frasers, but the shorter, steeper approach from Dash Falls.

Even though he was there on a solemn mission, when he reached the top, he was overcome with the beauty that surrounded him. Every day he was compelled to stop and stare at the beauty of the land he now called home.

Down below, beside the lucific lake, he could just see the roof of his cottage, hiding among the trees. He pictured his rowing boat, tied up at the lake's edge, always ready for a lazy afternoon's drifting, or a spot of fishing; the wild birds and animals on the lawn, and Helen, dear Helen, baking and cooking on her day off, humming contentedly, flour everywhere. He could smell the hot scones. Was ever a man so lucky?

From Skiddaw's highest point he moved along the ridge until he reached Little Man. He inspected the area where people were most likely to stop to take in the magnificent view.

He had remembered correctly. The top of the mountain was convex for a few yards before it became a sheer drop. The contour naturally forced people to stand away from the absolute edge. Even if you slipped at this point you would have a few yards of safety before you plunged over the edge. The chances of it being an accident were virtually nil. You would have to deliberately throw yourself off, or be pushed. It had to be suicide or murder.

As he turned to leave the area, he spotted something blue lying on the dark grey, loose shale, ground. Bending down, he found a badly chewed plastic top off a ballpoint pen. It found its way into the pocket of his body warmer, to share space with bits of wire, string, radiator key, numerous dog-eared bits of paper containing once vital notes, elastic bands, zip tag, and sundry electric fuses.

Helen no longer shook her head when she saw him studiously placing them in a pile while the jacket got washed. She had long ago accepted that some men never totally grow up.

*

During those three weeks, Ben had phoned Sophie Lund frequently. She had been waiting, which had reassured him that she was genuine, and he had passed on the snippets of information he had gleaned. When they had spoken, it had been very brief and to the point, except for one occasion when she sounded a bit down and confided in him that her 'project was not proceeding smoothly.'

Ben began to sense that he was wasting his time. Even if there was something to find out, he probably couldn't unearth it. A few more weeks, and he would phone Sophie to call it a day.

Chapter 6

'A child would destroy the world if it had the power,' Freud said. So it was with Hector Snodd as he moved into adolescence. He wanted to explode in a blaze of destruction. His years of loneliness, lack of affection, and rejection by his peers, had forged him into a morose loner. His years of pathetically trying to please were over. To hell with them. He would make them pay. He would make everybody pay.

He started to play truant from his new high school, where the boys called him 'Snoddy the Body'. He wandered the streets of Thurso town, stealing from shops. When at school, where he had been doing well academically, he became disruptive, deliberately played dumb.

At the croft, he became cruel to the animals he had once loved. He enjoyed hearing them cry out in pain. He set fire to his uncle's hay crop and to others. He fought back when his uncle tried to discipline him.

Each time he gave vent to his destructive forces, his sense of inadequacy and inferiority faded; his burning feeling of resentment was temporarily quenched. At that moment he was in control of himself, of others. He was powerful; he was worthwhile.

During this time, he made two life-changing discoveries. The first was normal: he loved girls. Even though they still snubbed him at school, they did not come into his circle of hate. With no experience of a mother or sister, he saw girls as beautiful, unattainable, angels from heaven.

One girl in particular filled him with longing. Kathleen Rinaldi had a gentle, fawn-like face, golden skin, deep brown eyes. She was small and slim, and seemed shy and quiet. He loved her desperately. At least he thought it was love. He wasn't sure what love was; it was outside his experience. If only he could hold her, he would protect her, and rest his cheek against her soft brown skin. He would take her to the cave and they would never leave.

A hopeless ache ensued when he thought like this: a lump in his throat, his lips tight, deep, terrible sobs. As the tears poured, he would get out the magazines he had stolen from the newsagent, and gaze longingly at their heavenly bodies. One day...one day.

The second discovery was unusual for a crofting youth. His uncle wouldn't allow television, 'the tool of Satan', into the house, but he did keep a small radio, which he used only for the news and weather forecast.

While his uncle was out working at night, Hector relieved his loneliness by listening to pop music on the many programmes that it offered.

He had been changing programmes when a dramatic sound grabbed his attention. He released the tuning knob.

Soaring, searing, music entered his head, and seized his mind. It took him on an emotional journey. It spoke of turmoil, pain, misery, resentment, anger, confusion, and finally, as it faded to a breathlessly quiet conclusion - of resignation and death. When it had finished, he found himself sitting on the bed, shaking, and crying uncontrollably. It had taken him on a journey through his own miserable life. Someone else had felt like him and, miraculously, described his feelings with music - without words.

He listened intently as the announcer told him that he had been listening to the final movement of the sixth symphony written by a man whose name sounded to him like Chykoski. Wiping his eyes, he found pencil and paper and made a note of the name. He wanted to know more about Mr Chykoski.

He was about to switch back to his usual pop programme, when a massive sound leapt from the radio, making his heart jump. As he recovered, he heard some simple notes, sounding like mice running about, take over. Gradually a simple tune built up to what, he thought, was its loud conclusion, but then it drove on, picking up more pace and volume.

His heart kept pace with the excitement. The music surged and swayed, driving on and on. It spoke about power, strength, achievement and joy. It ended in a massive blast of triumph. He paced the floor, his heart racing. He had to hear it again. He wanted to capture that feeling of power forever. He had his pencil ready this time to record that he had heard Beethoven's third symphony for the first time.

*

So started Hector Snodd's lifelong, obsessional love of serious music. The next day he went to Thurso library and, upon enquiring about Mr Chikoski and Mr Beethoven, was introduced to *The Groves Dictionary of Music and Musicians*. In it he found the brief life stories of Peter Ilyich Tchaikovsky, and Ludwig Von Beethoven. Even the strange spelling excited him.

After reading about their troubled lives, Hector began to understand. Tchaikovsky had described his feelings of loneliness and misery, while Beethoven had described his feelings of fighting back, winning, proclaiming victory. He had found two people who understood him exactly. He must learn more about them, hear more of their music; make them his friends.

*

From the library, Hector went straight to Begg's electric shop in Rotterdam Street and stole a Walkman. From there he went to The Music Shop in High Street and stole eight tapes. As well as Tchaikovsky, and Beethoven, he now had Sibelius, Mozart, Rachmaninov and Mahler to listen to and learn from.

During breaks at school he used his Walkman constantly, walking among the other pupils, lost in his own world of mighty music, feeling superior to those who had once frightened him.

Back at the croft, he hid the Walkman and tapes from his Uncle, in the same place as his stolen magazines - under the floorboards, under a rug.

Chapter 7

Hector left school without qualifications. After a few months of unemployment his uncle used his contacts at Dounreay to get him a job as a labourer in the concrete batching plant, which had been set up on site for the construction of a new waste, receipt, assay, character-isation and super-compaction (WRACS) facility.

His uncle, and the manager of the batching plant, Callum McDonald, both attended the same church on Sunday mornings, which is where the good word went in.

Hector found it difficult to socialise with the rest of the workers and, eventually, found a quiet hideaway in a corner of the laboratory mould store, making himself a seat with an upturned admixture container. Here he spent his breaks alone, listening to music on his Walkman. By now he had added Sibelius and Rachmaninov to his list of favourites.

*

For the next few months, the routine of work, and the novelty of having money to spend, brought some stability into his life. Then, during a rare cleaning spell, his uncle found his stash of magazines and tapes under the floorboards, and threw him out.

He had just enough money to pay the bond on a dingy flat in Thurso, above Harold's butcher's shop in Bank Street, next to the Central Hotel.

*

During the next three years Hector drifted into a routine of work and drink. During the day, the uncomplicated, physical work routine suited him. He kept his nose clean and the rest of the staff left him alone.

But at night it was different. The solitude he sought during the day became his tormentor at night. In the evening, alone in his flat, he listened to his music. But as the night progressed, he would begin to feel empty and desolate. He had nobody to share his music with. He wanted somebody to sit beside him and hold his hand while they listened. He wanted somebody to love. He wanted Kathleen Rinaldi.

He fantasised about abducting her. When he saw her in the street, holding hands with her boyfriend, he wanted to kill him. He would follow them just to keep her in his sight as long as possible. But it would become unbearable, and the night would end in the Central's lounge bar drowning out the pain, blotting out the malevolent world.

After a drinking session, he would lie in his bed, eyes closed, listening to an adagio, tears flowing, relying on the swirling, nauseous, numbness in his head to blot out thoughts of suicide or ...

*

He was still clinging to this fragile routine when his uncle died.

Hector had been asked by Dounreay Security to check on him, as he hadn't turned up for work for two days.

He found him at the back of the croft; face down in an overflowing sheep-dip bath, together with a dozen trapped sheep bleating their hunger. It was the first time Hector had seen a human corpse.

He poked it with his foot. The body suddenly turned over in the stinking organophosphate solution, stiff arms saluting the air, head fixed in a sitting up position, staring at him with pickled grey eyes. Fascinating.

Before the body could turn over again, Hector put his foot on the head and pushed it under. He watched with interest as rigid legs came up and kicked at the sky, then sank, bringing the arms and head back up, the whole body becoming a gradually faltering seesaw in a khaki liquid grave.

He released the sheep and played a few more body games before going into the house. Not knowing he would inherit the croft, he spent the next hour searching and looting.

He informed the police on his return to Thurso. Subsequently, they informed him that his uncle had died of a heart attack, and that a will had been found and passed on to a solicitor.

His uncle had left him everything - house and outbuildings, car, animals, and, surprisingly, savings of over eleven thousand pounds. The solicitor read out a statement from the will. 'I am leaving everything to my nephew Hector Ian Snodd, in the belief that this act of charity will inspire him to mend his ways and take the path of God to everlasting salvation.'

Hector took the path to the high street and bought the best hi-fi system available. He installed it and himself in the croft house, opened the windows, and introduced every creature for miles around to the majesty of symphonic music.

On that very special first evening, he wanted to play music that exactly matched his remote rural surroundings, and the new way he felt about it. For the first time, he was seeing it as a place of space and freedom, instead of a dour prison.

He started with Beethoven's Pastoral Symphony, but decided that it was too genteel. Perfect for the lush meadows and forests it described, but not bare and hard like the northern Scottish coast. It had to be Sibelius - any symphony.

The gulls took off from the fields, the sheep lifted their heads, as the shimmering, spacious, glorious sound surged over the rugged headland.

Later, he sold the sheep, bought some new furniture, and traded in his uncle's old banger for a newer car.

*

A few weeks after moving into the croft house, Hector was invited by Callum McDonald to train as a laboratory technician to replace a staff member who was leaving. Presumably, his boss felt some Christian responsibility for him after the death of his uncle.

He was sent to British Nuclear Fuels central concrete laboratory at Sellafield to attend a series of concrete technology training courses. He had never been south of Inverness, and found the whole business of travelling, finding accommodation, and attending courses, stressful. But he persevered, and managed to pass his examinations.

During the courses he became infected with his tutor's enthusiasm for concrete. It wasn't the boring, grey, man-made material he had thought. It was the scientific blending of natural materials - stones, sands, cements and waters, each with an infinite variety of sizes, strengths, porosities, viscosities, hardnesses, absorptions, colours.

Hector found the whole subject fascinating, and he threw himself enthusiastically into his work when he returned to his laboratory.

Things were looking up. Now he was a man of property, with a good job, and two absorbing passions - music and concrete. His third passion, Kathleen Rinaldi, still remained a fantasy of the night.

Chapter 8

The red squirrels were doing their early morning party piece, scrambling up the oars Ben had left leaning against the cottage wall. Near them stood his fishing rod, and two golf clubs. They were all supposed to reside in the garage, but they never seemed to get there until he brought the boat up from the lake for winter maintenance.

Ben filled up the bird nut holder and scattered grain for the pheasants that gathered around his ankles. As usual, the mallard ducks started to nudge the pheasants out and take over their food, until Ben scattered their breakfast on a different part of the lawn.

While they all tucked in, Ben took hold of a golf club and took a practice swing. A chunk of lawn flew up. As he retrieved the divot, a knock on the conservatory window attracted his attention. Helen sat at the window, drinking her morning coffee, waving her fist in mock annoyance at the damage to the lawn, then mimed that his coffee was ready.

Ben replaced the divot in the dew soaked grass, placed the golf club against the old stone wall, absorbed the recondite sunlight, the sweet dank smell of the yew hedge and the surrounding trees, the flitting, quacking, chattering life around him, and went in contented.

Time together was precious. Managing the leisure centre took a lot of Helen's time. It was open from six in the morning till ten in the evening, seven days a week, offering a multitude of facilities and training courses. Helen was always on call. When she wasn't at the centre she was usually taking calls at home.

It was because of this heavy workload that Ben had refrained from burdening her with his concerns about the deaths of Jack Fraser and his wife. But now his investigations had ground to a halt, he was keen to get her point of view. She always brought a pragmatic, down-to-earth approach to situations, compared to his more quixotic, facetious, approach. They made a good team.

Sitting beside her, sipping his coffee, Ben glanced at her to see if she might be receptive. Too late - her head was buried, as usual, in a wad of papers.

He shuffled to the other end of the sofa, lounged back, and watched her, deep in concentration. He liked her hair most of all. It displayed every shade of light brown, from milk chocolate to light gold. It was always clean and shining, and flowed in a curve to her shoulder like fresh molten lava. There was no make-up, no trinkets, just an everyday 40-something face that spoke of strength, serenity, generosity. She was beautiful, and he loved her, and more than this, he respected her.

Eventually, she put the papers down on the coffee table, and glanced at him. 'Fancy a walk? I've a couple of letters to post.'

The walk took them north along the lake's tree lined east shore, around Scarness Bay, skirting the grounds of Scarness Manor, followed the stream across the fields, and over the hump back bridge into the village; still farming, not yet given over to tourism; the smell of manure always in the air.

The post box stood in front of a group of farm buildings whose erratic confluence of rooftops and chimneys framed against the smooth shaped backdrop of Skiddaw always caught Ben's eye. He kept promising himself to capture it on canvas one day. Today, it reminded him of tragedy.

As they turned to go home, this time via the lanes, not the lakeside, Ben was still looking up at Skiddaw. 'Remember those deaths up there a few weeks ago?' he asked.

'The government minister?'

'And his wife.'

'Yes.'

'I was talking to someone who believes the minister was murdered by his colleagues...'

'Go on, get it over with,' Helen sighed. 'You know I can see your awful jokes coming. *And* you know I don't like cruel ones....'

'No ...it's not a joke. Somebody really thinks he was murdered...'

'By his colleagues?'

'Yes...well, by agents acting on behalf of his colleagues.'

'Acting on behalf? You make them sound like solicitors. Are you really serious?'

'Absolutely.'

'Who told you this nonsense? Somebody with a glass in their hand, no doubt.'

Ben latched on to the suggestion. 'Well, he had, but he wasn't drunk. It was a journalist with the Workington Herald. Their paper's part of a big group. He said the rumour was going around their London head office.'

'Well,' Helen scoffed. 'You know what they're like in London. Nothing better to do than make up rumours. Keeps the chattering classes entertained.'

'Maybe.'

'Oh! Come on, you can't.........what's the motive supposed to be...pinched their parking space, or slept with their secretaries?'

Ben winced. 'Bit more serious than that! Something to do with his involvement with the nuclear industry...look out.' He grabbed Helen's arm and guided her on to the grass verge as a tractor and trailer loaded with manure rumbled past.

Helen stepped back on to the tarmac. 'It all sounds to me like a load of what's just gone past on that trailer,' she said, pointedly. 'These conspiracy theories always come to nothing. Remember Kennedy, remember Monroe? Nothing is ever proved. If the police don't find anything, then there's nothing to find.'

'The police still don't think it was an accident,' Ben countered. 'But they have no evidence of foul play. The Coroner reconvened the inquest last week and they came up with an open verdict. So it looks like it's going to be just another unsolved mystery. I'm pretty sure they were murdered.'

'You might be sure, but you're not pretty,' Helen gibed, as she playfully slapped his bottom and started running down the lane.

This was her way of ending a conversation she didn't like. She had never been keen on politics, deep and meaningful discussions, or the darker side of humanity. Sometimes Ben found it frustrating when a serious conversation fizzled out, but he respected the insinuation implicit in her philosophy - that it is better to focus on the good things in life.

He gave chase. 'Hey! You...come here...that hurt...'

After a hundred metres, she let him catch her and they hugged, breathlessly, while he took gentle revenge on her bottom. Their breathing was so loud that they didn't hear the sniffs. Nor did they see the eyes that watched them from the nearby trees.

Chapter 9

The WRACS facility was nearing completion when Hector was summoned to the plant manager's office. He feared redundancy.

Callum McDonald said, 'Good news.'

Hector relaxed.

'Sellafield have started to build a new vitrification plant, the one that turns high-level waste into glass blocks. Well, they're having trouble designing a micro-concrete for the process position inserts. They've been working on it for three months at the Sellafield lab. All their theoretical designs have failed in practice and they're getting desperate for time. The micro-concrete has to be non shrink, flow-able enough to pump into narrow voids, achieve 3,000 pounds per cubic metre density, and its specified compressive strength.'

'They want us to help them with their testing programme. Which is where you come in. Work on WRACS is running down. You can start on this straight away.'

'What do I have to do?' Hector gulped, worried it would be over his head.

'Don't worry,' Callum said. 'They have produced all the designs.' He handed Hector a thin file. 'They are all in there. All you have to do is source the materials, follow their instructions, and carry out the tests.'

'Is it a question of adjusting the admixtures, or is there still some granulometry to be sorted?' Hector asked, feeling less nervous now.

His boss pointed to the file. 'You'll see in there. The granulometry is the same throughout. They obviously see it as an admixture issue. Their biggest problem, apparently, is settlement of the extra lead in the micro-mix. They have nominated a cocktail of five admixtures. It seems to be a question of finding precisely the right dosage of each. The permutations are endless, so you could be in for a long haul. It could get boring.'

'I won't get bored', Hector said. Inside, he felt excited. He couldn't wait to get started. It would be fascinating.

*

Within two weeks he had sourced all materials and commenced testing regimes. Such was his enthusiasm that they had to buy more steel cube moulds as he produced mix after mix and took up large areas of the laboratory with six inch cubes of cast micro-concrete in various stages of maturity.

But, eventually, his enthusiasm gave way to frustration as test after test failed to meet the criteria in one way or another.

*

At night, his life was lonelier than ever. Since moving into the croft he visited Thurso only once a week for shopping.

This always included three bottles of whisky, and a kerb crawl around the streets to see if he could catch sight of Kathleen Rinaldi. On the occasions that he did, she didn't appear to notice him.

By now, he was seeking solace in videos as well as music and alcohol. The late night viewing and excessive alcohol meant that he routinely started the day with a hangover.

*

It was a hangover that changed his life. It had been a heavy weekend: head throbbing, tongue coated, breath ignitable. It was Monday lunchtime before he realised that he had not added any admixtures to the six micro-mixes he had poured that morning.

'Shit,' as he pushed the six half-set cubes into a corner of the workbench. He would dispose of them tomorrow. Meanwhile, he hurriedly started on a new batch.

The next day he removed the six cubes from their moulds and threw them in the waste bin. Then, out of curiosity, he picked out one cube and placed it under the compressive strength-crushing machine. It met the strength criteria. He increased the pressure to break the cube in half. The lead shot was uniformly distributed. He weighed it. The density was 3,120. He was getting excited. He measured it. 'Shit.' Slight shrinkage had occurred. But he could probably adjust that. He had done the flow tests yesterday before pouring the mix into the moulds. He grabbed the book with the results. 'Shit' again. The flows were just short of the criteria. He sat down and thought hard. He had almost satisfied the design criteria without adding any of the five admixtures. It didn't make sense. According to his limited knowledge, all he had to do now was add a small quantity of super-plasticiser to increase the flow, and a lignosulphonate to stop the shrinkage. He grabbed the other five cubes from the bin and put them through the tests. All five showed similar results.

During the rest of that week, he carried out a series of tests on his own designs alongside the routine Sellafield designs. By Friday he had arrived at the optimum percentage of super-plasticiser and lignosulphonate to add, and was satisfying all test criteria except one - lead settlement.

He couldn't wait for Monday. He went to work over the weekend, and again followed basic principles. This time he adjusted the granulometry, reducing the fines and increasing the large aggregates to give more support to the lead shot. He poured five slightly varying cubes and left them for testing on Monday.

The only hangover he had on that Monday was due to lack of sleep, not alcohol. His mind had been racing throughout the night, unable to rid itself of the infinite formulations that had imprinted themselves.

He started his tests. One of the five cubes met all the criteria. Excited, but still unsure, he took his results and his explanations to his boss.

Callum McDonald was intrigued and supportive. He instructed Hector to make ten cubes of his formulation, and to carry out more tests with himself present. Two days later, he was shaking Hector's hand. All ten cubes were within the design parameters. Hector had cracked it.

Being a good Christian, and unlike most managers, Callum McDonald took no credit when he passed on the good news to Sellafield Concrete Laboratory.

Not only were they delighted that the problem had been solved, but they pointed out that Hector's formulation was also a lot cheaper than envisaged because of the reduction in the number of admixtures. They invited Hector down to Sellafield to thank him, to discuss his formulation, and to try to discover why their own designer's formulations hadn't worked.

Hector had hated the attention, the back slapping, the hand shaking, and he had felt out of his depth and embarrassed when he was invited to join in discussions with Sellafield's design engineers as they theorised about their formulation's failure. He contributed nothing as he listened to these confident men, all with degrees, go over their calculations, and find nothing wrong with them.

Much to his relief, the answer was found within three days by one of Hector's equivalents in the Sellafield laboratory, a humble lab technician called John Grey.

Hector's simple design, and hindsight, guided him to conclude that the five admixtures were not behaving as they should. He carried out tests and found that at the high dosages specified by the design engineers, who had based their designs on extrapolation of previously successful designs, the admixtures were causing unforeseen side effects within the micro-concrete, much like strong drugs do in humans.

For this design, the engineers should not have used extrapolation, but gone back to first principles. This was why someone with Hector's basic knowledge, and a lucky hangover, had come up with the answer.

The fact remained that, however lucky, Hector had saved them a lot of time, and money. Now they could proceed to invite concrete supply companies to submit quotations for supplying Hector's formulation in pre-bagged commercial quantities. They had decided to call it HD3000, everyone concerned understanding that the H stood for Hector as well as the High in High Density.

*

Two months later, with the WRACS facility complete, Hector was offered a permanent quality control position in the Dounreay Cementation Plant (DCP). This encapsulated old Reactor raffinate in a cementitious matrix within stainless steel drums.

Shortly after starting his new job, Hector heard on the grapevine that a small Essex Company called Amtex had won the contract to supply HD3000 to Sellafield.

*

Six months later, back in his old dissolute routine, glad to be anonymous again, he was surprised by a summons from his old boss at the laboratory. Callum McDonald came straight to the point.

'How do you fancy a trip to the Philippines?'

'Pardon?'

'Remember the HD3000?'

'Yes.'

'My boss, Eric Diller at Sellafield, wants you to go to the Philippines with the Sales Manager of Amtex Ltd at the end of this month. They have the opportunity to sell a lot of HD3000 for a new American waste facility to be built there. Amtex have asked Sellafield to supply some technical back-up to help them with their bid. Apparently Sellafield owes them a few favours, and Amtex will be footing the bill, so Eric agreed to help them. He reckons it will only be a PR job, nothing too technical, just flag waving. This is his way of thanking you for saving them money. The trip will last about three weeks, mainly because the Amtex man has other business there. Your bit should only take a few days, educating a Philippine import company and a few government officials. How you spend the rest of your time is up to you. Do you think you are up to it?'

Hector hesitated. He now felt confident about his technical ability, but he was still hopeless socially, and he daren't admit that he had never been abroad. The prospect terrified him.

'It's not really my kind of thing is it,' he said, looking for confirmation from the man he respected.

'Well, I don't think so,' Callum McDonald said frankly, 'and I told Eric so, and I asked him if he could send somebody else. But he insisted it must be you. He thinks he is doing you a big favour. He likes feeling magnanimous. I couldn't dissuade him.'

That night, Hector downed extra whisky and listened to Bach, but he still couldn't sleep.

Chapter 10

Cities sleep in different ways: some soundly, some fitfully. Manila has nightmares.

Leni and Vilma are late and running. Sales have been poor because they have been busy digging the company out of technical holes. Yul doesn't want to hear excuses, and has been threatening the sack.

Last night they worked till midnight in a food factory, trying to repair a damaged resin floor and a damaged company reputation. They arrived home at 1.00 a.m, exhausted. They were too tired to shower. They ate two bananas, drank water, made their beds and collapsed.

Now, as a morning mist softens the edges of the harsh city, they are running late.

They gasp into Tugatog Street and, knowing they are too late for their current free ride, wave down the first jeepney they see.

Leni has just got settled in her seat, her breathing almost recovered, when she notices the driver's eyes in the mirror. They are watching her. Her breath stops. They are familiar. She grabs Vilma's arm. Vilma jumps, then follows her gaze. The jeepney stops in the dense traffic. The driver turns and grins. The grin is broad and toothless.

Leni leaps to make her escape through the back door. A man in a red shirt leaves his seat and bars her way. Vilma rushes to the front. A tall man with a moustache stands up and blocks the exit. He smiles at her, knowingly, like a cat that is about to get the cream.

Leni slumps into a seat. There are no other passengers. It is a set up. The driver must have been waiting for this chance for weeks. The realisation has also dawned on Vilma. She grips Leni's hand as her eyes start to moisten.

They stare blankly ahead as the jeepney turns off Tugatog Street and heads southwards. They won't fight or scream. They had known this would happen one day. The driver had every right to claim payment. He wasn't a charity; he was struggling like the rest of them. It was just a pity that they would have to lose their virginity. Without it, or the money to have the hymen surgically restored, there would be no chance of marrying a decent man.

As the jeepney turns off the surfaced road and rattles through a shanty area, Vilma whispers 'I'm frightened.'

Leni squeezes her hand. 'There is nothing to be afraid of,' she says loudly, trying to be brave for both of them. Inside, she trembles. 'Don't resist. Try to imagine you are somewhere else, with someone else. It will soon be over. Time will heal our memories.'

The jeepney pulls up beside a large concrete bridge that spans a shallow valley. It is a sought-after location. The underside of the bridge provides a secure, dry, roof from which corrugated metal sheeting is hung, and fixed, to form the walls of better than average homes. The constant rumbling of the traffic overhead is a price worth paying.

The driver and his cohorts usher Leni and Vilma towards a corrugated door. The driver takes Leni by the arm. Close up, he looks a lot younger than she had thought. Behind the weary eyes and toothless grin, she senses a kindness. He was showing them no animosity for their failure to pay in the past. He was not a rapist. This was routine business; he was just collecting his debt.

As they step inside the door, Leni stops. 'Can we give you money...we are both virgins.'

The driver hesitates, then, 'Too late. My friends are expecting...'

'Your friends?' Leni was horrified, expecting that the driver would take a turn with each of them and then let them go. 'We don't owe them anything, only you.'

'I owe them for helping me catch you. Don't worry, they will go with her, only I will have you.'

'No,' Vilma shouts.

The tall man pulls her through the darkness. 'Come on.'

They pass through a small kitchen room into a larger room. The driver strikes a match and lights a paraffin lamp. Among sundry makeshift bits of furniture, two old double mattresses lie on the floor on top of polythene sheeting. Between the two mattresses, a blanket hangs from the roof to the floor in an attempt to create privacy between the two beds. Clearly two families live here.

The driver takes Leni to the left of the blanket. The tall man and his friend take Vilma to the right.

The driver sits on the mattress and starts to undress. Leni takes a deep breath and does likewise. She hangs her dress neatly over a chair and places her briefcase next to it. She will need both in good condition if she is going to make good sales that morning.

Naked, she moves closer to the paraffin light so that the driver can see her better. She stands straight, shoulders back, head high. She looks, unflinchingly, into his eyes. She sees him swallow, then lower his eyes.

'I give you respect,' he says. Leaning over, he pulls a packet of condoms from under a pillow.

'My friend also,' Leni demands.

The driver steps to the end of the mattress and throws the packet into the other bedroom. 'We show respect,' he shouts. There is no reply.

*

Leni lowers herself to the mattress. A fusion of rancid smells emanate from it. She lies beneath the driver, and studies the flickering shadows cast by the paraffin lamp on to the underside of the bridge, as he takes her virginity. She tries to imagine the shadows are clouds drifting over her mama's house. She tries to take her mind back to happy childhood days, but it is difficult to concentrate because of his unexpected urgency and the smell.

She is more concerned about Vilma than herself. Please God, they will be gentle with her. She prays to the Blessed Virgin Mary to give Vilma strength. Apart from slight shuffling noises, there is no sound from the other side of the blanket.

The driver is finished and rolls over to find a cigarette. Leni starts to rise. He holds her back. 'Just a little break,' he explains, his cigarette glowing in the semi darkness. Leni lies still beside him and tries not to listen to the shuffling beyond the blanket.

During the second session Leni counts the cars grumbling on the bridge overhead. A dudd-diff, dudd-diff, sound tells her that there is an expansion joint directly over her head. She can tell whether it is a car or a lorry going over by the volume of the dudd-diff. During one surreal moment she finds that a flurry of vehicles causes the dudd-diffs to keep exact time with the movements of the driver.

Leni glances at her watch, another 'gift' from her brother, as the driver finishes for the second time. Twenty minutes. They are almost an hour late for work. This time he lets her get up and get dressed while he lights another cigarette and continues to loll on the mattress. She looks down at him. She doesn't hate him.

'Will you give us a lift to work please. We will be fired for being late.'

The driver rises quickly, stubbing out his cigarette in his hand. 'Me too! Hey Pedro,' he shouts, 'we have to go. Come on...finish.' He is dressed in a flash. Clearly, he doesn't own the jeepney and has his own boss problems.

The two men appear, fastening their clothes. There is an awful, breath holding, delay before Vilma appears, blank-faced, wet-eyed. She stumbles over something on the floor, and makes a pitiable gasp. She looks at Leni, pleadingly.

'Don't forget your briefcase,' Leni orders. 'Come on, we're getting a lift.'

*

Twenty-five minutes later, after a visit to the washroom, Leni and Vilma are knocking on Yul's office door. They have travelled there holding hands, in silence, recognising that words were inadequate.

'The jeepney broke down, then there was a jam,' Leni lies, using everybody's stock, and frequently truthful, excuse.

Yul frowns while he searches for a suitable western cliché.

'You must think I fell off the plum tree yesterday,' is the best he can do. 'Jams don't last one and a half hours. Dallying with your boyfriends I bet. I am cutting yesterday morning's commission from your pay, and giving you just another two weeks to pull up your socks. Go.' He waves a dismissive hand.

Leni knows he is bluffing this time. He has no intention of getting rid of them because he needs them for next week's visit by the British company. They are leaving his office when he shouts, 'What's the names of the two men coming next week?' He always does this. It's his way of keeping his staff on their toes. And it works.

'Mr Elland and Mr Snodd,' Leni and Vilma say in unison, like trained parrots.

'And what is the name of their companies?'

'Amtex Limited and British Nuclear Fuels.'

'Right...off you go.'

*

Leni and Vilma step out into hot chaos. Across the city, a driver loses his job, fears about tomorrow; forgets the carnal morning. Manila's nightmare does not need the dark.

Chapter 11

Even the beautiful, diminutive, flight attendants of Singapore Airlines couldn't distract Hector from the discomfort of his first flight. Their constant procession of food and warm face towels served only to disturb him as he tried to find comfort and sleep. Their interruptions also meant that he had to listen to more verbosity from his travelling companion.

John Elland, Sales Manager for Amtex Ltd, was proving to be his antithesis. Tall, good looking, confident, smartly dressed, well travelled, and still only in his 30s. He hadn't stopped talking since meeting Hector at Heathrow Airport, a place that Hector found totally bewildering.

John Elland explained that he had many projects to visit, but Hector was only required to supply technical support when promoting HD3000 to Wayne Industrial Supplies and a few government officials. He could spend the rest of the time accompanying John on his visits or do his own thing - it was up to him.

He made it all sound so simple and easy, but Hector knew it was completely outside his experience or capabilities, and the thought of it made him sick with worry.

*

The first thing that struck him about Manila, as they entered the dingy airport terminal, was the smell. Had he been a traveller, he would have recognised the warm, damp, thick, smell that announces all tropical cities.

Then there were the crowds. It was as if all Manila had turned out to greet them. A confusion of hundreds of people babbled and waved beyond the barriers; a mixture of taxi drivers, relatives, friends, beggars, people offering to carry luggage, armed police.

Among this melee they finally spotted a board saying 'Amtex Ltd'. It was being held aloft by small, bare arms. The rest of the body belonged to the most beautiful young woman Hector had ever seen.

Leni greeted them with a practised smile and a firm shake of her tiny hand, then led them through the throng to a waiting company car. The company driver was not, apparently, worthy of introduction.

He drove at a speed and through gaps in the frantic, honking traffic that Hector found unbelievable. He gazed in shock at the soiled, noisy, decrepit, neon lit, people-plagued, city as it flashed past in the darkness of early evening. In the frequent traffic jams the car was besieged by limbless beggars and gaunt children offering one cigarette for sale. John, who had been to Manila before, advised him to ignore them, saying that they were mostly organised by gangs.

'We are here!' Leni announced.

Hector was dismayed to find himself looking out at ragged people sitting and lying on the pavement in front of corrugated iron structures, but then realised that the car was in a queue waiting to pull up in front of a large modern hotel called *The Sheraton.*

The adjacent poverty served to emphasise the opulence of the Sheraton. A huge entrance lobby containing open plan bars, restaurants, moving staircases, fountains, and an immaculately dressed group of musicians playing classical music, filled Hector's wondering eyes.

Leni escorted them, via the moving staircase, to reception, which overlooked the lobby below. Here, she helped them to check in, then announced that she would be back to pick them up at eight o'clock to take them to a Chinese restaurant for dinner, where Yul was waiting to meet them. Before they could protest, she was gone.

Without any sleep for 15 hours and with his stomach already heaving with plane food and tension, Hector hated the idea, but kept quiet.

Reading his mind, John Elland said wearily, 'They've obviously forgotten about the time difference. We'd better go - they'd be offended if we didn't turn up.'

*

The Chinese restaurant turned out to be another hectic, swerving, honking, 20-minute drive across the city, which left Hector on the verge of throwing up.

His face was almost as white as his clean shirt as he was introduced to Yul and the whole of his staff, who had congregated around a giant circular table. A sea of smiling faces made it very clear that he and John were honoured guests.

Amid the constant babble, an endless parade of small dishes of food appeared in front of him on the rotating table. He forced himself to take a nibble from each, even though their strange smells caused an upsurge of nausea. Thankfully, John Elland kept the conversation going while he tried to smile and nod in the right places.

Miraculously, he got through the meal without being sick, but back at the hotel, his upset stomach, and the constant whirring of the drinks fridge, wouldn't allow him to sleep.

*

He was lying in the dark, in the foetal position, wishing he were dead, when two sounds invaded simultaneously. One was the ringing of the bedside telephone, the other a series of knocking noises coming from outside the building. He grabbed the phone and found the bedside light.

A woman's voice said: 'Good morning Mr Snodd. Miss Gonzalez is waiting for you in reception.'

Panic. 'Thank you.' He leapt out of bed, looking at his watch. Seven o'clock. What time did they start here? He didn't remember arranging to be picked up at seven. John Elland would be all ready and smart and waiting impatiently...Christ!

He flung open the curtains. In the semi darkness of dawn he could make out 20 or so men chipping away with hammers and chisels on a flat roof about five floors below his room. Beyond them he saw armed security guards taking up posts outside a large superstore.

A fast shave, face splash, teeth rub on the towel, and ten minutes later he was breathing heavily in the reception area. John Elland was deep in conversation with Leni, who looked so small and delicate beside him.   Although her mouth was smiling, Hector noticed that her dark brown eyes weren't. In the hollows beneath them, he recognised the shadows of permanent tiredness. He wanted to kiss them better.

After a cursory greeting, he was left trailing behind as they headed for the waiting car. They were on their way to Yul's office where John Elland was to give the staff a demonstration of a new flooring product, which had been shipped over in advance of their visit.

On their arrival they found that the tiny office was too small to accommodate a demonstration, and decided to move out on to the pavement. Here, John Elland unpacked his sample product, which had apparently been held in customs for three days because they thought the loose, white, polystyrene packing might be drugs, and carried out his demonstration next to an old Chinese man sitting in the gutter cooking a foul smelling fish concoction on an ancient gas stove.

On the other side, hordes of young men mixed mortar and carried it up rickety bamboo scaffolding to bricklayers above. The scaffolding, and Yul's excited staff, protruded out on to the road, but the swarming traffic and heaving pedestrians didn't seem to mind.

Hector stood at the back of the group and took in the sights and sounds of the crazy city. Then he circled around until he could get a better view of Leni, who was watching the demonstration intently.

He watched her every movement. The big eyes concentrating, then blinking with tiredness. The generous lips pursed, then spreading at someone's joke. The pure white teeth flashing in the morning sunlight. The delicate hand brushing back her glorious hair. The flawless olive skin, smooth over high cheekbones. His heart ached with longing. Kathleen Rinaldi had been displaced.

*

The next day, after a fitful sleep, disturbed again by the whirring fridge and the seven o'clock chisel gang, Hector managed to be at reception before Leni arrived. The company car was not at her disposal today. It was being used by Yul who was taking John Elland, alone, to meet some of their mutually important customers. It was known in Manila as 'the bribe drive'.

Leni arrived looking worried and flustered.

'I'm very sorry to be late Mr Snodd. The jeepneys are not very reliable.'

Hector didn't know what to say. He had never been alone in the company of an ordinary woman, let alone a goddess like Leni. He could feel his face going red, his throat drying.

'That's alright,' he eventually managed.

There was a long silence as they waited, each expecting the other to take the lead.

Finally, Leni said, 'What would you like to do today, Mr Snodd?'

'I don't like being called *Mr* Snodd,' Hector blurted. 'Just Hector...sorry. I don't know what to do today. Can you suggest something? Have you not got other work to do...Leni?'

He had hesitated to say her name. Now that he had, it felt wonderful. This was what having a girlfriend must be like. So close, so intimate, so in love. She was listening, paying attention to him, not turning away. His head was swimming.

'Yes, I have a lot of work to do,' Leni said. 'But my job for the next three weeks is to look after you and Mr Elland..........'

'I could help you,' Hector blurted.

Leni hesitated. His behaviour was different to the other domineering westerners she had met. And he had a strange accent. Perhaps he was joking - the British sense of humour was famous. If he was serious, he would probably only get in her way. She was desperate to get out and make some sales.

She was regretting the three-week monetary arrangement she had made with Yul. Mama had serious money problems. If she hadn't been tied up with the two Brits, she could have worked harder and longer and hopefully made more money for Mama. As it was, she was having to rely on Vilma having a good spell, then try to pay her back. Maybe today, however, she could get rid of Mr Snodd and make some sales. He didn't seem to have any plans.

'It is kind of you to offer to help me...Hector,' she said, 'but Yul wouldn't like it. I am supposed to be looking after you. If you have no plans, why don't you relax by the hotel swimming pool or do a bit of shopping. I could go and do some work and call back later this afternoon to see if you are comfortable, and Yul would never know.' She added her sweetest persuasive smile at the end.

Hector was about to agree – he would have agreed if she had asked him to set fire to himself – when the hotel musicians started up in the lobby below.

Immediately, the sweet refrain made him clench his fists, and grit his teeth, to stop himself from crying. Madame Butterfly always had that effect.

'You don't like Madame Butterfly?' Leni asked, having noticed the change in him.

Yes...no,' Hector flustered. 'Do you know this music?'

'Of course,' Leni smiled. It is my favourite Puccini.'

'Can we stay and listen?' Hector asked in a dream. Now he knew Leni was perfect.

'We could go down into the lobby and listen, but we should buy a coffee,' Leni explained.

Hector nodded and followed her. On the large mobile staircase that took them down to the lobby, with the fountain playing, and the music soaring, Hector felt like a king making a grand entrance with his beautiful queen beside him.

Leni guided him to a seat in one of the open plan restaurants. No one seemed to be listening to the music. They were talking, eating, drinking, reading, but not listening. Leni ordered coffee for Hector, but hot chocolate for herself, there being little food value in coffee. She eyed the delicious looking food, but daren't ask, and arranged for the bill to go to Hector's room number.

Hector sat just a few yards from the musicians, enthralled, ignoring his coffee. He had heard this wonderful music only on tape before. To see the violinists move in unison, feel the glowing golden sound wrap around him like a warm blanket, was indescribable. He started to shake inside.

'They seem good,' he said, trying to distract himself from his emotions.

'They are part of the Manila Symphony Orchestra,' Leni explained. 'They do this to make a living in between concerts.'

Suddenly, Hector wanted to jump up to tell everybody to be quiet. How dare they speak when professional musicians were playing great music. How dare they ignore them. What else on earth, in life, could be as important as this. A master composer was ...superior. They knew the truth. They knew how we felt. They brought us messages...from...? They understood. They must be listened to.

The lobby chatter, created by the hotel's pre-dominantly western guests, continued. Now the orchestra started on Rachmaninov's 'Vocalise'.

Hector glanced across the table at Leni. She sat straight backed, head high, watching the orchestra - a glorious sight. She sensed his gaze and turned.

'Do you know this?' Hector whispered.

Leni smiled, and whispered back, 'Vocalise... Rachmaninov.'

It should have pleased him. It should have delighted him. It did for a second. But then the realisation that she had become even more desirable, and that he could never have her or someone like her, pulled a familiar dark cloud into his mind.

He tried not to feel sorry for himself. He turned away from the orchestra, away from Leni, and looked out through the window at the morning's dazzling brightness. The sun made him squint...close his eyes, reminded him of his tiredness...then his weakness...his social incompetence, his ugliness.

When he turned back and opened his eyes, tears discharged themselves. They had taken on a life of their own, tired of being held back.

He reached for his handkerchief.

'Is it the music?' Leni whispered. 'It often makes me cry, it is so beautiful.'

'Yes...it always does this,' Hector sniffed. It was only a white lie - he did usually cry when listening to 'Vocalise.'

Leni sensed his lie. There was something in his tone, his manner, his sad eyes that she recognised. She had seen much suffering, though never in western eyes.

'I'll get you some water,' she said, and left the table quickly.

She had left him alone deliberately, to give him time to recover his composure. Men didn't like an audience when they broke down. She had seen her father and brothers walk into dark corners when lips began to tremble and eyes moisten.

When she returned, the music had finished and Hector was standing at the main door, apparently recovered.

'Can I come with you to work,' he pleaded. 'I won't

get in the way. Maybe I could help you. Maybe we could talk about music.'

Now she was unable to refuse him. He had touched the soft centre that lay beneath her toughness. Yet, even now, her business-like brain reminded her to spend most of the time picking his brains about HD3000, as she had been ordered.

As they stepped out into the wall of heat, Leni opened her briefcase and took out a piece of cardboard of the same shape and size. She held it over her head, as did many of the people passing by. Like them, a sunshade umbrella was low on her priority list.

*

Hector spent most of the day trying to keep up with her as she dashed around the city calling at offices and factories. At times, she ran and jumped from one jeepney to another as she tried to make as many calls as possible. Only during a short lunch break in Jollybees, which he was glad to pay for, did he manage to talk to her about music. Even then, she soon changed the subject to HD3000. Surprisingly, he found it easy to respond to her endless questions about his special concrete, and watching her listening intently gave his confidence a boost.

He spent most of the day searching for shade as he waited for her outside her clients' workplaces. On more than one occasion he was questioned by armed security guards and asked to move on. Eventually, he found it easier and more welcoming to wait in nearby shops.

At the end of the day he was exhausted, but Leni looked remarkably fresh. She was about to escort him back to his hotel when he announced: 'I've bought something for you. I hope you don't mind.'

He gave her a small parcel from which she extracted a small colourful umbrella. Her hand went to her mouth in surprise. Even though she had been pursued by many westerners, none of them had ever bought her a present. They always assumed you were grateful just because they were hunting you. She sensed that this was a genuine gift, not a prelude to seduction. He seemed too shy for that.

'It's wonderful,' she said, giggling like a schoolgirl. 'It's beautiful.' She spun it around above her head, and swivelled on her toes like a ballet dancer.

Hector had never seen such a lovely sight.

'Thank you very much, Hector,' she beamed. 'I will use it every day, and I will take good care of it. Now I'm no longer a cardboard girl.' She giggled and smiled and admired the umbrella from every angle.

Her reaction surprised Hector. That such a small gift could generate such excitement and pleasure was unexpected. It had changed her from an efficient businesswoman into a charming, giggling, schoolgirl. For the first time he was seeing what lay beneath her tough veneer.

In accordance with Filipino custom, Leni now felt obliged to reciprocate with a gift or service, so instead of returning to the hotel, she invited Hector to her home for tea.

*

Vilma had just arrived home when Leni and Hector appeared.

'Look what I've got,' Leni smiled, flashing the umbrella into action. 'Hector bought it for me. Isn't it wonderful.'

Vilma took the umbrella from Leni and examined it as though it was precious jewellery. Holding her breath and smiling excitedly, she opened and closed it repeatedly. Finally, she giggled and the two girls embraced each other in a fit of happiness. Hector looked on in wonderment.

His next shock came when Leni pulled an upturned plastic container from under a steel shelf and invited him to sit on it, and then moved two paces to where a kettle sat on a small Calor gas stove.

Only then did he realise that this was their home. He had thought they were calling in the shed to pick something up before entering the nearby house, which itself was incredibly small and humble. A few dresses hanging from a string line caught his eye and confirmed that he was not mistaken. He felt ashamed and guilty. It was no bigger or better than one of his uncle's hen huts. He had always thought that life on the croft was basic, but this! The contrast with the luxury of his hotel now seemed obscene. And yet, Leni seemed quite at home in either. She made no apology for her home; she was not ashamed of it.

He watched her make three cups of tea, a long process involving fetching water in a plastic container, and saving the spent tea leaves into another. All the time, Leni and Vilma smiled huge smiles, giving the impression that this was the happiest moment of their lives.

Leni presented the tea to Hector as though it was

a special gift and then she and Vilma sat on their upturned containers, forming a close triangle with Hector, knees almost touching.

They drank in silence, the two women deferring to Hector, expecting the western man to dominate. Hector didn't know what to say and stared nervously at the floor. When, occasionally, he raised his head, he was met by beautiful smiles, and puzzled glances between them.

Suddenly, Hector got to his feet. The only way to end this embarrassment was to go. 'I'd better be getting back to the hotel', he mumbled. 'Thanks...thanks for the tea. It was nice...'

Had he been a Filipino, Leni would have been insulted by the abruptness of his visit, and assumed that he didn't like their company. But she was beginning to understand that, for a westerner, Hector was incredibly shy and reticent, and so she felt sorry for him.

'I'll come with you,' she said. 'You won't know the way or find the right jeepneys.'

Half an hour later they were back in the lobby of the luxurious hotel. Hector was aching to invite her to his room, and to tell the rest of the world to go away.

He wanted to take her away from that horrible shed, look after her, protect her, hold her. He wanted to buy her lots of things to make her happy, always smiling. He wanted to buy her a meal in one of the posh lobby restaurants.

But he knew it was no use. He didn't have the nerve to ask. And she wouldn't be interested. Instead, he would order a room service meal and go to bed early.

'Hector, I'll show you the layout at the Hyatt Regency tomorrow,' Leni was saying.

Hector was still in his own worrying mind. 'Right... what's happening there...what's the Hyatt Regency,' he said, absently.

'It's the hotel where you are giving your talk,' Leni explained.

'My talk?' Hector was paying attention again. 'What talk?'

Leni looked puzzled. 'Your talk to the government engineers about HD3000. Did nobody tell you it was tomorrow night?'

'Nobody told me I was doing a talk,' Hector panicked. 'I've never done one before. Where is it? What time? Who'll be there? I thought I was just sitting in at a meeting with them with John Elland. Who arranged this?'

Leni gave a rueful smile. This was typical of Yul. He loved to put on a big show. He had invited 50 government engineers to dinner in the penthouse suite of the best hotel in town, to be followed by presentations by his own company, then by Amtex, then by Hector for BNFL. And, typically, he had forgotten to tell the people involved.

She could sense the panic in Hector's voice. 'Have you got anything prepared?' she asked calmly.

'No...I wasn't expecting. I've just got a technical data sheet. Who's going to be there...how many....'

'Maybe I can help you prepare something,' Leni offered quietly. She was beginning to understand that Hector was very insecure. 'Maybe we can turn your data sheet into a speech. Is it in your room?'

'Yes.'

'Let's go,' Leni said, and held out her hand as if to a child.

Hector took hold, and trembled. He was actually touching her. Such softness, such warmth, so small. This was probably the greatest moment of his life. And yet, she was leading him to what promised to be the worst.

Up in his room, they sat side-by-side studying the technical data sheet, shoulders almost touching. Hector could hardly breathe. Being alone with a beautiful woman in a luxury hotel in a strange country, preparing to make his first public speech, was more than his mind could cope with.

It escaped into a dream-like state, and participated from a distance, as Leni gradually took over. She wrote down suggestions for introductions, flip chart displays, overhead projector drawings on acetate. She even ordered some food and drinks from room service. Hector simply listened and agreed and fell deeper in love with her.

Suddenly, she was saying something reassuring as she glided out of the room, and he was left alone, staring.

*

The following day, John Elland and the company car reappeared, and Hector spent the day sitting beside the driver while Elland and Leni shared the back seat. They lurched around Manila visiting customers and projects. From their intervening conversations it was clear that Elland had been told about that night's presentation at the Hyatt Regency and was well prepared, and confident as usual. In mid afternoon, Leni suggested that they call at the hotel to see if preparations were complete for the evening.

The Hyatt Regency proved to be even grander than the Sheraton, the huge interior being finished almost entirely in cool marble. As the lift reached the penthouse suite, Hector's stomach was churning. They walked into a vast room, its large windows providing a panorama of the city. Hector's heart almost stopped.

Beyond the many tables laid ready for dinner, was a raised table laid for six on which sat three microphones. On one side of the table stood a podium with a microphone mounted, and on the other side a screen and projector. On the wall behind the table, a very large banner proclaimed in red letters:

WELCOME TO PRODUCT SYMPOSIUM
AMTEX U.K. LTD WITH
WAYNE INDUSTRIAL SUPPLY INC.
SPEAKER: MR HECTOR SNODD
CHIEF ENGINEER, BNFL.
HYATT REGENCY, MANILA

Hector spotted a toilet sign, dashed for it, and managed to throw up accurately into a hand basin. He was literally sick with worry. Why had nobody told him about this? He wouldn't have come if he had known. He couldn't possibly stand up there and deliver a speech.

White faced, he returned to the room. Elland was engaged in conversation with hotel staff. Leni was fussing about the top table. He approached her and said quietly, 'what is going on, Leni? I'm not the chief engineer of BNFL. I can't do this. I can't make a speech.'

Leni glanced at the banner, then whispered conspiratorially, 'It's Yul trying to impress his guests. You will have to make a speech, Hector. It's not as hard as you think. I'll help you. If you put a drawing up on the screen, that will distract their eyes from you. I'll work the projector. Then I'll sit at the table directly in front of you, and you must only look at me and speak to me. Just give a brief introduction then read the information off the data sheet. Nobody has seen that yet. Don't worry, most people are only here for the free dinner, they won't be listening carefully.'

*

A few hours later, having produced a simple drawing on acetate of an application where HD3000 would be used, and having consumed the entire spirit content of his room's drinks fridge, Hector was back at the Hyatt Regency sitting at the top table alongside Yul and Elland.

Dinner was over, more drinks had been consumed, the white-shirted, brown-faced, guests had stashed away their gifts from Yul, and now sat facing the podium where Leni was re-welcoming them on behalf of Wayne Industrial Supply Inc. Even in a cheap blue cotton dress, she radiated beauty and confidence. Hector was amazed at how she and Vilma could be totally at ease in these five-star surroundings when they lived in such poverty.

After giving a short talk about her company, during which she praised Yul's leadership, as instructed, Leni introduced John Elland. He gave a confident talk on his company's range of products ending it with a brief introduction to HD3000, then called on Hector to come forward to give his talk on the unique properties of the product.

Hector rose from the table in a daze. It was all happening to somebody else. He saw Leni take his drawing to the projector, and noticed the sea of faces swivel to watch the image on the screen. On reaching the podium, he stopped his hands shaking by gripping the edges.

By the time he had placed the data sheet on the podium, Leni was back in a seat directly in front of him. She smiled and nodded encouragement. Hector concentrated his drunken stare at her then heard somebody say, loudly, 'Good evening ladies and gentlemen, my name is Hector Snodd.'

The same person went on to read out the whole of the HD3000 technical data sheet, after which there was silence, followed by stuttering applause led by Leni.

Hector floated back to the top table. Suddenly, people in the audience were standing up and asking technical questions about HD3000. Yul passed a microphone along the table to Hector so that he could answer. Fortunately, he knew his stuff, and somehow managed to give coherent answers to the blurred audience.

When it was all over he swayed to the toilet, and threw up again. When he came out, still feeling nauseous, Leni was waiting for him.

'You did well,' she said, putting a comforting arm around his shoulders.

Nobody had ever shown him such kindness; nobody had ever touched him. He thought he was going to burst into tears. Instead, he fainted.

*

The rest of his time in Manila was less stressful. Giving that talk, albeit in a drunken dream, had given him more confidence. Apparently, it had gone down quite well. Leni had been right. The audience were easily pleased. And they were quite used to seeing westerners fainting and throwing up as the local water and bugs took their toll.

He became more relaxed as he accompanied Elland and Leni on their visits to projects and customers. Eventually, he was even called in to offer advice on some concrete erosion problems the water companies had when tropical downpours swept stones down culverts, and his suggestions were well received.

He trailed around with them in the heat and the squalor rather than sit at the hotel poolside because he wanted to be near Leni. Every day she seemed more perfect; every night he closed his eyes thinking about her.

He had taken to staying in the hotel at night as Elland went with Yul on a tour of Manila's nightspots. One night had been enough for him. Instead of lusting after the girls, he had felt sorry for them. They looked so young and frail; he wanted to take them away to look after them. If only he could do that with Leni.

As the final few days approached, he grew more and more depressed at the thought of not seeing Leni again. He knew she couldn't possibly be interested in him, but he had to let her know how he felt about her. He must not leave without telling her how much he loved her. He would get drunk, that was the answer.

Two days before they were due to leave, he told Elland and Leni that he was going to have a day by the pool. Instead he went shopping and bought Leni a small battery operated radio cassette so that she could listen to their music. He couldn't find a shop that sold up-to-date classical music and had to make do with an old compilation tape of opera duets. At least it contained his favourite - the love duet from Madame Butterfly.

That evening, having spent the whole afternoon rehearsing speeches, while bathing, shaving, and generally trying to make the best of his appearance, and fortified with a few whiskies, he took a taxi to Leni's home.

The door of the shed was opened by Vilma. She didn't beam her usual smile as she invited him in. Leni sat with her back to them, head bowed. She didn't turn around. Vilma went to her and put her arm around her shoulders. 'Leni's brother has been arrested,' she announced over her shoulder. 'Leni is upset.'

'I'm sorry,' Hector said, feeling completely inadequate again, not knowing what to say or do. 'Shall I go?'

Leni spun around. 'No ...no ...stay ...I am alright.' Her beautiful eyes glinted with tears. She attempted a smile.

Hector couldn't bear it. 'I've brought you a present,' he blurted out, his voice too loud in the tiny space, the alcohol in charge.

'Thank you,' Leni said wearily.

Vilma said, 'I'm going to see if my uncle can spare some milk and I will make us a cup of tea.'

After she had gone, Hector took over her seat. He smiled at Leni. She bowed her head. There was a long silence.

'Sorry about your brother,' Hector said. 'What...?'

'He was caught stealing. A security guard shot him in the leg. He's not a bad boy. Now he'll go to prison and he won't get any medical help unless he has money.' She was on the verge of tears again.

'I can give you money,' Hector said, quickly, desperate to take the sorrow from her eyes.

'No....I didn't mean...I wasn't begging...'

'How much does he need?'

'I don't know...at least 5,000 pesos. Please forget it, Hector, it is not your problem.'

Hector did a quick mental calculation. It was only 75 pounds. He took all the notes from his back pocket, and counted them on the floor.

'No!' Leni insisted.

'Three thousand, one hundred and twenty five; I will bring you the rest tomorrow.' He forced the notes into Leni's hands.

'I can't take this,' Leni pleaded, thrusting the notes back at him. 'You are very kind, but I could never pay you back.'

Hector shuffled his seat out of range. Suddenly, the alcohol gave him the inspiration and the courage. 'You could let me look after you,' he said firmly.

The words hung in the air, like the dresses in the corner, waiting. Leni looked puzzled. 'I'm not sure what you mean, Hector?'

'You could come and live with me, and I would look after you,' Hector blurted, head down, eyes closed, fists clenched behind his back, waiting for rejection.

'You mean, go back to England with you?' Leni asked, disbelievingly.

'Scotland.'

'But I couldn't do that, Hector...'

'Why not?'

'Well...I cannot leave Mama and my family; they need my support. And, I have a religion that says it is sinful to live with a man outside of marriage.'

'But that's what I meant,' Hector insisted urgently, impatient with his clumsiness. 'I want us to get married. We could send money to your mother from Scotland.'

Leni was stunned to silence. He was proposing marriage, yet they didn't know each other; they hadn't even kissed, or been on a date? Maybe he was just like the other westerners who came in their thousands to pick up a Filipino bride as though shopping for a bargain car to drive and ride.

Well, she wasn't one of those girls and she would let him know it. And yet! Had she any right to feel superior? She had lost her virginity. Her chances of marrying a decent Filipino man were practically nil. Perhaps this timid, unattractive, but kind little man was the best chance she would ever get. He was offering to give money to her brother and Mama and he hadn't even met them. That was always the trouble with westerners - they had money. And in the Philippines, money is everything.

Now she realised that she was just like all the other pathetic Filipino women who have to chose between a future of unending struggle in their own country or risk selling themselves to westerners in the hope that life in their country will be better.

Most of them did it so that they could send money back to their families, which is why mothers were always encouraging their daughters to accept the offers. It was nearly always about money, not love.

She certainly didn't love Hector; there was no physical attraction. But she did like him. He seemed kind and gentle and he loved music, and best of all, he wasn't huge. She had learned from an early age that beggars cannot be choosers. Now, instead of following her initial impulse to reject his proposal, she decided to pursue the matter further.

'Thank you for your proposal, Hector' she said, finally, and very formally. 'You do me a great honour. But please forgive me for being practical. In the Philippines, we have to be. I assume you want to marry me because you need a wife, and you find me attractive. Can you not find an attractive wife in Scotland?'

'I don't need a wife,' Hector pleaded. 'I just love you. I've never met anyone so beautiful. I want to take care of you. You shouldn't have to live in a place like...'

'Do you own a house?'

'Yes...it's not very...'

'And a car?'

'Yes.'

'Would you sign a contract promising to send Mama 500 pesos every week?'

'Yes,' Hector agreed, even before he had worked out that it was only seven pounds something. He couldn't believe that she was asking these questions. She was actually taking his proposal seriously.

'We could send her 1,000 pesos,' he announced eagerly, 'and we could come back and visit her every year... or send her the money to come and see us.' The sound of 'we' and 'us' thrilled him.

'We could send money for Vilma as well,' he added, desperately. He would fund every relative and friend she had if only she would come with him.

With a hundred more questions still to ask, Leni now knew that she had no choice but to accept his proposal. The family always came first. A thousand pesos a week would give Mama and the children a much better life. She could picture the look on her face, the relief, the tears of joy and hope and gratitude.

'I will be pleased to marry you, Hector,' she said, simply. 'But we have two problems. First, I cannot go to Scotland with you without first being married. It would not be honourable. So, we would need to be married tomorrow. Second, I cannot leave without saying goodbye to Mama and my family on Mindoro, and that is a three day round trip.'

Hector had never been so focussed in his life. His adrenalin was flying. The impossible had happened. The most beautiful girl in the world had agreed to marry him. *Him!*

The shock brought clarity to his swirling brain. He must stay calm. He mustn't grab her. He must solve these problems.

One of the problems solved itself. He didn't have enough money with him to buy her a flight to Scotland.

He shuffled his seat closer to her and took hold of her tiny hand. His heart was thumping, his face burning.

'Why don't we get married tomorrow,' he rasped, hoarsely, his mouth dry with heat and tension, 'and then you go to see your family, and I'll fly home and send you the money for you to follow me later. Do you know anywhere where we could get married tomorrow?'

'What strange people westerners are,' Leni thought. 'They don't ask questions about virginity. They don't seem to care about morals or religion. They seem to believe in nothing except money. They value things as much as people, and treat them the same.'

'We could try Father Botaro. He does lots of quick weddings,' she said.

The shed door handle rattled loudly, and Vilma came in carrying an old bean tin half full of milk. She stopped, open-mouthed, when she saw them holding hands.

'I am getting married to Hector tomorrow,' Leni announced.

Vilma dropped the tin, and the milk surged across the floorboards, percolated through the joints, and fed the loitering cockroaches.

*

The next day, Father Botaro managed to fit them in at 4.30. Leni wore Vilma's newest dress. Yul gave her away. John Elland was best man. Vilma cried.

At the end of the ceremony, Hector kissed a woman for the first time in his life. Still trembling, he was ushered, along with John Elland, into the company car to be hurtled towards the airport where the 6.15 flight took him home to anxiously wait for his new bride.

Chapter 12

It was a perfect day for Tessa Coleman. Early morning rain had left small clouds hanging low above the lakes and in the valleys, floating about like islands of smoke. Above 2,000 ft, mist screened the fells, but she knew from experience, and a quick listen to the local weather forecast, that there was a chance of the sun breaking through by lunchtime.

This was her kind of weather. The kind that brings mood and drama, making a masterpiece of an already transcendent landscape. She liked to capture that magic moment when the sun breaks through the mist and lights up a mountain-top or sends a shaft of light down to a cloud-filled valley, or best of all, to a precipitous crag face.

Her watercolour paintings were full of swirling mists, dramatic clouds, and shafts of sunlight highlighting the main subject, usually a high crag face. Not for her the gentle, pastoral views of the Lake District that dominated the towns' gift shops, pandering to the tourists who viewed it all from the windows of their cars.

She was a climber as well as an artist. Her paintings were born of her love of the high places where she set her small, athletic frame against the might of the mountain. There was nothing more fulfilling than climbing a difficult crag, then capturing it forever on paper. Both were experienced through your fingertips. A lack of concentration, determination or skill, and both ended in disaster, albeit with greatly differing consequences. She enjoyed the challenge; she loved taking risks; it made her alive.

Winter was her favourite time, when rust-coloured bracken and reflecting snow added yet more colour and drama. Being on the tops, in the snow, in the silence, with only her sketchbook for company, was her idea of heaven. Her winter sketches provided her with the backbone of a year's work, which she completed in her studio, an ex-post office in the village of Patterdale, overlooking Ullswater.

Today, she was heading for Dale Head, from where she hoped to capture the sun casting dramatic light into a cloud-filled Newlands valley. To give herself as much sketching time as possible, she decided to drive up to the top of Honister Pass, and take the short route from there.

She parked her car at the top of Honister Pass, in the slate quarry car park, and armed with her sketchbook and climbing rope, started the easy ascent of Dale Head's south-facing slope.

Within an hour she reached the summit, a simple mound with a magnificent cairn marking the highest point. She was planning to include the cairn in the foreground of her composition, sitting as it does only a few paces from the precipitous north face drop into Newlands valley.

The valley was just discernable through the mist, and the sun had yet to break through, but it still looked promising. Tessa sat with her back resting against the cairn, looking down the valley, absorbing the atmosphere, the mood. This was more important to her than graphic accuracy.

She was still absorbing her surroundings, in preparation for sketching, when she heard someone sniff behind her. Turning, she saw a small man standing a few paces away. He appeared to be carrying a small sketch pad. She assumed he was a fellow artist.

Chapter 13

'Don't tell me, Margaret,' Ben said to the middle-aged woman standing behind the counter in Keswick Police Station. 'You've had three missing cats, two thefts from cars, two sprained ankles on the fells, the Chief Constable's ran off with his secretary, and you've won the lottery.'

'Spot on,' Margaret said, straight-faced, while pushing slips of paper towards him.

Ben was making his regular call at the station to pick up the week's events, to include in his column in the Tribune. He glanced at the mountain rescue slip. 'MR's been busy,' he noted.

'Aye - usual charities nonsense,' Margaret said.

Ben knew she was referring to the annual mass invasion of well-meaning charity organisations doing sponsored walks and climbs. They might be saving the whale, but they were eroding the fells and making life difficult for villagers as they clogged up the narrow valley lanes with their parked vehicles. A lot of them were inexperienced on the fells so there was always plenty of action for the mountain rescue team when they were visiting.

'Nothing too serious,' Ben observed, reading the slip. 'Have they all gone yet?'

'I think so,' Margaret said. 'But the team's getting no rest. They've just been called out again. There's a woman missing. I think she's a local artist.'

'Thanks,' Ben said, hurriedly, as he took his leave.

He wanted to get to the mountain rescue headquarters as soon as possible to find out who it was. As a member of the Keswick Society of Art himself, he knew most of the local artists, and had interviewed many of them for a series of articles he was writing for a county magazine.

A brisk ten-minute walk took him through Keswick's narrow streets to the headquarters by the lake, and a dash up the stairs brought him, breathlessly, to the controller's office. As ever, Ian had his head down, filling-in some paperwork.

'Good morning Ian,' Ben breathed. 'Do you mind telling me who you are you looking for?'

Ian didn't raise his head. 'Somebody called Coleman. She's a climber.'

Ben knew immediately. Tessa was a leading light in the Art Society - exhibition organiser, and probably its best artist. He had interviewed her last year for the magazine and been captivated by her climbing exploits and zest for life, as well as her painting.

'Should know better than be on her own,' Ian mumbled. 'We've just got rid of that charity lot. Save this, help that. Now we've got a local behaving like a prat.'

'How long has she been missing?' Ben asked.

'Could be a few days. They found old mail in her flat when the alarm was raised. Looks like she didn't tell anybody where she was going.'

'So you don't know where to look!'

'Nope,' Ian sighed, resignedly. 'We've put out a general call to all the other teams to come and help.'

'I'd like to help,' Ben said. 'I know her. Is there anything I can do without getting in the way?'

Ian shook his head, then hesitated. 'Her car is missing. You could help to look for that. Hopefully, it will lead us to the area she went climbing in.'

He glanced at his notes. 'It's a red Astra, Reg. number J658 TEF.' He wrote it down on a scrap of paper and handed it to Ben. 'We're searching the central climbing areas, so it would be best if you concentrated on the northern outer peripheries. Thanks.'

*

For the next two days, Ben spent every spare hour scouring the highways and byways of the northern limits of the national park, concentrating on the places where a climber like Tessa might park her car before setting off to the high crags.

Throughout his search he phoned in to MR control to let Ian know the car parking areas he had covered. At the end of two unsuccessful days for both him and the mountain rescue teams, he filed the following report at the offices of the Tribune:

MISSING CLIMBER

Fears are growing for a local climber and artist who has not been seen for more than a week.

Tessa Coleman is still missing in spite of a two-day search by members of several mountain rescue teams, including teams from Teesside and Ribblesdale as well as from other parts of the Lake District,

co-ordinated by the Keswick Mountain Rescue Team.
In spite of two days intensive search by
150 volunteers, 17 search and rescue dogs and
an RAF helicopter, Mrs Coleman was not found.
Sergeant Bill Unwin of Keswick police said the
searchers returned on Friday evening extremely tired
after their long hours on the fells.
It has been estimated that the search has
involved more than three and a half thousand man
hours, many spent looking for Mrs Coleman's car.
It is hoped that the discovery of her red Astra,
Registration No. J658 TEF, will pinpoint her
location within the national park. Police are again
reminding people not to go on to the fells without
informing someone of their destination, and, preferably,
not to go alone.
Mrs Coleman, who lives in Patterdale, is 5 ft. 2 ins.
tall and has distinctive long brown hair. She is
a well known local artist specialising in paintings of the
high crags she climbs, being a member of the Patterdale
Climbing Club.
It is assumed that she left her studio, early last
week, to set off on one of her many painting expeditions
to the high fells.
Keswick police would like anyone with a lead
as to her whereabouts to contact them on Keswick 79003.

Two days later, the Manager of the recently re-opened Honister Pass Slate Quarry Company reported finding the red Astra in his car park, tucked away behind a large stack of newly palletised slates, which had obviously hidden the car from the view of the search teams.

From the car park, the re-assembled search teams spread out into the three main climbing zones in that area - around Great Gable, Haystacks, and Dale Head. Again, after three more days searching, they were unsuccessful.

Ben was about to submit his piece to the Tribune, confirming these facts, when a phone call from Bill Unwin told him that she had been found by two climbers.

Follow-up enquiries at the police station and mountain rescue headquarters enabled him to file the following report for the Tribune.

MISSING CLIMBER MYSTERY SOLVED

A disturbing Lake District mystery was brought to a conclusion this week with the identification of a body, found on Dale Head by climbers at the weekend, as that of 39-year-old Tessa Coleman from Patterdale. Two full-scale search operations during the past two weeks had failed to find Mrs Coleman, a well-known local artist, who had apparently set out on a climbing/ sketching expedition and failed to return. Despite an extensive sweep of the area by mountain rescue teams from all over the north of England, 5 ft. 2 ins. tall Mrs Coleman was never found.

However, on Wednesday two climbers from the Liverpool area spotted a body on a narrow ledge about 340 feet from the summit of Dale Head.

They notified the authorities and PC Adrian Low, a member of Keswick Mountain Rescue Team, was winched by helicopter on to the ledge to confirm that what

*the climbers had seen was indeed the body of a woman,
which had been there for some time.*
*The following day, members of the Keswick Rescue
Team returned to Dale Head and recovered the body,
leaving the police with the task of formally identifying it
as that of Mrs Coleman.*
*It was evident that Mrs Coleman had fallen over steep
ground on to the narrow ledge.*
*Police are currently trying to contact relatives of Mrs
Coleman to obtain confirmation of identity.*

Ben finished the piece with moist eyes. She had been so full of life, so friendly, so vital; even inspiring when giving her risk-taking painting demonstrations to the Art Society. And, he had inadvertently seen the photographs taken at the scene of death, temporarily unguarded on Ian's desk. Nature is indeed pitiless. To the ravens and carrion crows, she was just another carcass. Both of her beautiful brown eyes had gone. One socket had been left intact; the other had suffered severe attack leaving a void through to the brain filled with maggots. Dried blood and lesions around the mouth, tongue and ears told of pecking and tearing. Her long brown hair was matted with blood.

As she lay on her back, arms and legs spread wide, she looked like a discarded scarecrow, though her clothes were incongruously clean and tidy. Through all this horror, Ben could still see her sweet, youthful, face shining through, and he kept this image with him as he tore himself from the photographs.

As he did so, his brain flashed: *'Something's wrong.'* There was nothing more. He searched for it, but it wouldn't come.

Back at the police station, Bill Unwin told him that Tessa had been found with her rope unused and her sketch materials still in her backpack. Obviously, she hadn't been climbing or drawing when she fell.

'She must have fallen from the top,' Bill surmised. 'She must have slipped or tripped while looking over the edge. Even the most experienced...'

'Have you had many falls off Dale Head,' Ben interrupted.

'None that I can remember; MR have all the records.' Bill turned his back and blew his nose into his handkerchief. He was a big softy at heart. 'You never get used to this,' he said.

*

Ben arrived home that night planning to check the MR records the next day. His antennae were twitching. Something wasn't right.

Helen came in late as usual. She looked exhausted.

'I've booked us a holiday,' she announced in a tone that rejected debate.

Ben held out his arms and took her into a big cuddle. She still managed to smell nice even after 12 hours in a sticky, chlorine filled atmosphere. He felt at home against her soft cheek.

'When and where?' he whispered

'Tomorrow. Sutherland.'

Ben watched her slump into the armchair beside the fireplace. 'Good,' he said.

Chapter 14

After Cumbria, Sutherland is their favourite county. Its unpopulated, barren, wilderness of moorland, rock, and water is the perfect place to escape from work, renew your natural senses.

Its grotesquely shaped bare rock mountains, suddenly rearing up from bleak, heathered plains, looking like giant thimbles, seem to have been transported from the Arizona desert.

When all these elements reach the sea, they produce scenery of stunning natural beauty. Here, the craggy, luminous, rock plunges steeply into pristine water, made light green by unsullied white sand beaches. Massive sea lochs, hewn over centuries, play host to wild life and nothing else.

*

Ben allowed himself a yawn and a smile as he passed a sign saying 'Dornoch 4 miles'. He had been driving a long time since picking up the motor home in Edinburgh, but he was delighted to be back. He glanced at Helen, to share the moment. She was still asleep in the passenger seat, catching flies as her mouth lolled open, ridding herself of exhaustion.

Though still enthusiastic and motivated at work, she had simply ran out of energy after a long tiring spell of teaching courses, and the inevitable staffing problems.

As the motor home buzzed across the bridge over the spectacular Dornoch Firth, Ben could no longer contain himself. He nudged Helen. She moaned. He nudged her again. She opened her eyes.

'We're here,' he exclaimed.

Helen slowly shuffled into an upright position and surveyed the moving scene like a drowsy, brainless kitten. 'Lovely,' she purred, and sank back into oblivion.

*

Helen was back to normal the next morning. She took the wheel and started singing: 'ye tak the high road' as they pulled out of Dornoch. Ben joined in the discordant duet, and settled back to enjoy the scenery from the motor home's high perspective.

After picking up some supplies in the east coast village of Helmsdale they took the A897 for a diagonal cross-country drive to the north coast. An hour later, they arrived at the north coast village of Melvich, turned west on the A836 coast road, and soon were pulling-in to the Strathy Inn for a cup of coffee and the last chance to use a civilized toilet.

After coffee, they left the motor home in the pub's car park, and walked the three miles to Strathy Point headland: past the dotted, lonely, crofts, to stand on the cliff tops and feel the eagerness of the North Atlantic wind.

The seals were still there, lounging on the rocks below, the gulls were still agitating along the cliff face, and along the coast to the east, in the distance, the Dounreay nuclear plant still looked inappropriate.

Back at the motor home, lunch had to be jock pie and beans, then it was off again along the A836. In late afternoon they arrived at their first major highlight - the Kyle of Tongue. The massive sea loch, penetrating deep into the interior, opened its vast mouth to shout a greeting to the arctic, lurking somewhere beyond the horizon in cold infinity.

Driving around the Kyle's coastline they eventually came to the scattered community of Talmine. They parked up for the night on a grassy knoll above a pristine beach, and went for a stroll.

On their way back to the motor home, they were enticed into the village pub by the sound of traditional Scottish music.

A large, bearded man was playing the piano accordion and a tall, thin man was playing the fiddle. Three regulars, judging by their glazed stares, propped up the bar, and a group of men were gathered in conversation around a large table in a corner of the dingy room.

Ben risked a pint of processed beer, there being no real ale on tap. Helen sat with a dry sherry. She tapped her feet in time with the music and got into the swing of things, while Ben, grimacing at every gulp of his beer, found himself listening to snatches of the conversation going on in the corner.

He heard them talking about 'hill familiarisation', 'casualty evacuation', 'stretcher rigging', 'first aid'. From this, he gleaned that the men had been carrying out a training rescue that afternoon, and they were now comparing notes, and discussing good and bad practice. Clearly, they were part of a local mountain rescue team.

Ben's next trip to the bar, this time for two non-risky drams, coincided with the arrival at his side of one of the men from the corner table. He was young, wiry, weather-beaten, with strong hands impatiently waving a ten-pound note.

'Six halves here, Willy,' he shouted to the landlord, who had temporarily disappeared to serve someone in the snug.

'Had a good day?' Ben enquired, conversationally.

'Aye.'

'Thirsty work - lugging stretchers about.'

'Aye.'

'Is there a collection box in the pub? I'd like to contribute.' That did the trick.

'Aye. Over there, at the end of the bar.'

Ben followed his directions to see that the box was being obscured by the well-worn Harris Tweed elbow of one of the regulars. Ben sauntered across, put some pound coins in, and returned to the young man.

'Thanks,' the young man said. 'On holiday?'

'Yes,' Ben said. 'Just a few days. I couldn't help overhearing. What rescue team are you in?'

'Assynt. We're from the base at Thurso. We cover the north coast area. The main team operate out of the headquarters at Inchnadamph near Lochinver.'

'So, how many's in your team at Thurso?' Ben asked.

'Fourteen at the moment!'

'And have you got a full set-up, with base control and all that?'

The young man laughed. 'Naw...we've just got an equipment store behind the police station. It's all controlled from Inchnadamph. Mind, it's not much better there. Just a garage with a store and a common room in it. Are you in a rescue team yourself?'

'No ...no,' Ben smiled, pleased that the young man thought he looked young enough and fit enough. 'I'm from the Lake District. I work for a little newspaper there. I do a weekly report on the local rescue team's call outs.'

The landlord returned and took their orders.

'My name's Ben, by the way,' Ben said, holding out his hand. 'I've got a lot of respect for you blokes. You do a great job.'

The young man shook his hand. 'Alec...Alec Gordon. How come a Sassenach gets named after a Scottish mountain?'

'My mother was a Scot.'

'So you can't be all bad,' Alec joked. 'Who's your local rescue team then?'

'Keswick.'

'They must be busy if you have something to report every week.'

'Virtually every week,' Ben corrected. 'It's a very busy holiday area. I don't suppose you're quite as busy up here.'

'No, thank God,' Alec said, gathering the six halves on to a tray. 'I don't suppose we have more than ten incidents a year. Mostly walkers getting lost. And the odd sea cliff rescue, usually over at Dunnet Head. I believe they get very busy down at Glen Coe, but not many people come this far north.'

'Do you get many fatalities?' Ben wasn't sure where the question came from. Something at the back of his mind must have pushed it forward.

Alec held the tray of drinks, and turned to leave the bar. 'There's usually one or two. Usually walkers getting lost in the winter...hypothermia.'

He started walking towards the corner table.

A raised voice came from behind Ben. 'What about that time, three years ago. There was a lot dead that year.'

Obviously, one of the regulars had been listening to their conversation.

Alec returned to pick up his change from the bar. 'Aye, it was a funny year that year right enough.'

'What happened?' Ben asked.

Alec pocketed his change, and stared in recall. 'We had about eight deaths that year. And they weren't the usual walkers getting lost. They were all fallers off crags. All badly damaged. There was some couples.' He shook his head. 'It was bad.'

'Did the doctors or police have anything to say about them?' Ben pressed on.

'How do you mean?'

'You know, when they came out to the scene to certify them.'

'We can't do that up here,' Alec said. 'We don't have enough doctors or police and the distances are too great. We bring the bodies in to the nearest police station, and they call in a doctor for certification.'

'Do you take photographs at the scene?'

'Aye - they go to the police.'

'And, no doubt, you keep a written record of each incident and do an annual incident report.'

'Aye.'

Ben searched his pockets and found an old bill and a pen. 'Look, Alec,' he said. 'I don't want to keep you from your mates any longer. I'm putting my home address and E Mail address on the back of this bill. Would you mind sending me a copy of your annual report for that year?'

'Aye - nae bother.' He took the piece of paper, and didn't ask Ben why he wanted the information, presumably because he wanted to get back to his meeting.

As he made his way back to Helen, Ben shouted to Alec: 'where's the next mountain rescue team south of Inchnadamph?'

'Torridon,' Alec shouted back. 'It's in the Torridon youth hostel.'

Ben raised his hand in acknowledgement, as he sat down beside Helen, and proffered the long-awaited dram.

'What was that all about?' Helen asked, patiently.

'Oh! It's just the local MR team...he's going to send me some stuff down,' Ben said, dismissively, not wanting to spoil Helen's enjoyment of the music or her holiday.

Helen sensed that there was more to it than that, but knew he didn't want to interrupt the holiday atmosphere. She could read his mind, and was grateful for his thoughtfulness. Her feet started tapping again.

*

Three days later, after a magical drive down the west coast of Sutherland, revisiting the wonderful beaches, the weird mountains, and the vast panoramas, they arrived in the more conventional, though still spectacular, landscape of Wester Ross where the daunting Torridon Mountains throw down their challenge.

At the eastern end of Loch Maree, Ben stopped to check the map.

For the past three days, he had been so wrapped up in the enjoyment of the holiday, that he had forgotten about his chat with the Assynt Mountain Rescue man. Now it all came back. Was it fate, or just a strange coincidence, that he was about to drive past the next mountain rescue team's headquarters?

*

Ben dropped Helen off at the Torridon visitor centre, while he went in search of the Torridon youth hostel.

There was no one in the room, set aside within the youth hostel for the Torridon Mountain Rescue Team, but the man running the hostel was a team member and very helpful. He let Ben read through the last few years' annual incident reports, and allowed him to take a photocopy of the report of two years ago. Ben had noticed a spate of deaths in that year, mostly falls from high crags.

*

After returning the motor home to the hire company in what now seemed to be a disagreeably noisy and overcrowded Edinburgh, Helen, now back to her energetic self, persuaded Ben to end the holiday by spending the night in one of the city's best hotels. She also persuaded him to leave his seventh-floor view of the city lights, to join her in bed early. It was her way of ensuring that their holiday came to a satisfying climax.

Chapter 15

Back at the cottage, they were greeted by hyperactive pheasants and ducks, like children who had been deserted by their parents for a week - excited, noisy, and hungry. Ben hoped that there was still some bread in the freezer.

He had difficulty in opening the cottage door because of the mail on the floor. Among the diatribes from insurance and credit card companies, miraculously offering to save you money while taking it off you, he spotted a Thurso postmark. Alec Gordon had kept his promise.

Later that night, with the unpacking finished, the washing machine whirring, the birds and humans fed, he settled down to read the Assynt team's annual incident report of three years ago. It got off to a humorous start:

25th March   Shin Falls
Call out for missing child (3 years) who had wandered off from visitor centre play area. Found safe and well by RAF SARDA at 08.30, having been looking for dinosaurs.

9th April   Ben Klibreck
Call out to search for owner of rucksack abandoned at col. Owner identified from passport as —————————,
an American. Despite an extensive search involving 12

*AMRT, 14 Kinloss MRT, 8 SARDA, and helicopter,
nothing was found. After reports of various sightings,
eventually found by police in Thurso the following Tuesday
and bollocked rigid!*

Ben's guffaw made Helen jump. She was already
back to the grind, poring over papers taken from her
briefcase. He apologised and carried on reading.

*10th May   Inchnadamph
Call out to search for six missing Dutch women. Found by
helicopter on path behind Beinn Uidhe cold and wet but
unhurt.*

*2nd JuneScourie
Call out for missing fisherman. Walked out to Lower
Badcall having become completely disorientated in the area
around Loch Mhuirt. No map or compass.*

*11th July   Golspie
Call out for missing person, probable suicide. Nothing
found.
Body found in sea off Peterhead two weeks later.*

*18th July   Achmelvich
Call to assist Police in search for person thought to be 'On
the Run'. Nothing found.*

*3rd August   Ben More Assynt
Call out for missing woman on Ben More Assynt. Body
found below top section of south ridge east of Dubh Loch*

Mor. Sustained extensive injuries to body and head. Helicopter unable to reach the casualty because of low cloud. Body evacuated to a pick up point with some difficulty.

29th August   Fannichs
Call out to assist Dundonnell MRT with search. Body found.

18th September   Ben Hope, Central Gully
Call out for missing man on Ben Hope. Body found among boulders 250' below Central Gully. Sustained various multiple injuries consistent with his fall. Taken by helicopter to Inverness.

The usual mixture of stupidity, tragedy and a little humour continued to unfold. Ben had seen it all before. But, the man in the pub had been right. The difference with this one was that it contained eight deaths out of 15 incidents, compared to an average of one or two in other years. And six of them were falls from high crags.

Next, he studied the photocopy he had picked up at Torridon Mountain Rescue headquarters, reporting on incidents of two years ago. Again, it contained an exceptionally high mortality figure of nine, with five being falls from crags.

Maybe they were just freak years, he reasoned. Statistical blips. But it was strange that the years came one after another. What were the odds on that? Something itched at the back of his mind. He knew he wouldn't be able to rest until he'd scratched it. He was stubborn, and stupid, like that. He had chased up many a blind alley in his time; spent hours and days on a detail others couldn't or wouldn't be bothered with, often to find that he had wasted his time.

But, just occasionally, he hadn't wasted his time, and he had found great satisfaction when his persistence paid off. This is what kept him going, like the good golf round remembered, the bad ones forgotten.

Tomorrow, he determined, he would visit Keswick Mountain Rescue HQ to check on their annual fatality statistics, and he still had to check whether Tessa Coleman's fall from Dale Head was a one-off, or was it a regular accident black spot?

*

There was only one car in the Keswick Mountain Rescue headquarters' car park. Ben recognised it as belonging to Ian the Controller.

'One day I'll remember to ask him his surname,' Ben thought to himself as he walked across the empty yard. Clearly, there was no call-out or training taking place.

Ian was sitting with his back to him when he entered the Control Room. He jumped, and shuffled some papers, as Ben greeted him.

Probably caught him reading a dirty book, Ben thought, smiling inwardly.

'You frightened the life out of me,' Ian barked. He was renowned for stating the obvious. A crumpled anorak and muddy boots lay close to his stockinged feet.

'Been far?' Ben asked, conversationally.

'Not really,' Ian said. 'Just along Friars Crag, down to Lodore and back along the valley.'

He was one of those strange characters you can never get close to, Ben had decided some time ago. He answered questions or made pronouncements, but he didn't hold conversations. And he was always on his own. He never joined in the camaraderie of the rest of the team and never went to their fund raising events or annual parties. But, he was a very good controller: meticulous, accurate, reliable, fastidious with paperwork and records, often nagging team members to speed up and improve their written reports.

Most organisations have an Ian, Ben thought, remembering his work days, at the same time realising he didn't know what Ian did for a living. That was something else to ask him - one day! Right now, he wanted to make use of Ian's meticulous records.

Ian produced them with great alacrity, and spread them neatly on the control room table, obviously proud of their perfection. There were pie charts and graphs and lists and reports. All were colour-coded and bound in protective plastic sleeves.

Ben took out his notebook and pen as he glanced at last year's Incident Report. As well as a written, detailed, summary of each of the 69 incidents, there was a pie chart showing the 'Type of Incident', and three graphs showing 'Times of Day', 'Days of The Week', and 'Months of the Year'.

At a glance he could see that the most common incident was a lower leg injury, occurring between 13.00 and 16.00 hours, on a Saturday, in September. 'Must remember not to walk on a Saturday afternoon in September', he joked with himself.

The inner smile vanished when he returned to the pie chart. Opposite the large orange segment declaring 22 lower leg injuries, with a red hypothermia segment on one side and blue paragliding segment on the other, was a green one announcing 15 fall fatalities.

He turned the page to find a chart summarising the number of incidents and fatalities since the team was set up in 1948. Scanning across the green and red columns he found that the highest number of fatalities before last year had been in 1989 when there had been nine fatalities. An average across the whole period was four fatalities.

Last year's 15 fatalities now looked like yet another, very large, statistical blip. It now seemed to him beyond coincidence that a statistical blip could appear in successive years in three different rescue teams. So if it wasn't coincidence, what was it?

He was going to have to dig much deeper, try to find out more about each fatal incident. Could there be a common link? Did other unfortunate victims work for the government, like Jack Fraser? Was Sophie Lund right after all? Was this how they got rid of the government's perceived enemies? His mind was starting to whirl with alternatives. His imagination was up and running, and he didn't like where it was taking him.

The obvious starting place was Tessa Coleman, tragically the most recent statistic, and known personally. Clearly, she didn't work for the government. Clearly, she had no enemies. Hers was probably a genuine accident. And yet, something still niggled him.

'Have you any statistics on the most common fatality locations, Ian?' he asked. 'I was wondering....'

'Right here,' Ian said, proudly pulling out a folder from his desk.

A glance along the columns showed that Sharp Edge on Blencathra had claimed the most victims, followed by Striding Edge on Helvellyn. These were dangerous places where ordinary fell walkers sought adventure.

The rest of the statistics confirmed that it was mostly fell walkers who perished, not climbers, even though they tackled far more hazardous routes.   Dale Head, where Tessa had died, didn't appear. Nor did Little Man, where the Frasers had died. As he had suspected, these were not inherently dangerous places. You would have to be blind not to see where the summits dropped away on one side, into the valley. The edges were clearly visible. The only other explanation was that the victims were suicidal, or had been pushed.

Maybe Tessa had been suicidal. She had suffered a marriage breakdown. She led a lonely, insular, life working and living in the same building.

But why take your climbing gear and your sketch pads with you if you are going to commit suicide? There had been no suicide note left in her flat, or at the scene of death. Anyway, he knew her well enough to be almost certain that she wasn't the suicidal type. He had rarely met someone so full of zest and confidence.

So, if it wasn't suicide, or a climbing accident - the rope was still on her body, unused - that left an accidental slip while near the edge, looking for a subject to paint.

Her sketch pad was still in her backpack. Even if she had been sketching near the edge, she would probably have been seated, and therefore safe. And, she was an experienced, very fit climber, and the edge is not sudden but gradual. Had she slipped, he felt sure she would have been able to grab hold of something before the ground fell away completely.

That left one more alternative. She was pushed. But who would do such a thing? What was the motive? How could such a beautiful, harmless woman have any enemies?

Ben let these thoughts settle in his mind. Things like this didn't happen in the Lake District. Motiveless murder happened on squalid city streets. It didn't happen to beautiful people in beautiful places...did it?

Now he recalled that sudden feeling that something was wrong when he saw the photographs of Tessa lying like a discarded scarecrow. It had been transient, but strong. He had returned to it in his mind many times since, usually when first waking, when he was at his sharpest, but nothing had revealed itself.

He handed the folder back to Ian. 'Thanks.'

Then he found his voice assuming a quiet, reverential, tone. 'Do you still have the photographs of Tessa Coleman?'

'Naw. We don't keep photos. They go to the police. They keep them.' Ian's reply was irritatingly brusque, as usual.

Ben pocketed his notebook and headed for the control room door. 'Thanks for your help,' he said, as he left the room.

Ian waited until he heard the main door close, then stood at the window to watch Ben walk across the car park. He returned to his desk and took out an envelope from the back of a drawer. From it, he carefully picked out a negative of a photograph, and held it up to view via the light from the window.

Chapter 16

On the morning that Ben set out from his cottage to ask Sergeant Bill Unwin to help him dig deeper into the recent fatal incidents, a few miles away, in a small flat in the town of Cockermouth, on the northern fringe of the Lake District, Professor Manfred Metternich was studying a copy of Wainwright's 'Guide to the Far Eastern Fells'. He always consulted these unique, hand-written, sketch-filled guides, when planning the day's walk.

Although in his 60s, he was still very strong, with massive thighs and a bull like neck. But English wife, Joan, was not so strong, and so he had to look for fells that were not too strenuous.

He turned a page and found Place Fell - 2154 feet. They had done it a few times over the years - it was one of their favourites. Again he read Wainwright's description of it, just for pleasure: *'It occupies an exceptionally good position in the curve of Ullswater, in the centre of a great bowl of hills; its summit commands a very beautiful and impressive panorama. No other viewpoint gives such an appreciation of the design of this lovely corner of Lakeland. Many discoveries await those who explore: in particular the abrupt western flank, richly clothed with juniper and bracken and heather, and plunging down to the lake in a rough tumble of crag and scree, boulders and birches.'*

The Professor knew that the way to the top from the north or south was not abrupt, thankfully, but a delightful, gradual, walk.

'Do you fancy doing Place Fell again?' he asked.

Joan was only three paces away, preparing their packed lunch in the small kitchen area of the open planned flat they had bought as a retirement present to each other.

'Is that the Ullswater one?' she queried, having done so many fells in 40-years of walking.

'That's the one.'

'That'll be fine.'

Although their home was a small town near Munich, only 25 miles from the Bavarian Alps, and they had lived all over the world, because of Manfred's work as a senior officer with the United Nations, they still only headed for one place when free time came round - the English Lake District. And now that they had nothing but free time, they had bought the flat so that they could spend as much time as they liked in their favourite place.

Shortly after their arrival at the flat, a next-door neighbour had asked them why they came to the Lake District, when they lived so close to the Alps. Manfred, who had taken a couple of drinks, and was not normally so verbose, had said: 'When I retired, I calculated that I had worked in 48 countries. In all my travels, this is the most beautiful place I've seen on earth. It is wonderfully unique. So much variety of hills, lakes, streams, woods, contained in so compact an area.'

He continued: 'You don't have to travel vast distances as in other countries; there is beauty and variety at every turn. It is all so accessible. The mountains are friendly. The Alps are too high, frightening. But the mountains here can still provide a great challenge. A sudden weather change, and in an instant you are alone in the clouds. But it is a nice loneliness, a loneliness to relish - peaceful, not frightening. Nowhere else have I seen these short-lived weather changes. Next, the sun suddenly bursts through the clouds, and your peaceful loneliness turns to joy as you see again the beautiful valley below you.'

Manfred concluded: 'it is like a religious experience. And it is so unchanging. I've seen bad development all over the world, but when I come here it is always the same. There is a wonderful continuity of nature and life style. I know that here, the best of nature will be preserved. This is a very precious and unique place. If you keep it unchanged; if you keep the spirit of the Lakes alive, then people will continue to come from all over the world, to relax, recharge their batteries, appreciate nature.........'

The neighbour, whose travels were limited to the local pub and betting shop, had made a sudden excuse, shuffled away, and vowed to himself never to ask the strange foreigner another question.

*

Manfred and Joan put their packed lunch, walking boots and waterproofs, into their Mercedes, and enjoyed the drive over to the eastern fells.

They also enjoyed the slow amble to the top of Place Fell, the incredible views, and the chat with the small man they met there.

But soon, they were not enjoying 'Place Fell's abrupt western flank, richly clothed with juniper and bracken and heather, and plunging down to the lake in a rough tumble of crag and scree, boulders and birches.'

They had told their neighbour where they were going for the day, so the mountain rescue team was called out that evening.

Joan was found first, cold dead, badly disfigured, with a shattered birch branch passing through her neck.

Manfred was higher up the slope, wedged behind a large boulder. He was still warm. The team used a defibrillator on him. On the third shock, Manfred shuddered, opened his eyes and said quite loudly: 'Summer sniffs.' He never spoke again.

Chapter 17

'Problem solving is a savage pleasure and we are born to it.' All the way, on the drive to the golf course, Ben had been unable to remember who wrote it. But he knew it to be true.

He now had the bit between his teeth and he wouldn't let go until he had found some answers. Unfortunately, the answers probably lay somewhere within the files, records, autopsies, photographs, databases, held by the police on each fatal incident. Which is why he was going to have to be very friendly and persuasive with Bill Unwin after their round.

And, even if Bill came good, there was still all the Scottish incidents to investigate. It all looked very daunting. Hopefully, he reasoned, the answers to the local incidents will also provide the key to answering the Scottish questions. 'I have to start somewhere,' he sighed to himself, as he pulled into the golf club car park.

A few hours later he was placing a pint of ale in front of Bill, on a polished wooden table in a corner of the club house lounge. His four-wood hadn't worked its usual magic. His mind had been elsewhere.

'Cheers Bill...well played. Top form today, eh! Well and truly thrashed.'

'It's no use buttering me up, Ben,' Bill said firmly. Then he lowered his voice to a conspiratorial whisper: 'I just can't help you. It's more than my job's worth.'

Ben had broached the subject on the way up the 18th fairway, given Bill his reasons for suspicion, asked Bill for as much information as possible on each of this year's and last year's 20 fall fatalities. He needed to know everything possible about the victims when alive and everything about their subsequent deaths.

'I'd like to help if I could,' Bill was still whispering. 'But you haven't given me enough to go on. Just statistics, speculation, theories based on personal knowledge of one person, and, god help us, your *feeling* that something isn't right. Can you imagine me taking that lot to my boss and asking him to forward it to Penrith CID? They already have a backlog of current cases to deal with, without opening old ones without good cause, such as hard evidence.'

There was a hint of condescension in his voice as he finished. Its irritation, added to Ben's rising feeling of frustration at having to deal with a large bureaucratic machine, made him take a long slug at his ale.

'Could you not do this on a personal basis,' Ben pleaded. 'Without involving your boss or anyone else?'

'Look,' Bill said. 'Even if I tried, I doubt if I could get my hands on all the information you're after. I don't have access to all the stuff you want. And if I did, and you uncovered something worthwhile, it would have to finish as police business wouldn't it, and somebody upstairs would want to know where you got your initial information from. I can't risk that. It could mean my job.' He had stopped whispering now.

Ben understood Bill's dilemma, but, after draining his glass, made one last plea. 'You know I'm not asking for fun, Bill. There's nothing in it for me, just hard slog' ... not quite true - Sophie's money...'but I genuinely believe that there is something bad happening here, and I ...we... should try to do something about it.'

Bill nodded his acknowledgement while draining his glass. But his silence said everything.

'I'll leave it with you,' Ben went on, hesitantly. 'If there is any snippet of info you can supply, without risk to yourself, I'd be very grateful.'

They rose from the table together, Ben hoping that he hadn't smudged the polish on a good friendship. After all, what was more important than good friendship, a round of golf, and a pint of ale. You have to get your priorities right.

Ben felt a sense of relief as he drove away from the club house. Yes, he was frustrated. But the barriers that Bill had put in front of him were just too high to climb. He had no choice but to let go, to let the bit slide, to get back to routine.

*

His routine over the next two days consisted of some housework; it had been due for a clean when they dashed off on holiday; some boring gardening, a bit of journalism, and a start on a new oil painting based on a couple he had seen fishing from the jetty down at the lake.

He was busy diluting burnt umber with turpentine, to use on the outline sketch, when the phone rang.

'Ben...its Bill Unwin. I've just heard that Patterdale Rescue Team recovered two bodies a couple of days ago. They're in Penrith morgue at the moment. As you know, it's outside my area, so I don't have much detail. But I can tell you...you got me thinking the other day...and as soon as I heard about this one I rang around the other five MRT's and they all reported an increase in fatalities last year and, proportionately, this year as well. There's not a lot in it, just ones and twos. But, for what it's worth, I pointed this out to my oppo at Penrith...I'm not bothering my boss yet... and told him about the big fatality increase in the Keswick area, and mentioned that a member of the public...I had to give them your name...felt that these statistics warranted an investigation...' There was a pause, waiting for a reaction.

Ben was surprised. Not only by Bill's efforts on his behalf, but also by his own stupidity at not checking the other five Lake District MRT's himself.

'Thanks Bill,' he said. 'I appreciate what you've done, and letting me know about the Patterdale incident. Do you know where the bodies were found? Were they badly injured?'

'They were at the bottom of Place Fell...you know... overlooking Ullswater.'

'Yeh!'

'And the woman was severely injured, I understand. Why do you ask?'

'Just a theory at the moment Bill...so I won't bother you with it.' He hadn't intended to say the last bit; his subconscious must have spat it out to pay back Bill's previous condescension. Hurriedly, he went on: 'Do you think there will be an investigation?'

'Who knows. My oppo said he would pass it on to CID. After that it's anybody's guess. They may take it up, or they may decide that they have covered most of the ground with that massive investigation they did into the government minister's death, or they may have other priorities.'

'How long does it take to decide these things,' Ben asked.

'A week, a month...who knows...sometimes it's a case of who shouts loudest.'

'I'm sure my shout would be deafening if I had all the information I asked for,' Ben said, impatiently. 'Any chance you might change your mind, Bill. Get some of that info to me?'

'Sorry mate...still no can do...got to go...see you on the course next week...leave that four-wood behind.'

Freshly frustrated, Ben didn't slam the phone down. Instead he took his newly mixed paint and vigorously daubed 'SOD IT!' on the canvas.

*

An hour later he had calmed down, and sat with a cup of tea and one of Helen's home made scones, having saved his canvas by wiping the daub off with more turpentine.

Another double death had occurred. What if the police didn't investigate? He was undecided whether to let the whole thing go again, or to drive over to Ullswater, to give Place Fell the once over. It was some years since he had persuaded Helen to walk up it on a bleak autumn day; that the rain would stop before they got to the top. It hadn't, and all he remembered was being up to his oxters in mud, and a vague view of Ullswater somewhere below in the mist. However, he felt sure it wouldn't feature as a regular accident spot in the MRT's statistics.

As usual, his inquisitiveness won the day. He would have to go. If nothing else, it was a beautiful drive over there.

The phone rang.

'Hello....'

'Are you alone. Can you speak?'

Ben recognised the husky voice of Sophie Lund. 'Here we go again, more cloak and dagger stuff,' he thought, dejectedly.

'Ben, don't mention my name, and don't hang up. I want to help with those questions you've been asking Bill Unwin.'

'How the hell...'

'Are you alone,' she insisted.

'Yes...my wife is at work.'

'You've been very naughty, Ben. Finding things out, but not telling me. What about our agreement?

'I haven't got anything new to tell you,' Ben retorted.

There was a pause, a suck and a blow, as a cigarette helped her consider her response. 'You still don't take me seriously, do you Ben? Maybe I should withdraw my offer.'

'You can do what you like,' Ben said, confidently. 'Remember, you came to me for help. Before you go, just tell me how you know I've been asking Bill Unwin questions.'

'Isn't it obvious?'

'You haven't bugged my house?' Ben's slow fuse was starting to burn.

'Christ, do I have to spell it out? Computers, Ben, computers...you know those little boxes that sit on our desks. Didn't you know they have become indispensable? All the little key tappers around the world are speaking to each other with them, keeping records on them, firing missiles at each other with....'

'Okay...okay...I get the message. But I haven't contacted Bill Unwin by computer?'

'Maybe not, but your Sergeant Unwin recently E-mailed a Sergeant in Penrith confirming their telephone conversation. They are so thorough, bless them! Apparently, you have been asking for all sorts of information, and for an investigation into other Lake District deaths, not just Jack Fraser's. If there's something going on, I want to know. What have you found...?'

The fuse was getting shorter. 'Have you nothing better to do. Surely you are too busy with your book to bother about two small town policemen talking to each other. You realise I'm going to have to tell them you've listened in to their conversations.'

'I wouldn't do that, Ben. Not that they would ever be able to trace anything back to me. But I always take out insurance just in case. It's the best there is. It's based on human frailty, and guess what, it has never failed me yet. Put simply, you tell the police about me, and I tell your wife...Helen isn't it...about our copulation at the Keswick Hotel.'

Ben sniggered. 'But we didn't.'

'I would say we did.'

'It would be your word against mine. Who is she going to believe? A woman with your reputation or her devoted husband?'

'Ben...Ben,' her voice became patronising. 'You don't understand women, do you? My reputation would *ensure* that she didn't believe you. Anyway, I always make sure my insurance policies are foolproof. Listen.'

He heard a button being pressed, a slight hiss, and then Sophie's voice: '...are you married, would you like to sleep with me.'

Then his own voice: 'I'm extremely married. I would like to sleep with you.'

Then Sophie: 'Now Ben, be a good man, get dressed, and come and have a drink with me.' Again a button was pressed and the tape stopped.

'Heard enough?' Sophie's voice was now flat and businesslike. 'Now you know how I operate. You can't deal with complete strangers without insurance can you.'

She was always one step ahead. She had even anticipated his reaction, and had the tape ready to play. Ben had to concede that she was operating in a different league, a league he didn't want to join.

'As for being too busy with my book,' she went on. 'You are quite right. I don't have the time to listen to two small town policemen. But my computers do. Whenever Jack Fraser's name or yours passes through the Keswick/ Penrith system, my computers are alerted. Aren't my hackers clever! I had to keep track of any contact you might have with the police, both for my own security and because I'm still desperate to know what happened to Jack Fraser.'

She had him. He couldn't risk hurting Helen.

'Okay,' Ben conceded. 'I'm not telling the police about you, so what...'

'Listen, Ben,' Sophie had switched to her conciliatory tone. 'Now that we know where we stand, why don't we forget all this sniping and try to help each other. I understand that the police won't or can't give you the information you're after. My hackers can get it for you. If it's on a computer system, and most things are these days, then my boys can access it, anywhere in the world. As long as it leads to the cause of Jack Fraser's death, I don't mind how much time they spend on it. That would be your intention, wouldn't it? You seem to have been sidetracked by these other deaths'?

'I think they might be linked.'

'So tell me. What have you got,' Sophie pried, patiently.

'Very little,' Ben said. 'There's nothing concrete. Just theories based on statistics and something I can't put my finger on. That's why I needed all that information, to help me test my theories, try to find the links.'

'You wouldn't be holding back on me, Ben?'

'Why should I?'

'So let's talk turkey. What kind of info are you looking for?'

She was doing it again, trying to control him.
'Look, you couldn't possibly get all the information I'm looking for. I need police records, autopsy reports, photographs, mountain rescue reports, concerning people and places scattered all over Britain.'

'You haven't been listening, Ben. If it is recorded on computer systems, we can get it, and fast. My boys have already found the trapdoor in the Metropolitan serious crime system. They have already checked the national BADMAN database.'

She was indomitable. He would try another tack. 'How can your hackers cope with the new Anti-Cyber Crime Unit set up by the Home Secretary recently. What was it...40 officers specifically employed to fight against hackers?'

'Bureaucratic plodders,' Sophie scoffed. ' Oh, they'll sort out a few criminals and virus freaks, but they are no match for my boys! I have the cream. My boys are interested in becoming legends, not plodding wage earners in a government department.'

She had an answer to everything. He decided to humour her and, hopefully, call her bluff. 'Okay, you win. Let's give it a go. But I can't do it over the phone. I need to sit down and write a list, and then I'll e-mail it to you, or wherever you want me to send it. If you don't want to give me your e-mail address over the phone, send it by e-mail. My address is: benhelen2@aol.com.'

Sophie sighed. 'That's more like it. Now we're getting somewhere. I'll send an e-mail contact address as soon as I put the phone down, and I expect to have your list within 24-hours. Let's get cracking on this thing. I think you'll be surprised at how much we can help you. And I really do need to get this Jack Fraser thing sorted, Ben. It's not just about me, it's about our country's future.'

'Pompous bitch,' Ben thought. 'I'll start on the list now,' he said.

'Good. Bye,' Sophie concluded.

'Goodbye,' Ben concluded.

He left the conservatory, where he did his painting because of the light, and walked upstairs to the spare bedroom, which doubled as an office. All the communication paraphernalia of the immediate age sat on a black desk in the corner, looking incongruous in the high ceilinged, corniced surroundings of an unhurried age.

He dropped into the well-padded swivelling chair, switched on the computer in the same movement, and started to type.

He was about to bombard Sophie Lund and her 'boys' with a list so long it would be impossible to cope with. He would ask for every conceivable report, statistic, photograph, compiled by every police force, MRT, doctor, coroner, pathologist, for every fall victim in every area, including Scotland, over the past three years.

It would look as though he was trying, and although he was aware of his vulnerability as long as she had that tape, he was sure it would call her bluff, and get her off his back once and for all.

Chapter 18

He sits in a dark room, Walkman earphones clamped to his head. He has to have the music, can't be without it; has to feel it throbbing against his skull, filling his mind, drowning his thoughts. Sibelius's fifth is doing the job at the moment, shaking him with emotion. When it finishes, he knows the seventh will start immediately.

The fleshiness of contentment that filled his face during the first few blissful years has gone. Skeletal looks have returned, gaunt cheeks, thin lips barely covering large teeth, sunken eyes. The eyes are glazed; an empty whisky bottle on the floor claims responsibility.

A bridging passage in the third movement allows the attention to drift - even Sibelius isn't perfect. For a moment he is in reality, aware of his surroundings, the time of day.

'Have I fed her', flashes into his mind. He can remember leaving her food and drink in the morning, but did he do it when he came in that night, or did he head straight for the bottle. 'Better check.'

He sways as he stands and moves the chair to one side. An unsteady flick of the right foot and the rug concertinas across the floorboards. He grasps the steel handle of the trapdoor, and swings the door up and over, and lowers it again to the floorboards.

He steps down into the faintly lit void. At the foot of the stairs, he moves along a dark passage towards the source of light. He reaches a large door. Before opening it, he takes a few steps to the left and looks through a window into a well lit room

She lies on a mattress on the floor, her back to him, as usual.

Her nakedness is well concealed by her foetal position and her long, tangled, waist length hair.

In the shadows he can see the breakfast leftovers and her bucket. He was getting worse. He had forgotten to feed her that evening. It was unforgivable; he would see to it straight away.

He moves to the door and turns the key. While opening it, he removes his earphones. An explosion of sound greets him. He doesn't flinch. Instead, he smiles. The love duet from Madame Butterfly always makes him smile...initially.

He moves into the room and picks up the breakfast things and the bucket. He holds it at arms length while he stares down at her. Light and shadow highlight her buttocks. He doubts if he will hold them tonight. It is getting late and he is tired, and there is still a meal to make.

For a moment, he puts the bucket down, and bends and gently strokes her hair, and whispers 'Leni', and feels the pain move in. He rises quickly, picks up the bucket and leaves the room.

Outside the door, he takes one more glance through the window. She hasn't moved.

Chapter 19

Two days after e-mailing his 'mission impossible' list to Sophie Lund, Ben has forgotten about it. He is walking among his beloved fells, the weather is fine, and best of all, Helen is with him.

She is having one of her rare days off from any kind of work. As always, she leaves the choice of walk to Ben, being delighted to stretch her desk-bound legs along any route he takes her.

They are heading for Dale Head along one of the Newlands Valley routes. He can't get Tessa Coleman's death out of his mind. He keeps re-living the moment when he saw the photographs, when he felt that something was wrong. He still can't find it.

He has given up on Jack Fraser and the others, but Tessa won't let him rest. He knew her; he liked her. Somehow he feels it is his responsibility to find out what happened to her. 'So, if I'm heading out for a day's fell walking, why not head for the place where she died,' he had reasoned.

Following the footsteps of the old miners, the first two miles along the flat valley floor is easy, yet spectacular. All around, the amphitheatre of the famous Newlands Valley Horseshoe encompasses them - Hindscarth Fell to the right, Maiden Moor to the left; Dale Head straight ahead at the end of the valley.

Past the site of the old Castlenook mine, where the main path rises to the left to take in the tarn before reaching Dale Head summit, Ben veers to the right and searches for an ill-defined path he last trod many years ago, on his own.

'Where are you taking me now,' Helen shouts with mock horror, being well used to Ben leading her off the normal tracks.

'It's the old path to Dale Head mine.' Ben leans on his thumb stick as he pauses to explain. 'It was made by the copper miners centuries ago. It hasn't been used for over a hundred years, but you can still just make it out if you look up to your right, and then follow it as it zigzags up and along Hindscarth to the mine, just to the right of that main crag on Dale Head.'

Helen screws up her eyes and follows his directions. 'Yes...I think I can see bits of it.'

'Can you believe it,' Ben enthuses. 'Miners used to drag horses and sleds up there. That's why it zigzags so much.'

'Looks a bit tough to me! Why do you want to go up there?'

Ben wished that she hadn't asked. He wanted her to enjoy a normal, mind-emptying, walk. He always tried to keep her precious days off as mindless as possible, allowing the physical challenge and great beauty of their surroundings to work their restorative magic.

'I hope you don't mind,' Ben started, apologetically. 'There's a shelf above the mine called Bilberry Shelf. That's where Tessa Coleman was found. I still think there's something strange about her death....'

'But what do you expect to find?' Helen interrupted quickly, though her tone was not unsupportive.

'I don't know...I just want to learn as much as I can about where she died. Eventually, I might be able to put my finger on something...who knows.'

'Well, let's get going.'

'Are you sure? It is pretty tough going. I could go up on my own another day....'

'You heard me...let's get going.'

It was typical of Helen. Never questioning. Always supportive. Always ready for a challenge.

*

A gasping hour later they reached the derelict buildings of the old mine, dramatically sited high on the fell-side, in the lee of precipitous Gable Crag. It was difficult to believe, and humbling to know, that men had daily climbed to work at this lonely place.

With the track now ended, they made their way up from the mine, walking and scrambling up a rough grassy slope, then traversing to the left, until they reached Bilberry Shelf. It was like a giant foothold in the upper slopes of Dale Head, being about twelve feet long and five feet deep.

Ben helped Helen scramble onto its flat, moss flecked, surface where she immediately helped him to offload the backpack containing their packed lunch.

As she started to lay things out, Ben examined their surroundings. There was nothing to indicate where Tessa's body had lain. The moss, which, he remembered, had made a surreal background in the horrific photographs, seemed undisturbed.

He looked upwards. A wall of smooth rock travelled all the way to the summit of Dale Head, about 300 ft above him. Only the best climbers came here; the challenge being its lack of holds and its pure verticality, culminating in a slight outward lean near the summit. The lean probably explained why the search parties hadn't spotted her from above.

Ben imagined poor Tessa's terrifying plunge direct from the top to the shelf's unyielding rock. He saw the photograph again, how she lay like a scarecrow; this time - spread-eagled at his feet. What was it that was wrong? He closed his eyes in concentration. But he still couldn't find it.

He moved to the edge of the shelf and looked down. It was vicious crag all the way to the valley floor.

At least she was spared complete disfigurement, Ben thought, knowing what crag impact did to peoples' bodies. The damage done by the birds had been bad enough, but it was nothing compared to what the crags below him would have done had she missed the shelf. Many fallers were unrecognisable.

He knew it was ridiculous for him to find consolation in this thought. Death was death, however it happened. Yet, somehow, it seemed better that someone so beautiful should not die unrecognisable. He returned to Helen's side.

'Find anything', she asked, kindly, as he sat down beside her.

Ben shook his head. 'I don't think so.' He felt dejected, and found himself staring blankly at the ground between his knees.

'Never mind,' Helen said, cheerily. 'At least you've been here. You now know the layout. You might be able to make use of it later. Come on, cheer up, have a sandwich.'

They ate their lunch in silence, small talk seeming inappropriate amongst such tragic surroundings. The only sound came from the ravens circling in the thermals above them, outlined against the blue sky, black as their deeds.

After lunch, they retraced their steps for a few hundred yards, then climbed left to the summit of Hindscarth. From here, a long gradually descending ridge would take them back to the floor of Newlands Valley.

As they started down, so Ben's spirits went up. It was impossible not to be enchanted by the panoramic views and the delightful, heathery, track that lay ahead.

After a mile of blissful ridge walking, scanning distant fells he knew so well, watching miniature life in the valleys below, he was counting his blessings again. What beauty, what joy. He was in an earthly heaven and his angel walked beside him.

A mile later, as they passed the pan holes of the old Goldscope Mine, nearing the valley floor, Ben spotted a dead herdwick sheep lying among the boulders. He was particularly fond of this small, tough, yet gentle looking breed that was unique to the Lake District. As they roamed the fells in their thousands, the sight of a dead one was commonplace.

Even so, Ben could never pass a body without pausing to look. 'Men's morbid curiosity,' Helen had called it. And she was probably right, it was a male trait; probably the child within them that never got round to leaving.

Helen stayed on the track as Ben tiptoed among the boulders to get a closer look. The smell was strong. The animal had been dead for some time. This time, one glance was enough to satisfy Ben's curiosity. He was used to the empty eye sockets in the head, the birds having visited, but the sight of heaving maggots in its back passage was too much.

He turned away quickly. Suddenly, the thing that had been trapped in the back of his mind bobbed to the surface. He looked back down at the sheep, then rushed back to Helen.

'I think I might be on to something,' he said, in a measured manner, trying not to get too excited.

'What is it?' Helen sensed his undertone.

Ben was silent, thinking. 'Damn,' he exclaimed. 'If only I could get my hands on those photographs and autopsy reports.'

'What is it, Ben?' Helen repeated.

'I need to check with Tony Williams....' Ben mumbled, still deep in thought.

Helen gave up. She looked around and found a place to sit. Ben remained rooted to the spot, both hands on his thumb stick, his chin resting on his hands. What he needed to check with Tony Williams, their neighbouring farmer, was a mystery to her. But she knew that all would be revealed when he came out of his thinking trance.

Eventually, he returned, and moved to sit beside her.

'It's the eyes,' he said, quietly. 'I think I can prove that Tessa's death wasn't an accident. But I need access to information only the police have, and they won't release it.'

'What was that about Tony Williams?' Helen asked, keen to keep Ben rolling.

'I just want to confirm something with him...about how his dead sheep look after the birds have been at them. I'm pretty sure they remove the eyes cleanly...I mean they leave a clean socket...they don't dig deeper...they're only interested in soft, edible, tissue.'

'And the significance of this?' Helen prodded.

'I saw photographs of Tessa lying dead on Bilberry Shelf.' Ben explained. 'Both of her eyes were missing. But I'm sure that one eye socket was clean and intact, whereas the other was severely damaged. I don't think birds, not even ravens, do that type of damage. And, before you ask, it couldn't have been crag damage. It's a clean drop from the summit to the shelf...there's no outcrops. And, judging by the photographs, she landed on her back. That's why I need to see the autopsy reports...to confirm that the cause of death was due to impact to the back of her head and body, and not to the front.'

Helen was puzzled. 'But even if the autopsy concluded that she did land on her back, and it caused her death, they would still have to show a reason for the damage to her eye, that's their job.'

'Exactly,' Ben expounded. 'My guess is that, because the pathologist didn't visit the scene - remember nobody is suspecting a crime here, it's a routine mountain fall - and because he is well aware of the damage mountain falls can cause, he will have theorised that the severe eye damage was caused by crags during the fall, just like many others, while the other eye was clearly the victim of bird attack. He is not to know that there are no crags on this fall.'

'Wouldn't mountain rescue have said something in their report,' Helen queried.

'It's very unlikely. It would just be routine to them, however sad. Like the pathologist, they wouldn't be expecting a crime. My guess is they would take their photographs, make some measurements and notes, then stretcher her off. Again, that's why I need to see their reports and photographs. To make sure that I'm not barking up the wrong tree.'

'So, how do *you* think Tessa came by those injuries?' Helen asked, reluctantly, not keen to hear the expected reply.

'I think she was attacked by somebody on the summit and was probably dead before she was thrown over the edge.'

Helen shuddered and frowned. 'You mean a sex attack? There couldn't be any other motive, could there? Perhaps she put up a fight. Maybe the man hit her with a rock or something, then panicked when he found she was dead, and threw her over, hoping the fall would hide the injuries he had inflicted....'

'No,' Ben interrupted. 'I don't think it is as simple as that. Her clothes were undisturbed. Sex wasn't the motive. I believe we have something worse than an isolated sex attack gone wrong. I believe the attack was premeditated. But, yes, the killer did assume that the fall would disguise the injuries he had caused. In this case his luck ran out. He hadn't spotted the shelf.... probably because of the outward lean....'

'What do you mean 'in this case'? Do you think there's been others?'

Instinctively, Ben put a protective arm around Helen and took hold of her hand. 'Believe it or not, sweetheart....' he paused as he took in their beautiful surroundings.... 'I think our little bit of heaven has been invaded by an habitual murderer...what do they call them these days...?'

'A serial killer?' Helen gibed, incredulously. 'You must be joking.'

'I wish I was. I think we have a murderer who believes he is committing the perfect crime time after time. He beats his victims to death on a mountain top, then throws them off, knowing that the fall injuries will disguise the attack. He also knows that the body will be picked up routinely, without suspicion, by mountain rescue teams, and that the murder scene will not be visited by the pathologist carrying out the post mortem, (a) because no crime is suspected and (b) because of inaccessibility.'

'How on earth have you made the quantum leap from Tessa's slightly suspicious death to mass murder?' Helen queried, disbelievingly. 'I think it's time you went back to a proper job. You need to occupy your mind...stop that imagination of yours....'

'Look,' Ben interrupted firmly. 'One thing I learned when I had a proper job was that statistics don't lie, contrary to what Mr Disraeli is supposed to have said. Here's a few: a marked increase in the mountain rescue teams' fatality figures in the last year and a half, an increase in crag fatalities, an increase in couples' fatalities, deaths in unexpected places, of unexpected people...'

He stopped suddenly. He knew it was a hell of a leap from statistics to where he was, and that Helen was sure to point out there could be any number of innocent explanations for the statistics. No doubt, she would go on to ask how murders on a mountain top could possibly be premeditated. How could anyone know that their victim was going to be on top of a mountain at a given time. Then she would ask what could be the motive to kill such a diverse group of people.

He had already asked himself these questions many times, and failed to find an answer. The reality was that he was working mostly on intuition aided by a fertile mind, and Helen was on to him.

Nevertheless, he had faith in his intuition, and now that he had something to go on in Tessa's case, he intended to pursue it as far as humanly possible.

However, it was time to disengage Helen. He had never wanted her to become involved; she had enough on her plate. And, anyway, she was far too pragmatic to accept his intuitive theories. She needed hard facts to convince her of anything.

'Forget the statistics,' he said, eventually. 'You're right, apart from this thing with Tessa's eye, I haven't got much to go on. Let's forget the whole thing. Let's drop it...it's your day off. Let's enjoy the rest of the walk. Then, how about driving round to that pub at Loweswater for a pint and a bar meal. And because I've spoiled your day, I'll treat you to a sticky toffee pudding.'

'You haven't spoiled my day,' Helen squeezed his hand. 'But I'll hold you to that pudding. Come on, let's go.'

She stood up and offered her hand to help Ben rise. As always, she was only too glad to see the end of dark tunnels.

*

The next day, having seen Helen off to work, Ben went to see Tony Williams. He always enjoyed the mile walk to see his neighbour - down to the lake, along Scarness Bay shore, skirting the grounds of Scarness Manor, back up the fields to the farmer's beautiful 18th century dower house, overlooking the lake.

He found Tony in the large barn where he used to winter his cattle. Last year he had given them up for economic reasons and concentrated on his sheep herd. He now brought his sheep down off the fells at lambing time and watched them deliver in the barn, to the accompaniment of middle-of-the-road pop music echoing from speakers placed in two corners.

He reckoned the music relaxed them while they gave birth, and he knew that he was increasing his yield by not losing lambs to death on the fells from weather and predators.

In spite of losing his cattle and in spite of having his sheep destroyed during the foot and mouth epidemic, Tony Williams always seemed cheerful.

'Morning Tony!' Ben shouted, as he moved towards him through the mud and straw.

Tony's large, overall-clad frame turned, a beaming smile already in place. 'Ah! Mornin' Ben; what can I do you for today?'

Ben usually bought eggs and pheasant food from him, but today was different. 'It's information I'm after today, Tony,' he said. I wonder if you can help me. I'm doing a bit of research for an article I'm writing. It might seem a bit strange, but can you tell me what happens when a raven takes the eyes from a dead sheep. I mean...is it slow or quick...do they take anything else...' He paused, not wanting to put words into Tony's mouth.

Tony came straight back, without querying the strange question. It wasn't often he was made to feel like an expert.

'It's the carrion crows more than the ravens,' he started. 'They take the eyes in seconds. And it's not just dead sheep. At lambing time they attack the newborn lambs. If a mother sheep has twins, while she's looking after one, they'll attack the other. If the mother isn't quick enough, they'll kill it. I used to lose quite a few.'

'And do they do any other damage? Ben asked.

'Oh aye! They attack the tongue, and the navel and the rear end. Anywhere that's soft.'

'What about ears?'

'No, they're too hard.'

'You said they take the eyes in seconds. Do they attack around the sockets afterwards?'

'No...they're only interested in the soft tissue... anything that can be removed and eaten quickly. They don't hang about.'

'So the eye sockets are usually left untouched?'

'Aye. But it's just usually the one. The dead lamb is usually lying on its side. The crow can only get at one eye.'

Ben thanked Tony for the information and made an excuse to get away quickly. Normally, he would have stayed for a chat. He enjoyed learning about life on the farm, and usually came away thinking how lucky he was to have such an easy life compared to Tony Williams. But today, having had his hypothesis about Tessa's eye sockets confirmed, he wanted to get over to Glenridding to talk to someone in Patterdale Mountain Rescue team about the recent deaths on Place Fell. His enthusiasm for the hunt was beginning to return.

*

Ben's luck was in. A phone call to Patterdale HQ found the team leader. Dedicated as ever, John Simpson was working at the HQ during a school holiday period. He was a teacher at the village junior school who Ben had met on a number of occasions, when all the Lake District teams get together for a major search. 'Pop in anytime this afternoon,' John had said.

The drive to Glenridding was a joy as ever; the first, breathtaking, view of Ullswater as you crest a brackened hill, never failing to make Ben slow down to gaze in wonder. Such beauty almost demanded that you slow down, then continue in quiet respect.

At the foot of the hill, across the serene water, Ben took in the familiar sight of Place Fell, towering above the lake. It had been climbed by thousands of tourists because it was relatively easy and afforded wonderful views. But now it had claimed two lives. Once again, the combination of walkers, not climbers, falling off a relatively safe fell, raised doubts in Ben's mind.

Arriving at the team headquarters in Glenridding, he found John Simpson busily heaving gear about in the equipment store. After exchanging a few niceties, John took him into the control room and hunted out the relevant Place Fell incident file.

Ben sat at the long table, used for team meetings, and opened the file. Regrettably, he noted that the photographs had already gone to the police. He started to read.

It was all routine stuff - date, time, location, weather conditions, personnel present - until he came to injuries sustained.

Among other things, he read of 'a tree branch protruding through Mrs Metternich's neck, and heavy facial damage in the region of the left cheek and eye.' No mention was made of the right eye. Presumably, if it was still intact, she must have been lying so that the birds couldn't get at it, or, because the team had found her quickly, the birds hadn't yet got to her. Ben cursed to himself. If only he could see the photographs.

Professor Metternich had not, evidently, suffered such severe external injuries. Heavy facial abrasions, cuts and bruises were noted, as well as an apparent broken right leg. Eyes were not mentioned, and therefore presumably intact.

Towards the end of the report, Ben suddenly became aroused when he read that the professor was still warm when found, and that a defibrillator had been used in an attempt to re-start his heart.

When he read that the professor had momentarily recovered and said 'summer sniffs' before dying, he was positively excited. Here was something to work on - a clue at last. Or was his overactive imagination simply running away with him again? They could be, and probably were, meaningless words dredged from a childhood memory - they say you revert to childhood when you are about to die. Certainly, there was nothing in the words themselves to suggest that they were a clue.

However, Ben knew that from that moment he would assume they were, and that he would be spending an inordinate amount of time trying to solve it, just like he did with difficult crossword puzzles, when he would work on an irritating clue in his head for days, not wanting to be beaten by it.

The crazy thing was, there was still no evidence to suggest the deaths of the professor and his wife were not accidental. Maybe that was the reality. Maybe all these deaths were perfectly innocent. It was him that was going crazy.

Chapter 20

He is remembering. That is all he does these days. He has tried to stop. He has tried everything to make it go away. But it won't. It is unrelenting. Sometimes he remembers a fragment, sometimes the whole thing. When it gets too much he needs special relief.

As soon as he is unoccupied, the memories begin, as though on a screen in front of him. Then, on go the earphones, and out comes the whisky to drown the pain. Tonight, sitting alone in his high back rocking chair, he is at the beginning...again.

It is a cold, grey, day at Inverness airport. But it isn't the cold that makes him shake as he stands watching the plane taxi in, close to the terminal building. He has been excited and terrified ever since she phoned to say she was coming, giving him the flight numbers.

The door of the plane opens. Passengers come down the steps, hugging their coats, turning their collars up. Then she is in the doorway, small and dark in a large white frame, hesitant as the colour of her over-washed dress.

Across the tarmac she marches, carrying her hand luggage, head high, shoulders back.

She enters the terminal building, shivering, eyes searching. He steps forward, trembling. She sees him and smiles, nervously. He tries to smile as he holds out his hand to take her hand luggage. She mistakes the gesture and takes his hand in hers, and, dropping her luggage, dutifully slips in close to hug him.

He can feel her shivering in his arms. He can feel her softness through the thin dress, her hair against his cheek. He must stop trembling. He is holding a beautiful woman in public. She is his wife. She is Mrs Snodd. Dare he kiss her? He turns his head and kisses her gently on the cheek. Suddenly, she moves and kisses him on the lips. How can this be happening to *him* - Snoddy the body! He can't believe it. If only they could see him now. He hugs her fiercely. He doesn't want to let go. He will never let go.

*

Now, after a car journey of awkward silences and nervous laughs, they are in the croft house. He had spent two weeks tidying and cleaning, making it ready for her.

Leni smiles a lot as she moves around exploring, hiding her dismay at the bleak, treeless, landscape showing through the windows. Hector sits watching her. He can't take his eyes off her, forgets to offer her the soup and bread he had prepared.

Eventually, Leni stops prowling and stands in the small kitchen.

'Can I make you a drink?' she asks.

Hector leaps from his chair. 'I'll get it. I've got some food ready for you. You sit down.'

Leni, puzzled at the role reversal, does as she is told.

At the table, hesitant small talk accompanies the meal. Hector insists on washing the dishes, and while doing so, is relieved to see Leni move to a chair at the fireside, and quickly fall asleep.

Soon, he is sitting in the chair opposite, watching her, captivated by her beauty. The perfect contours of her body show through the flimsy dress. She doesn't seem to have anything else underneath. He remembers the present he has bought her, a quilted, red dressing gown to keep the cold out, fetches it from the bedroom, and lays it across her.

Back in his chair, he throws some more peat on the fire, settles back to watch her, and feels the tension of the day gradually drain out of his body. He doesn't remember falling asleep.

*

Now, it is the next night. Leni has spent most of the day apologising for falling asleep. She is ashamed that she was not available for her husband on their first night together. Hector can't understand her anxiety. He is thrilled just to be in the same room as her, to be able to see her, to say her name, to know that she belongs to him.

That night, as they sit facing each other, sharing the fire as an arctic wind rattles the windows, Leni stands up and undresses in front of the fire. Her movements are routine and business-like rather than erotic. Hector is spellbound.

She puts on her red dressing gown, and takes Hector by the hand and leads him to the bedroom. Here, she kisses him, slowly undresses him, and holds back the bedcovers for him. Soon, she joins him in bed, and places his trembling hand on her breast. Then she put into practice the sexual instructions given to her by her mother, who had taught her and her sisters how important it was to give your husband satisfaction in bed.

That was the night, Hector remembered, he was taken into a new world. A world of ecstasy.

Chapter 21

On his return from Glenridding, having spent the entire journey trying to find a hidden message in the dying professor's 'summer sniffs', without success, Ben headed straight for his computer. He had been neglecting his Tribune work, and needed to catch up.

His first routine was to check for incoming e-mail. Usually, there were one or two leads from editor Sue Burrows. He typed in his password - FREEDOM. After all this time it still felt good. It was a regular reminder that he had escaped from the bad old days, when he had worked for soul devouring companies. Then, he had used the password PRISONER.

There were two items waiting for him. One, from Sue, gave him the location and date of a forthcoming hound-trailing event, suggesting that he cover it. He downloaded this immediately.

The second item waiting was from a sender address he didn't recognise, and it looked like it was going to be long. He clicked and sat back.

For a moment he wasn't sure what he was looking at as the screen filled with an official looking document, but then, among a column of data giving name, sex, age, height, weight, colour of eyes, hair, he saw 'Post-Mortem No. 97A-187' followed by an ID No, a PM date, and a Death D/T.

He didn't recognise the persons name, but as he read on, he realised that he was looking at the official post mortem report on a man who had been recovered from the foot of Blencathra's Sharp Edge 13-months ago.

It started: 'The body is that of a muscular, well-developed and well nourished adult Caucasian male measuring 71 inches and weighing approximately 160 pounds. There is beginning rigor mortis, and early algo mortis. The hair is brown and abundant, the eyes are brown, both pupils measuring 6 mm. in diameter. There is clotted blood on the external ears but otherwise the ears, mouth and nares are essentially unremarkable. The teeth are in excellent repair and there is some pallor of the oral mucous membrane.'

Over the next three pages, the report covered the external appearance of the body and it's wounds, the condition of the internal organs and abdominal cavity, and the thoracic cavity and skeletal system. Photographs had not been taken in this case, but the next two pages contained anatomical drawings and diagrams relating to the man's injuries. A summary page containing the 'Pathological Diagnosis' found that the man had died of
'multiple injuries associated with cranio-cerebral trauma.'

As Ben stopped reading, he could see that there was a lot more to come. It looked as though Sophie Lund's boast had not been idle after all. Her 'boys' *were* able to produce the goods.

The thought had him excited and worried in equal measure. Excited at the prospect of delving into masses of information to tease out a morsel that would confirm his theory. Worried, because he knew he was breaking the law by gaining access to the information, and because it meant he was still tied in with Sophie Lund.

For the moment, he put these thoughts to one side as he loaded the printer with paper and started to download. An hour later, a deep pile of documents lay on his desk. As they came through, he could see they were all post-mortem reports, from Scotland as well as from Cumbria, some with photographs, some with drawings. His pulse quickened when he saw the names John William Fraser, and Tessa Marie Coleman. He extracted their reports before they became part of the pile. As the printer stopped, a message came up on his monitor: MORE TO COME LATER - SL.

The full implication of what was happening slowly took root. This was getting serious. He didn't like that. He thought he had left serious behind when he left work. He was now backed into a corner. Somehow, events had conspired to put him there.

It looked as though he was going to get all the information he wanted, but he wouldn't be able to discuss any of it with the people he most wanted to - Bill Unwin and, to a lesser extent, Helen. For different reasons, neither must know that he was in possession of the pile of papers that lay, tantalisingly, on his desk. He was going to have to go it alone.

*

He read Jack Fraser's post-mortem report first. It extended to five pages compared to Tessa's three. Were ministers, he wondered, considered worthy of more thoroughness?

'Cranio-cerebral Injuries' seemed to take up the majority of the report. He read of 'Linear, comminuted fracture of right side of skull. Linear pattern of contusions of right cerebral hemisphere. Abrasion of right cheek. Sub-arachnoid and sub-dural haemorrhage. A lacerated wound measuring 14 x 5 mm. above the external occipital protuberance. This wound exhibited small fragments of stone and other detritus, which have gone for microscopic examination and will be the subject of a supplementary report

Later, the paragraph ended: 'The complexity of these fractures tax satisfactory verbal description and are better appreciated in photographs which are prepared. Ben glanced at the photographs. They confirmed that Jack Fraser had suffered severe damage to his skull.

'Poor sod,' Ben thought, as he read on, looking for the eyes.

They were both there. 'The eyes are blue, the right pupil measuring 7 mm. in diameter, the left 6 mm. There is oedema and ecchymosis of the inner canthus region of both eyelids measuring approximately 1.4 cm. in greatest diameter.' A quick check in his dictionary told Ben that they were nothing more than swollen, black, eyes.

He concluded from this that Jack Fraser's body had been recovered before the birds had attacked or he had been found lying face down. Only the mountain rescue team's photographs would show that. He wondered whether he could look forward to seeing them in the near future, courtesy of Sophie Lund's 'boys'.

Ploughing through two more pages giving the findings of the dissection of the internal organs, Ben reached the 'Summary'. It read: 'Based on the above observations it is my opinion that the deceased died as a result of blunt trauma consistent with a fall from a mountain.'

On the final 'Report' page he found: 'Pathological Diagnosis: Cause of death of this 57-yer-old male is multiple injuries to vital organs.'

Ben let the report slide from his hand on to the desk. He was disappointed. There was nothing remotely suspicious contained in it. It began to look as though Sophie Lund's conspiracy theory and his own serial killer theory were both implausible.

He picked up Tessa's post-mortem report without enthusiasm, and with some trepidation. He didn't want to picture her as pieces of meat scattered all over an autopsy suite, in various stages of dissection. He wanted to remember her sweet, characterful, face, her bubbly personality.

With the aid of his dictionary and an old medical book called 'Everybody's Family Doctor', which had been on their bookshelves for years, neither he nor Helen knowing how it got there, he worked his way through the report, 'translating' medical terms into plain English.

Tessa had suffered fractures to the back of the skull, the base of the skull, the brain stem, the spinal column, and numerous bones in her arms and legs. Rigor mortis was, of course, advanced.

The right eye orbit was 'empty of all vitreous and aqueous tissue, consistent with removal by birds after death.' The left eye had suffered fractures to all the bones surrounding the orbit. The orbit was mostly empty, containing only particles of eye tissue as well as particles of stone, and other detritus. This was consistent with the soft tissue of the eye being disintegrated by impact before being removed by birds after death. The left ear was badly lacerated, mostly detached from the skull, the wounds containing particles of stone and other detritus.

An examination of the vaginal mucosa confirmed there had been no recent sexual activity.

The 'Summary' and 'Pathological Diagnosis' were almost identical to that of Jack Fraser, namely - death was consistent with a fall from a mountain, and was due to multiple injuries to vital organs.

This time, Ben was even more dejected. The post-mortem had confirmed that the left eye had been damaged *before* being taken by the birds, but it had also pointed out that particles of stone were present in the empty socket, suggesting that Tessa's head had struck a crag on the way down. Clearly, that is what the pathologist had concluded, as he had raised no questions about it. At least Ben had been right about that - the pathologist had made assumptions.

Ben dropped the papers on to the desk and trudged to the window. Though he could see the beauty outside, it didn't register. His mind was still preoccupied. He was convinced that Tessa could not have hit a crag on her way down - the fall was sheer and clean. And there was nothing sharp on the ledge that could have caused that injury to her left eye.

Then he remembered what Helen had said, when she had theorised about Tessa being attacked for sexual reasons. She had said that Tessa may have fought back and that the attacker had panicked and hit her with a rock. Maybe he had hit her in the left eye. Maybe she was right; maybe the killer was clever enough to know that a blow caused by a man-made tool like a hammer or a steel bar would leave a different wound; one that would raise questions at post-mortems. He would have to hang on to that remaining possibility. It was all he had left.

A harsh squawk from a male pheasant on the lawn below momentarily distracted him, but he was soon back inside his head. Suppose Helen was right, he thought. Suppose a killer struck Tessa with a rock before throwing her off the top. There would be a blood-stained rock somewhere, and possibly some blood-stains on the summit of Dale Head. But how could he find them? The odds on the killer leaving the rock on the summit were astronomical, and he didn't know how to recognise an old blood-stain, and he couldn't call in the police to do it without exposing the source of his information. He was quite prepared to do that, and take the consequences, when he had collected sufficient evidence to motivate them, but, right now, that potentiality seemed a distant fantasy.

He returned from the window and flopped in his chair. Stubbornly, yet resignedly, he wrote on his desk pad: 'Visit Dale Head summit – blood stains?' He had, at least, to go through the motions or his mind wouldn't give him peace.

As he stared at the blank computer monitor in front of him, his focus shifted. If she had been struck with a rock at the summit, she might have been dead before the fall, before she hit the ledge. Would that not show up at the post-mortem?

The question came from deep in his brain's database. Like millions of others, it had been filled with a morass of, up till now, useless information resulting from too many hours watching television police series. He was almost certain that the timing of injuries could be accurately calculated by pathologists. There were no timing discrepancies mentioned in Tessa's post mortem-report. Could the pathologist have skipped through his routines because he was certain he knew what he was looking at - a fall victim? Had he not made an incorrect assumption about the cause of the eye wound? It wouldn't go away. Ben would have to double check.

Five minutes later, he was putting the question, suitably disguised, to local GP Dr Philip Grearson, on the telephone. He had consulted him on a couple of occasions, and met him socially at the golf club. He was one of the new breed of approachable young doctors.

His answer was: 'If an injury occurs causing death, i.e. the heart has stopped pumping blood, and then the body suffers further injuries shortly afterwards, the pathologist will recognise this by different contusion patterns and colours, and thus he will be able to say which injuries occurred first and which injuries caused the death. However, if an injury just renders a person unconscious, i.e. the heart is still working, and all the injuries occur within a short time frame, then the pathologist will not be able to distinguish between the timing of the injuries.'

Ben thanked the doctor and returned to his ruminations. The method of distinguishing between injury times sounded relatively simple and obvious. It was very unlikely that the pathologist in Tessa's case would not have spotted the difference in contusions had she died at the summit, before the fall injuries occurred. Therefore, if she had been attacked at the summit, she was still alive, but possibly unconscious, before the fall.

Ben had to admit that all the post-mortem evidence pointed to an accidental fall, and he could see why the pathologist had not raised any questions. His own murder theory was quickly becoming one of diminishing possibility. Now, for it to be true, the killer would have had to use a rock, a clumsy tool compared to a hammer, smash it into Tessa's eye with enough force to shatter bones and splatter the eye, yet judge it so that she remained alive, though possibly unconscious, until he threw her down.

Even if this unlikely sequence happened, there were still the big questions to be answered - why would a killer look for victims on mountain tops, and what was his motive?

Ben's mind began to blur. He was going round in circles. It was time to get on with some Tribune work; he would return to Tessa later. Before starting, he went through the pile of post-mortems on his desk, collated them into individual reports, stapled them together, then hid them among a large pile of old Tribune papers that lay in a corner; a constant source of annoyance to Helen who liked to see things kept tidy.

Finally, he tore a fresh sheet from his desk pad and wrote the heading - 'CLUES.' Under this he listed - '1. Fatality Statistics. 2. Tessa's left eye damage. 3. 'Summer sniffs'.'

'Not a lot,' he sighed, as he stuffed it into his personal correspondence file in the desk Then, realising that he was allowing himself to get disheartened, he recalled his old motivational motto - 'There's always tomorrow.'

Chapter 22

The good people of Thurso were shocked. You could see it in their faces; they couldn't hide it. Those that didn't know him stared because they rarely, if ever, saw a non-white face in town. Those that did know him stared in disbelief that 'Snoddy the body' was walking down the street holding hands with a stunningly beautiful foreign woman.

Few would know where she came from, and many would resent her presence. The good folk of the north of Scotland have their own ways, and like to keep them unsullied by outsiders.

Their isolationism had been sorely tested by the 'invasion' of engineers from England to work in the Dounreay nuclear plant. That was bad enough! But, a local man bringing a foreigner to live there was beyond the pale. It was unheard of. Hector could hear the whispering swirling around the streets like car exhaust fumes - polluting.

The first time he took Leni into town was one of his favourite memories. It always came to mind when he heard the triumphant trumpet introduction to Sibelius's first symphony pounding in his headphones. It epitomized exactly how he felt when he marched down the street, hand-in-hand. Now he was showing them. Now he was somebody. The explosive, exultant, music said it all.

They had been together for a few weeks, clumsily getting to know each other, stumbling through the days like newborn foals. But the nights brought magic - when darkness hid shyness, when touch replaced words. Then, each seeking comfort in an alien world, they joined in a desperate joy.

He had bought her some new clothes and shoes from a mail order catalogue. He had watched her smile with delight when she turned the pages, then giggle infectiously when he had indicated she could order more than one item.

When she had finished making her choice, Hector added a scarlet dress he had spotted, with matching scarlet shoes. It was these he insisted she wore on their first parade along Thurso's main street.

In that grey town, under a grey sky, she had looked like a dazzling, exotic, butterfly. Madame Butterfly! And wonder of wonders - she belonged to him.

Chapter 23

It was two days before Ben got back to 'Tessa business'. At the behest of Sue Burrows, he had been charging about covering a number of events, from the annual jazz festival to the opening of a new equestrian centre. When driving between assignments he had occasionally put his mind to the 'summer sniffs' enigma, but for the most part it had been head down for the Tribune.

On the second day, during his lunch break at home, he checked his e-mail and found another pile of data waiting to come through from Sophie Lund. They turned out to be all the fatal incident reports from every mountain rescue team he had nominated, including Scotland's teams. Her 'boys' were indeed remarkable.

Now, having stapled each mountain rescue report to its relevant post mortem report, and having sorted them into datal order, he sat with a very large stack of paper in front of him.

He intended to visit the summit of Dale Head as soon as possible, to go through the motions of looking for blood-stains, but it wasn't going to be today. Heavy rain tapped at the bedroom window, and through it he could see dense mist and cloud obscuring the fells on the other side of the lake. As he looked, it occurred to him that the

Lake District's heavy rainfall might make it difficult, even for experts, to find any blood-stains that had been deposited. Even more reason to stay inside, fill a coffee cup, grab a scone, and plough through paper.

He decided to start with the most recent and work back. His pad and pen were ready to note any similarities, coincidences, mutuality. Taking a deep breath, as though he was about to start a marathon, he picked up the first set of papers - the reports on Professor and Mrs Metternich.

Having already seen their mountain rescue reports at Patterdale team headquarters, he skipped through them briefly, noting again that Mrs Metternich had suffered extensive injuries to her face, and Professor Metternich had said 'summer sniffs' before dying. He moved on to their post-mortem reports.

The first thing he noticed was that the pathologist was not the one who had carried out Tessa's post mortem. Tessa's body had been taken to Whitehaven hospital, while the Metternichs had gone to Penrith morgue. Clearly, with the Lake District being ringed by six hospitals, bodies found in different areas were being taken to their nearest hospital or morgue. So, if there was any overall suspect injury pattern to be found, it would not be obvious to several individual pathologists. Only someone with an overview, like he now had, would be able to spot it. He jotted on his pad - 'No Post-Mortem Overview'.

Translating from medical to layman's language, he found that Professor Metternich's post-mortem report more-or-less confirmed the information contained in the mountain rescue report, adding, of course, the extensive internal injuries to major organs, which were stated as the cause of death. Both eyes were intact, and there were no queries raised. Once more, he was looking at a totally non-suspicious document.

Mrs Metternich's report was different. He was immediately attracted to a number of photographs. They showed where the tree branch had penetrated her neck, but having been taken from varying positions, they also showed the damage to the rest of her face, particularly to her left eye, cheek, and ear. The type and location of these injuries were very similar to those sustained by Tessa, though they didn't look quite the same, presumably because Mrs Metternich had been found within 24-hours, while Tessa had been missing for many days and the birds had been at her.

Ben found his sheet of paper headed - 'CLUES', and wrote '4. Mrs Metternich's left eye damage.'

He picked up the report again and started to read the detail. The bones around the left eye had been fractured and the soft eye tissue had been dispersed into liquid particles. These, together with stone fragments were still present within the socket, suggesting, once again, that the head had struck a crag on the way down, and also indicating that the birds had not paid a subsequent visit. The left ear was, again, severely torn, and almost severed from the head. Ben added '5. Ear damage - Tessa, Mrs Metternich' to his 'CLUES' list.

The Summary and Diagnosis were by now familiar - 'injuries consistent with a fall from a mountain', and, 'death due to multiple injuries to vital organs.' As with the others, the pathologist had found nothing to indicate that this might be a suspicious death.

Ben, however, was beginning to think he was getting somewhere. He now had two people with very similar injuries; too similar to be a coincidence, and too rare to be commonplace, he hoped. While he had no hard evidence that these were anything but accidental, he still had faith in his judgement that Tessa's left eye injuries had not been caused by the fall or by the birds.

At least, he now had something specific to look for in the daunting pile of reports that lay in front of him. If he found anyone with similar injuries, then, surely, he was on the right track.

He placed Mrs Metternich's reports face down on top of her husband's reports, which already lay on the desk. He found himself doing this with great care and gentleness, finger tipping the pages together until they looked like one, as if lying their bodies together in a final, perfect embrace.

His eyes misted, and he swallowed hard. This was bloody awful. A retired couple, out for a day's walk, lay in front of him in pieces. It could have been Helen and him. It didn't feel right, reading about the intimate condition of their bodies at death. He felt like an invader into their privacy. Worse still, he had been *hoping* to find terrible, matching injuries.

He got up from his chair and opened the bedroom window, somehow hoping that the fresh air might clear the bad taste in his mouth and the sad fog in his mind. Instead, the cloud and mist and rain that greeted him served only to deepen his gloom. He glanced back at the pile of papers on his desk. He didn't want to read them. He didn't want to wade through dozens of intimate reports that only families should see.

Yet, that was the thing wasn't it - there were dozens of them. If there was a killer out there...he needed to be stopped before the pile grew higher.

He didn't have to spend much time on the next two sets of reports. They covered the deaths of two young male novice climbers found at the foot of Castle Crag, a well-known training crag in Borrowdale. Ben had covered the incident for the Tribune. They had been roped together and fell together; the evidence was all there.

Sadly for all concerned, it was a routine case of a dangerous sport claiming two young lives. Its 'routineness' did, however, serve to remind Ben that the deaths of Tessa and the Frasers, and possibly the Metternichs, were not routine. Reinforced by this: he needed all the encouragement he could get: he picked up the next set of reports. They came from Scotland.

A lone walker had perished on Liathach, a severe mountain in the Torridon range, and another on Ben Hope, the most northerly Munro in Scotland; a Munro being a mountain over 3,000 ft in height, named as a tribute to Sir Hugh Munro who, in 1891, published a meticulous record of all Scottish mountains over 3,000 ft.

Both sets of reports pointed to routine tragedy rather than anything suspicious. It was what Ben had expected. If his theory was right he didn't expect to find anything questionable in the Scottish reports until he had gone back at least two years - to when the fatality figures had suddenly leaped in the Torridon and Inchnadamph MR team reports.

Again, he placed the papers carefully on to the finished pile, face down on top of the young novices reports. It was like building a wall of death.

The name John Fraser took him by surprise when he picked up the next reports. For a moment he wondered if it was another Fraser, not Jack Fraser, Secretary of State for Trade and Industry. Then he remembered that he had filed Jack's reports in datal order along with the rest. A quick glance at the wording of the post-mortem confirmed that he had already read it - it was Jack Fraser's. He added it carefully to the finished pile, then picked up the next report - Mrs Elaine Fraser - Jack's wife.

There appeared to be no photographs or drawings attached, so, stifling a yawn, he went straight to reading the post-mortem report. Within a minute he was wide awake, sitting up in his seat. There it was again. Amongst all the other injuries the poor woman had suffered were fractures to all the bones surrounding the left eye orbit. The orbit contained remnants of soft eye tissue and particles of stone, and the left ear was lacerated and had a 95 per cent disconnect with the skull.

With his mind now racing, Ben reached for his 'CLUES' list and wrote '6. Mrs Fraser - left eye damage.'

Chapter 24

'Smile, Leni, smile,' Hector shouted above the roar of the wind. Leni sat on a rock, posing. Hector was on one knee, having found the right angle for the photograph. He ignored the moisture soaking up from the sand into his trousers.

They were on Strathy Point beach on a bright but wild summer afternoon. Unlike the beaches of Sutherland's west coast, which are a match for any in more exotic corners of the earth, the northern beaches are plain and conventional. Nevertheless they had become a favourite playground for Leni and Hector. In spite of the cold, Leni had grown to love the feeling of space and freedom they offered, compared to the beehive activity of Manila. She had never had the time or money to visit the beaches of her own country, life there being about survival rather than pleasure.

Now, she had all the time in the world, as Hector would not allow her to go out to work. It wasn't that he wanted her at home, cooking and cleaning like a dutiful wife. He was prepared to do all that as well as work at Dounreay nuclear plant He just didn't want to share her with anyone. He wanted her beauty all to himself. He wanted to capture it, hold it, bottle it, cage it; keep it always within arms reach. That is why he had taken up photography.

Almost daily, he took a photograph of her. Anything would do as a subject, from eating her breakfast to reading a book, from bringing in the peat to running along the beach. He took them zealously, as though, at any moment, she was going to run away and leave him.

Such was his obsession that he set up his own developing unit in what had been a large pantry. Every room in the house now had photographs of Leni on every wall. Everywhere he went, his camera went with him, even though his only subject, so far, was Leni.

Leni shuffled slightly on the rock and gave him yet another dazzling smile, her perfect teeth white against her tanned skin, her black hair flying across a white cloud.

The rock was situated just outside the cave where Hector had fantasised about living with his animal friends when he was young; the cave where he dissected the fox to make it his first permanent friend. It was one of the first places he took Leni to see. To have her with him in the place where he had dreamt of living with Kathleen Rinaldi was like a dream come true.

The photograph had turned out brilliantly, and with so many attached memories, it was no wonder it became one of Hector's favourites.

Now it came back to him as he listened to Elgar's 'In the South', a joyous and beautiful tribute to the colour and vitality of Italy. It was as close as western music could bring him to the essence of Leni.

It brought a half smile to his thin lips, though such was his emaciation it looked like a skeletal grimace. After all those years, and though numbed by alcohol, the memory of Leni sitting on the rock was as clear as ever.

When would it fade? He needed it to fade. He glanced at the whisky bottle. It was empty.

He rose from his chair and swerved across the room to a sideboard. On his way, he stopped suddenly. He thought he felt a slight vibration in his stockinged feet. He removed his headphones, momentarily abandoning Elgar. He stood still...listening. There was nothing...there couldn't be.

The pause made him search his swirling mind. Yes, he decided eventually, he had fed her tonight. He continued to the sideboard, took out another bottle of whisky and returned to his chair. He half filled the seven-sided glass, noticing for the first time that the knuckles on his left hand were as prominent as the edges of the glass. He must eat more, he told himself, as he gulped some more pain killer. 'Tomorrow...that's when I'll eat ...tomorrow.'

It was getting late. He needed his sleep music. Music that soothed his mind, music that said the world was a beautiful place full of beautiful people who loved each other, music that engulfed him with its soaring passion and tender sweetness, then wrapped him up, tucked him in, and stroked his brow until he went to sleep.

He didn't have to look far. It was always to hand. With reverence, he ejected Elgar and replaced him with Rachmaninov. He put the headphones back on. The adagio from the second symphony came down from heaven and took hold of his soul. His head fell back and his eyes closed.

Chapter 25

The discovery that Mrs Fraser had the same left eye injuries as Tessa and Mrs Metternich was the stimulus Ben had been looking for. Up till then, he had been blowing hot and cold about the whole thing. Up one day, down the next; always feeling that it might not be worth the candle; always aware that he could pack it in and go fishing. Now he couldn't. Mrs Fraser had changed all that.

Now he had something tangible to work with. Two people with the same injuries could be coincidental, but not three. And it hadn't escaped his notice that all three were female. Was a second pattern starting to emerge? Time would tell. He jotted down: '7. All three female so far.'

This also kick-started the possibility that Jack Fraser had not been the main target. Maybe the fact that he was a government minister was totally irrelevant. Maybe, to the killer, he had been just another member of the public out walking with his wife. And it was his wife who interested the killer.

If this proved to be the case, it would be a big shock to Sophie Lund. She was convinced it was all about Jack, and politics, and the nuclear industry. She was counting on it.

At this stage, he decided, he wouldn't be passing on any of these thoughts to Sophie Lund. As long as she didn't have an answer, she would still be useful to him. He was still waiting for her 'boys' to send him the police records on each fatality, and maybe they could help with some future queries, as yet, unforeseen.

Ben had always felt that not enough attention had been paid to Mrs Fraser's death; the media and the police being so absorbed with her famous husband. Was there something special about her? Was there something she had in common with Tessa and Mrs Metternich? Or was it just because they were female? Was there another sick Ripper-type out there?

It was probably going to be a long, painstaking, journey to find out. But now that he had something to really get his teeth into, he wouldn't let go. He would work at it and worry it until he found the answer.

Before he could pick up the next set of reports, however, the phone rang. It was Bill Unwin making his routine call to check if he was okay for golf that afternoon. For the first time in his life, Ben felt he should forego the pleasure of a round of golf and a pint of ale. He should stay at his desk and get stuck into the remaining reports. But it was only a fleeting aberration. 'See you on the first tee at two,' he said.

*

Bill was waiting for him, practising his swing on the first tee.

'Sorry I'm late, 'Ben breathed, dragging his trolley alongside the tee. 'Got caught up in something.'

The 'something' had been the arrival, by e-mail, of

a huge quantity of police records relating to all the fatality incidents. Once again, the 'boys' had succeeded.

Before leaving for golf, Ben had quickly flicked through the pile and discovered that a large proportion of it was concerned solely with Jack Fraser's case; the rest being mostly brief notes and statements covering, what were assumed to be, routine accidental deaths. It would seem, from what he had recently learned, that all that police effort had probably been misplaced.

He had managed to staple each police record to its relevant batch of documents already on his desk, and hurriedly hid them away, before dashing off to the golf course.

On the quiet drive to the course, the full implication of having those records surfaced again. He was certain that he was now a criminal.

He had got himself into this situation, initially due to his own inquisitive nature and a soupcon of lust, and later through underestimating Sophie Lund's capabilities. Now, he was not only a criminal by deed, he actually felt like one. He felt guilty, and not a little sordid. He hoped none of it would show when he met his mate - the policeman.

*

After four holes of equal scoring, but unequal conversation, they set off after their drives down the long tree-lined fifth. Bill said: 'You're a bit quiet today...you okay?'

'Yes...yes...' Ben mumbled, as he made an exaggerated gesture of looking ahead for his ball. 'Just a bit tired I think. Don't know....'

'Not getting enough sleep eh?' Bill interrupted. It'll be the worry of stealing all those police records.'

Ben stopped in his tracks, utterly shocked. He didn't know what to say. Bill had continued walking ahead. He turned when he realised Ben had stopped. He could see by the look on Ben's face that he had been taken seriously.

'Just joking, Ben...sorry...no offence,' he stammered. 'It was just...with you asking me to get all that information for you, and Penrith telling me that we've had a few cyber hits recently...I mean, I knew it couldn't be you...'

'A few what? Cyber hits? What the heck are cyber hits?'

'See,' Bill laughed, slightly nervously, apparently bothered about upsetting his friend, 'you don't even know what cyber hits are...I knew it couldn't be you.'

'But you have just tested me, haven't you?' Ben was thinking quickly now, desperate to walk through the door Bill had left open for him. 'I'm a bit surprised,' he said firmly, trying to take the initiative. 'I thought you knew me better than that.'

'Yes...well...sorry mate...but you did push me hard for that information. Anyway, let's forget it eh? I shouldn't have brought it up on the golf course.'

Ben's heart started to slow down. What incredible luck. He had been let off the hook. Just to make sure, he decided to go on the offensive to try to clear the suspicion once and for all. He picked up his step, and put on his most friendly smile.

'I know as much about computers as you do about sinking putts over ten feet,' he joked.

'Hey, steady on,' Bill laughed. 'I have been known to sink a few. Let's think...there was that one in 1983...and that one...'

'Okay, I'll grant you that,' Ben said quickly. 'You know *more* about putting than I know about computers.'

An unsteady silence followed. It was as though the subject had suddenly been closed by mutual consent, and neither knew what to replace it with. Ben sensed that Bill wished he hadn't raised the subject in the first place, and was now feeling uncomfortable. Now was the time to ram home his 'innocence' and be magnanimous at the same time.

'Tell me about this cyber hit business, Bill. Sounds intriguing. I take it from what you said that some unauthorised person has been accessing, or should I say stealing, some of your records. Does it happen often?'

'You'd be surprised how often it's happening,' Bill explained. 'I don't see much of it myself, but the boys at Penrith HQ are always on about it. They reckon we should now treat the World Wide Web and the Internet as virtual city streets. They say that every criminal activity that takes place on our city streets is now also on the web, plus a few new ones. Apparently, we now employ a full time computer whiz kid at Central Records to watch out for cyber invaders would you believe. He's nicknamed the cyber sleuth. It was him who informed us that our records had been hit recently. He is supposed to spot these attacks in advance and ward them off. Don't ask me how; it's all double Dutch to me. Seems he didn't see the latest hits coming, says there's some very clever opponents out there; computer boffins who've been lured into crime with big money.'

'It sounds incredible,' Ben said convincingly. 'So now you've got virtual crime as well as real crime to deal with.' He paused as they approached his ball and he took his shot with a two-wood. A low slingy slice left the ball well short of the green. 'Still, it's good for the old job security,' he said lightly, trying to jolly things along. 'Sounds like you'll never be out of work.'

'You can say that again,' Bill agreed, tersely, before slamming a three-wood miles down the fairway. He seemed to have put extra venom in the shot.

They set off walking again. 'I suppose it's a pretty serious offence - stealing police records?' Ben asked, trying to sound casual.

'Very serious.'

'What are we talking? A heavy fine?'

'Let's just say - if it had been you, you wouldn't be tasting a Cumberland ale for a long time.'

'My God! That is serious.' Ben said it jokingly, but registered it with full gravity in his mind. He really could not afford to let Bill know anything about his dealings with Sophie Lund, or about his continuing investigations. Bill was already suspicious and was obviously as straight as a die. He would arrest him - friend or no friend.

He had been going to ask him if CID had reached a decision on whether or not to investigate the Metternich deaths, and if anything had happened since he brought the increase in fatality statistics to the notice of his oppo at Penrith HQ. But now he thought better of it. It would be wiser to let Bill think he had given up on his private detective work, and anyway, Bill would probably have offered the information by now, had there been anything to tell.

With a burgeoning workload, it was very unlikely that the police would drop their current priorities, which were no doubt based on sound evidence, to go chasing cases based on a member of the public's concern about a few statistics.

The rest of the round passed pleasantly enough, the conversation finding its way out of the rough, back on to the smooth green of small talk. Not surprisingly, Bill won easily, and Ben had to buy the ale.

They had almost finished their pints when Bill said casually: 'I take it you've dropped all that detective stuff about Tessa Coleman and the other fallers. You haven't asked me anything about it today? I didn't hear anything back from my oppo in Penrith by the way. To be honest, I didn't expect to - they're up to their eyes down there.'

'Well, I've had to drop it haven't I,' Ben lied. 'No information, no can do, it's as simple as that. But I am keeping my eyes and ears open. I'm still convinced there's something very suspicious about some of those falls.'
Bill leaned forward, and lowered his voice. 'Look, mate, you might be right for all I know. And if you are, and you get involved, you could find yourself in danger. I haven't been able to help you very much with the paperwork, but if you ever need any physical assistance, don't hesitate to shout. We're good at the strong-arm stuff.'

With that, he downed the dregs of his beer and took his leave.

Ben sat holding the remainder of his pint, puzzled. He didn't know whether he had just had an offer of help or a warning to keep his nose out. Surely the police weren't involved in a government cover-up, as Sophie Lund had suggested. He didn't want to underestimate Bill Unwin the way he had Sophie Lund. Maybe the solid station sergeant was cleverer and more subtle than he seemed. Then again, maybe he was getting paranoid. He finished his ale quickly. He needed to get back home; to a warm fire and a cuddle from Helen; he needed a strong dose of normality.

*

Back home, the cuddle from Helen was comforting but brief. She had her usual pool staffing problems to deal with and was busy phoning around her existing staff, telling them about two new temporary pool lifeguards she had just taken on. Rearranging the shift rosters to accommodate the newcomers seemed to take ages, as each temporary staff member had other work and family commitments to take into account. Ben admired the way she went about it all calmly and persuasively, and usually came up with a satisfactory conclusion.

*

The following morning, after an unavoidable two-hour spell for the Tribune, Ben hastily retrieved the pile of documents from their hiding place and sat them on his desk. In spite of what might have been a warning from the police, he couldn't wait to resume his examination of them.

Now that he had the police records, which contained the photographs taken by the mountain rescue teams, he possessed virtually all the records he had asked

Sophie Lund to supply. He still found it hard to believe that she, and her 'boys', could produce such results.

From the police records he extracted the mountain rescue photographs of Tessa, Mrs Fraser and Mrs Metternich. In gruesome, bloody detail they confirmed that similar violent damage had been done to their left eyes. Tessa and Mrs Metternich also had similar left ear injuries. Mrs Fraser's left ear was missing. The photographs of the two husbands, Jack Fraser and Professor Metternich, showed no such damage. So far, his theory was holding up.

Three laborious hours later, as he continued through the pile in datal order, occasionally recognising fatal incidents in the Keswick area he had already reported on, he came across another likely case.

The incident had occurred 11 months ago, on Glaramara fell in Borrowdale valley, about six miles from Keswick. At the time, he remembered reporting it as a 'routine' fall tragedy. Now, the deaths of Mr and Mrs Harris, on holiday from Lincolnshire, warranted a different, sinister, category.

The photographs said it all. Found at the foot of Bull Crag's steep cliffs, after a three-day search, the bodies had been visited by the birds. All four eyes were missing. Three had been taken cleanly by the birds. Mrs Harris's left eye region was severely damaged. Her left ear hung on a dry sliver of flesh. Mr Harris had no similar injuries. Again, the eye; again, the woman.

Ben found his CLUES list and wrote: '8. Mrs Harris (11 months ago) left eye/ear damage'. He moved up the page to No. 7 and changed it from 'All three female so far' to 'All four female so far'.

Towards the end of the day, Ben's own eyes were struggling. He left his desk and moved to the window. A flock of the lake's geese were wheeling in the sky, ready to land in a lakeside field. Outlined against a multi-coloured sunset over the western fells, they were a gloriously normal sight.

He had found one other possible case that afternoon. But the body of the lone woman had been found face down, and no photographs had been taken at the post-mortem. However, the post-mortem report spoke of left eye and ear damage. So, he had added the documents of Miss J Hudson to the separate, small, pile on the right side of the desk, and noted her as No. 9 on his CLUES list.

Rubbing his tired eyes, he returned from the window and started to put the documents back in their hiding place. As he did so, he noticed that the next set of reports were from Scotland. He had covered over a year of Lake District incidents and was now moving back in time to the information he had picked up from the Torridon Mountain Rescue headquarters and sent to him by Alec Gordon of the Assynt team.

They would have to wait until tomorrow. He was about to go for a stroll down to the lake before the sun disappeared, to see the red sky reflected in the still water, to watch the mallards glide and squabble, to see the fishermen measure their catches, to watch a buzzard take its final hover of the day, to listen to...silence. He would count his blessings and eventually stroll back to the cottage to prepare the evening meal, and wait like a lovesick teenager for the return of Helen.

*

For the next three days Ben maintained this routine. A few hours for the Tribune, the rest of the day studying the incident documents, ending with an evening stroll to the lake.

At the end of the third day he had read through the entire pile of documents. He had found four more cases in Scotland, two in the Torridon area and two in the Assynt area.

The two cases in the Torridon area had occurred 18 months and 21 months ago. In both cases, couples had been found at the foot of crags on Beinn Eighe and Liathach. In both cases the women had suffered left eye and ear damage, while the men, though severely injured in other ways, did not have the same left eye damage.

The two cases in the Assynt area had occurred 26 months and 30 months ago. The first case involved a couple being found on Conival. As usual, only the women had suffered left eye damage. The second case involved a man found at the foot of An Caisteal; the only man to show relevant left eye and ear damage.

At the end of it all, Ben felt totally drained and very depressed. He was, of course, gratified that his theory was looking increasingly plausible, but the horror he believed he had unearthed swamped any feeling of satisfaction. Out of the 43 deaths that had occurred in the three regions over the past three years he had extracted 15 that he believed had been perpetrated by a murderer. One man and eight women, whose left eyes and ears were severely damaged, and six accompanying husbands or boyfriends.

The fact that the men did not show any particular pattern of damage, left the door open to the possibility that other men, apart from those husbands and boyfriends, had also been murdered, but it was not obvious. And though he had gone back through three years of records to the times of increased fatalities in the three regions, how could he be sure that this was the full extent of the killer's range and time. The thought that there could be more than 15 victims only added to his sadness.

Ben battled against his tiredness as he took a breather at the window. There could be no stroll to the lake tonight; there was thinking to do.

With the first attacks taking place over a 12-month period in Assynt in the north of Scotland about three years ago, followed by attacks over the same period in the Torridon area approximately two years ago, the killer had probably lived in those areas and then moved on to the Lake District.

He had apparently now been in the Lake District for over 15 months, and had killed at least eight people in that time compared to seven during two years in Scotland. Clearly, he was speeding up. Or was it that there was a greater supply of the kind of people he liked to kill in the Lake District compared to the small population and number of visitors in the north of Scotland?

What was particularly worrying to Ben was that all the Lake District deaths had been within a ten mile radius of Keswick, and it had to be assumed that the killer was still in the area. What was it that was holding him here?

Suddenly, he experienced a feeling of panic. It was all up to him. He was the one who had to sort it out. Either that, or take it back to the police and have Helen find out about Sophie Lund and the stolen records. That would have to be the very last resort.

Yet, who was he to gamble with people's lives. If the killer struck again, before Ben had discovered his identity, he would find it impossible to forgive himself for not going to the police. But, was there any guarantee that the police would take up the baton again, and if they did, was there any guarantee that they would be successful in finding the killer before he struck again.

Perhaps he was the best bet after all. He now felt totally absorbed in the matter; he had read through every incident; he had felt empathy with the victims, being a fellow lover of the high places. Maybe this closeness he felt to the victims and the mountains on which they perished gave him a better chance of finding the killer than an uninvolved detective brought in from the city.

He was going around in circles again. He had to make a decision. Just then, he heard Helen's voice from downstairs. She must have come home early. Or had he forgotten the time? He glanced at his watch. He had forgotten the time. He bundled the documents out of sight and went downstairs.

Helen smiled her usual warm hello as they kissed. He held her a little longer than usual. The softness of her cheek matched the tenderness of her nature. She was all that was good in his life. She must not come to harm. The decision was made. He would go it alone. If someone died in the future because he hadn't gone to the police, so be it. It would be him that suffered, not Helen.

Chapter 26

He stares out of the window. The grey evening light is fading to darkness. A passing cormorant spreads its gothic wings against the sky. Another day's work is over. He doesn't feel so bad tonight.

He has fed her and emptied her bucket and even pecked at some food himself. Maybe, tonight, he can get through without drink. He has yet to put on his walkman earphones; enjoying, while he can, a rare blankness in his mind. Maybe some light Mozart will see him through. Maybe a piano concerto.... A noise from outside the window; a cat is meowing. A mournful cry against the passing of the day? A cry for a mate? Hungry? To Hector, it sounds like one thing only: the cry of a baby.

He rushes for his tapes. Only Mahler can cope with this. Soon he has the achingly poignant sound of the adagietto from the fifth symphony glowing in his head. He knows where it will, inevitably, take him. He takes a bottle from the cupboard and settles into his rocking chair.

*

Leni had smiled when she said: 'I think I'm pregnant, Hector.' He had been shocked to silence. In his naivety;

in the magic whirl of his first few months with Leni, he had never even thought of children, of fatherhood. That was something that happened to other people, to normal people. Not to misfits like him; to someone so uncertain, nervous, frightened, that he still felt like a child himself.

'Are you not pleased?' Leni said, querying his silence with a frown.

'Yes...yes,' Hector hurried, hating himself for causing the frown. It's...wonderful.' He had never used that word before. It didn't sound right...try again. 'It's magic.' That sounded better. He just wanted to say the right thing to please her. He didn't know what his feelings were; he didn't have any yet.

Somehow he muddled through the next few hours, trying to say the right thing, agreeing with everything Leni said, trying to match her excitement. She was obviously thrilled and couldn't wait to let Mama and Vilma know her incredible news. In his mind, Hector could picture Vilma leaping up and down, dancing around, laughing and shouting, and then crying because she was not with her best friend to share the moment.

Days later, when the full implication of fatherhood had finally sunk in, though exceedingly nervous about the prospect, he decided, emphatically, that this would be the best cared-for baby in the world. It would never have to suffer the neglect he had. Even now, the thought of those years of loneliness, and lack of affection, brought tears to his eyes. He couldn't remember anyone touching him in the first 20 years of his life.

Leni had changed all that and brought him the joy of physical contact, and more than that, made him feel he was worthwhile. When the child came, he decided, he would look after it as he looked after Leni - with complete devotion. It would be kissed and cuddled from dawn to dusk.

The lonely house on the windswept headland heard the baby's first cry at ten o'clock on a fine spring morning. Like most babies, it had wanted to arrive during the night. At Leni's request, Hector had phoned for the midwife at 5.30 a.m. He wouldn't allow her to go into hospital; he didn't want her out of his sight. Yet, when the delivery started, he had to leave the room because he couldn't bear to see Leni in pain.

When the midwife came out of the room and placed the tiny bundle in his arms, he almost fainted. It was so small he could have held it in his hands. The tiny face had been blessed with its mother's large eyes and generous lips, and he was glad there was none of his own ugliness to be seen.

'It's a girl,' the midwife smiled.

Hector stared at the angelic little face, and worried and swallowed hard. This little miracle was his. She was already depending on him...*him!* He would try not to let her down. He lifted her slowly to his face and kissed her gently on her brow, then, with his quivering lips trying to smile, he carried her back to her mama.

Grace had brought them truly together. No longer two individuals trying to please each other, they became a team, two acting as one in the shared joy of caring for their offspring. Leni had chosen the name Grace in memory of her sister who had died in childbirth. A perfect name, Hector often thought, as dotingly, he watched his baby grow into a graceful, happy little girl.

*

Hector pours himself another drink, then slumps back in the rocking chair, and closes his eyes as he recalls those blissful early years.

A keen swimmer, Leni had persuaded him to take them to Thurso pool to teach Grace to swim as soon as she could walk. He had been reluctant at first, not only because he couldn't swim, but also because it meant other people coming into contact with Leni, in a swimming costume. His initial reaction, to show her off when she first arrived, had long since been replaced by a desire to keep her to himself, away from lustful eyes. He worried also that Leni would tire of him and be tempted by a more attractive man.

But he need not have worried. With great patience and a thousand smiles, Leni had taught them both to swim, and she seemed totally unaware of the admiring glances of those around her. Always, her eyes were either on Grace or himself.

The daily trip to the pool, either early morning, or after work, had become a highlight of each day. He could still see Grace shouting 'Daddy' as she jumped from the poolside into the water beside him. He could still feel her wet little arms around his neck.

Lost in sweet recollection, he is suddenly startled by the searing finale of the adagietto. Now his head is swimming with heartbreaking thoughts and music. His face contorts its resistance, his body shakes with tension, but nothing can stop the bottomless pit of grief from erupting again.

The desperate, painful, sobbing leaves him exhausted and shivering, as though he has a disease.

Vaguely, he wanders how much more he can take before he must seek special relief. Shakily, he fills his glass and replaces the fifth with the fourth hoping that Mahler's lighter and most tender slow movement will take him to a better place.

The glorious music starts, like a waltz in slow motion, and soon has him sailing over the headland as though on a cloud. Leni is with him, holding his hand, smiling as always. They are looking down on the beach, the cliffs, in the distance - Dounreay, his place of work, over the fields to hover over the house, the door of the house opens and a little girl runs out and waves up at them, quick, away from there, inland to the mountains - ah yes - the mountains!

Again, Leni had been the instigator. Whereas he had been content to relax or potter around the house at weekends, Leni, after being in the house all week, was eager to spread her wings. Used only to overcrowded houses, streets and cities, she was tempted by the vast emptiness that lay inland from the house. She wanted to visit the bare hills and the peaked mountains. As usual, with a smile and a kiss, she got her way.

Carrying Grace in a special harness on his back, and later walking by his side, Hector had grown to love the empty mountains he had ignored as a child. He loved them because Leni had shown him how. She was so happy there, enjoying the space, the freedom. With Grace trying to keep up, she ran and climbed like a child. She never complained when the weather was bad, and made lots of hot soup, which they hugged when they huddled together for a picnic. She had even persuaded him to join the local mountain rescue team.

Ben Loyal, a corruption of the Gaelic Ben Laoghal, became her favourite mountain. 'Big Ben', she called it. With its five sculptured summits rising in complete isolation from the flat moorland, it compelled her to walk along its skyline ridge linking the five summits.

Although a long car ride from the house, they never tired of driving there, parking the car at Ribigill farm, and following the shepherd's track that led to the foot of An Caisteal - the castle - the highest of its peaks.

From the summit, the view of Sutherland's vast, empty, hinterland and the imposing Kyle of Tongue sea loch kept them captivated until sunset, which, in summer, didn't take place until midnight. Then, a fast asleep Grace would have to be carried back down to the car. He could still feel her dead weight on his back. No! ...He mustn't....

Clumsily, he removes Mahler's fourth and grabs the nearest tape. Suddenly, the mighty music of Sibelius fills his head. The second symphony reveals its wondrous grandeur, as though heaven has been brought to earth. There had to be such a place. Sibelius had seen it, and was letting ordinary mortals know it was there. Nothing else could explain this sound, this mysterious majesty. Hector travels on its familiar journey, following every chord, every nuance.

It was a favourite of Leni's as well as himself. Often, as they sat on a bench outside the house, watching the evening sunset, they would open a window and let it explode through and past them, to soar across the bleak headland, filling the emptiness of the scene, filling their hearts with emotion, confirming that heaven existed, that love was everything, that their love was true.

Now, the soaring strings rise to an immense, triumphant, unbearable, finale. Its intensity wrenches the last
ounce of sorrow from Hector's trembling frame. His face
contorts grotesquely as he lets out an ape-like scream, and
he curls up into a foetal position, hugging himself and
rocking himself into the night.

Chapter 27

The daunting prospect of single-handedly trying to hunt down a murderer stopped Ben in his tracks for a while. What chance did he have on his own when the police, with their teams of detectives, forensic scientists, profilers, often struggled for years with a case, and didn't always succeed. For two days he achieved nothing as myriad thoughts and concerns surged through his mind.

That he should be doing something, and quickly, he had no doubt. Like it or not, it had become his responsibility. But what to do? Where to start? Who to talk to?

How could he, a small town, part-time journalist, with no detective training, hope to track down a serial killer. A serial killer! How he disliked that description of a murderer. Its incessant use by Hollywood, television and the rest of the media, as a subject to sell their wares, had made the mass murderer's fiendish activities seem commonplace. Somehow, it had almost taken on a badge of respectability, as though it was a chosen profession.

He had to admit, however, that initially, he too had been absorbed by the horrendous stories played out on his television screen. He had always been a sucker for a good detective story; preferably a who-dunnit, investigated and solved by a world weary British chief inspector who had personal troubles at home.

The new, hard-hitting breed of programmes from America had come as a shock. But, like the rabbit in the headlight, he hadn't been able to tear himself away from them. That is, until they became so frequent that they became routine, and then, in search of ever increasing horror, banal.

He had stopped watching them some time ago, but now he wondered if all those hours might not have been wasted. Perhaps some of the investigation techniques and methods, which were reputedly authentic, had registered deep in his subconscious. Maybe he would be able to recall and use them. He closed his eyes and tried. Nothing.

Maybe he had been thinking too much lately, maybe his brain was tired. He couldn't remember a single episode from any series, not even a single plot. So much for my powers of retention, he thought.

He had now reached a point, which he recognised: the point where no amount of extra thinking gets you anywhere; the point where you have to start doing something, however trivial or, in retrospect, stupid, in the hope that the activity will kick start you on another route towards solving the problem. He decided, therefore, to start at the absolute beginning. He went upstairs to his office and picked up his favourite book.

Helen had bought him 'The New Shorter Oxford English Dictionary' for his last birthday. The 3,767 beautifully bound pages, in two volumes, were a joy to peruse. In it he looked up the definition of 'serial killer'. It read: 'a person who murders repeatedly with no apparent motive.' *Great,* he thought, as he took in the last three words; I have just confirmed the impossibility of my task. If there is no motive, where do I start looking? He hoped the word 'apparent' might prove the let out.

Now the word 'serial' started to bother him. He looked it up on its own and found, as he had expected, that it referred to events taking place in *regular* succession or intervals. He knew that the murderer he was looking for did not operate on a regular basis, and he suspected that most mass murderers did not follow a regular pattern. So he concluded that the word 'serial' had been misused and should be replaced with something like 'repeat'.

Having established that he was now looking for a 'repeat killer' rather than a 'serial killer', and knowing that all this playing around with the semantics of the English language was nothing more than procrastination while he put off taking the plunge into the unknown, he came to the realisation that he needed professional help.

If the murders were motiveless, then the only way to find the killer was to start by looking for the *type* of person who might commit them, and that was a psychological profiler's job. But how could he find a profiler, and, if he did, how could he ask for advice about murders which were just theoretical at the moment, and with which the police were not involved? Maybe he could consult on a hypothetical basis. Fat chance.

He remembered recently reading a feature article in a Sunday paper. It mentioned that there were only 20 accredited profilers in the country, all busy psychologists or psychiatrists who tried to fit the police work around their normal laden schedules. They were definitely not going to find time for him.

There was only one thing for it. He would have to try to pick up some basic profiler knowledge and methods himself. He would visit the library and try to find books on profilers, police detection methods, and serial killers.

In the meantime, he would work on the assumption that there was a link between the victims and their killer, that there was a motive, and he would try to find it by studying the lives and backgrounds of the victims. He would also put his mind to the 'summer sniffs' clue at every available moment, and finally get round to visiting the summit of Dale Head to look for blood-stains.

Now that he had a plan to work to, however small or inept, he felt better. He had always found that if he worked hard at something, even though he appeared to be getting nowhere, something relevant would come out of the blue to assist the cause, as though the very act of working at it set up some invisible vibrations that triggered something somewhere else. It was all very mysterious and other-worldly, and he didn't believe in that, yet his 'vibrations' hypothesis had never failed the test.

That afternoon he visited Keswick library and found exactly the book he was looking for. 'The Serial Killers - a study in the psychology of violence' by Colin Wilson and Donald Seaman, proved, on reading, to contain all the elements he was looking for.

After reading its horrific contents, he felt almost ashamed to be human. Its graphic accounts of the heinous acts carried out by people who, unfortunately, were now household names, showed that there was no limit to human depravity.

However, its main purpose was to shed light on the work and methods of the psychological profilers, and to publish their insights into the minds of serial killers. Ben read with alarm that apart from a few isolated historical cases, serial killers have only been appearing, in ever increasing numbers, since the 1960s.

Making copious notes as he went along, Ben felt that he had gained a fundamental understanding of the terrible subject by the time he closed its 349 pages. He then studied his notes, and using a highlighter pen, highlighted the essential basics that he must try to absorb, and work to, and to which he could refer at a glance.

The first lesson he had learned was that in order to find the type of person who kills repeatedly, the usual first step is to identify the type of victim the killer chooses. Although the killings are apparently motiveless, with the killers not knowing the victims personally, usually the victims had something in common and, could therefore also be categorised by type.

However, finding the commonality could be very difficult as it ranged from the very specific - prostitutes with red hair - to the very broad - they liked shopping in the evening. All this confirmed that he had been right to put the investigation of the victim's backgrounds as his first step.

While continuing to study his notes and the book, Ben also determined to watch every police programme on television. His patience was rewarded when the second of a Thursday evening's crop of four threw up a scene in which a harassed police chief stood in front of a board on which he had written in large letters:

WHY
WHEN
WHERE
HOW

He was berating his team of detectives for not concentrating on basic investigative procedure. 'We know the When, the Where, the How,' he snarled. 'My goddamned grocer could tell me that from reading the papers. But we are not even getting close to the Why... and why not? Because you've forgotten the first rule of investigation! And what might that be Baker?'

He glared at an unsuspecting rookie detective sitting at the back.

The rookie stood up, swallowed, and said: 'Identify the victim, Chief. Then link the victim to the killer ...somehow.'

'Smart boy,' the Chief shouted. 'Now let's get out there and do it for Christ's sake. You know what to do - don't ya? Knock on neighbours' doors, visit friends, talk to her frigging dentist. I want to know everything about this poor woman by tomorrow night...got me.'

Miraculously, by the next scene, the Chief had all the information he wanted, and he eventually went on to capture the killer after the inevitable car chase.

Ben knew it wasn't going to be quite as easy as that, but once again, he had confirmation that the victim was the right place to start. Initially, that meant ploughing through all the police records again to see if there was any victim commonality. He was beginning to think that, as with so many difficult endeavours, it might be perspiration rather than inspiration that eventually brings results.

Before starting his examination of the police records he typed some headings into a database on his computer: Name. Address. Sex. Age. Height. Weight. Nationality. Married. Single. Retired. Divorced. Children. Religion. Politics. Member Of. Hobbies. Travel. Sport. Military. Relatives. Enemies.

He felt sure that he hadn't covered everything, but knew he could add to it as he went along.

The journey through the police records, extracting and typing the relevant information on to the database, was long and painstaking. And eventually it was disappointing. The information held on most of the victims was very sketchy, leaving many of his database columns incomplete. The exception was Mrs Elaine Fraser. Presumably because she was the wife of a government minister, whose death had caused a big investigation, she had warranted special attention. Indeed, reading through the files, the police had paid much more attention to Mrs Fraser than Ben had given them credit for. They had looked in depth at her life as well as that of her husband's, but clearly, had found nothing that warranted a suspicion of murder, or a motive for murder. Not surprisingly, the proposition that she and her husband could be the random victims of a serial killer had not been mooted.

In Mrs Fraser's case, Ben had been able to fill every column of his database, and add some more that the police had covered, such as Medical History. On the face of it, there was nothing in Mrs Fraser's data to suggest that she was any particular type of person, and there was nothing to link her with any of the other victims at this stage.

Ben now knew that he would have to contact the families of the other victims to obtain more background information. As he contemplated this unwelcome task, his natural reticence was cast aside when he read in his notes that there was 'always a connection between victims, usually simple in retrospect, because the killer is usually simple-minded.' He was also encouraged to 'study the minutiae of events in all cases.'

He felt as though he was about to embark on a very long journey. He decided to start it close to home, by visiting Tessa's friends and neighbours to see if they could fill in her data gaps, and then he would head for the place of her death - Dale Head.

*

After a morning for the Tribune, a clear afternoon saw Ben taking the same route as Tessa on her last walk up Dale Head. He parked his car at the slate quarry and trudged the hour-long steep climb to the top.

As he climbed, he recalled some of the con-versations he had had with her friends and neighbours as he collected information from them, in the guise that it was going to be used in some future article about her.

Nothing surprising had come out of it. They all confirmed she was a beautiful, gifted person. His questions had brought tears to the eyes of an elderly neighbour who recalled that she had been 'a lovely girl', a term Ben thought very fitting for the ever-youthful Tessa.

Having filled almost all her database categories, he compared them with those of Mrs Fraser. Apart from the obvious commonality of sex, and height, he could see no apparent connection between the two of them and, as yet, no indication of the joint characteristics that would group them into a particular type of person.

As he approached the summit, his mind switched to the constantly nagging riddle of 'summer sniffs.' After days of contemplating it at every spare moment, and coming up with some bizarre, and fruitless explanations, he was beginning to dread putting it back in his mind. He was finding it hard to get to sleep because of it, and was waking up with it still gnawing away.

Arriving at the summit, 'summer sniffs' was temporarily abandoned as his eyes took in the familiar views. Though no lake or tarn could be seen, the panorama was still magnificent, with the northern prospect of Newlands Valley fading into the distance, to be stopped by the Skiddaw massif, being his favourite.

As he approached the summit cairn, dramatically perched on the brink of the great downfall to Bilberry shelf, he started his 'impossible' search for blood-stains, and any other clue that might reveal itself. The ground consisted of sharp upturned stones embedded in the surface and sharp, loose, stones that had obviously been prised from the ground by boots and weather. Any one of the stones could have been used to inflict Tessa's terrible eye injuries.

After 15 minutes of bending and examining what he thought might be blood-stained stones, he knew he was wasting his time. Most of them had some kind of colour variation, which might have been inherent or caused by the weather, or even the spilled tea from a walker's picnic. He would never be able to tell the difference. He did find a stained piece of paper stuffed into one of the gaps between the stones of the cairn. It read: 'Tim loves Lisa

- July 2002.' Apart from that, there was nothing to attract his attention.

He wandered over to the edge of the drop into Newlands Valley and looked down. It appeared to be a sheer fall on to the vicious crags a few hundred feet below. Cautiously, he leaned forward slightly. Only now could he see Bilberry shelf jutting out from the sheer rock face. He could see why the killer had been fooled, and the search parties had missed it.... footsteps behind him. Adrenalin rushed to his heart, hitting like a hammer. He threw himself sideways, every sinew and muscle taught, mind flying. The killer must have followed him. Why had he been so careless?

As he hit the ground, he intended to do one of those kung fu rolls, bounce back on his feet, and take up a defensive stance. Instead, he roared with pain as the upturned stones dug into his body and caught him a glancing blow on his right cheek bone. He finished lying on his back, like a stranded seal, moaning and gasping. The figure of a man loomed over him, outlined against the blue sky. Instinctively, he crossed his arms in front of his face, waiting for the attack.

'Good God!' a cultured voice said. 'Are you alright?'

Ben relaxed his arms and slowly propped himself up into a sitting position. He was looking at a grey-haired man with a concerned look on his benign face. For a moment his throbbing bruises took second place as a feeling of utter embarrassment took over. 'I'm fine...I'm okay...' he stumbled.

The grey haired man offered a hand to help Ben up. 'You gave me such a shock,' he panted, as he pulled

Ben on to his feet. 'I thought you were throwing yourself over the edge.'

'Sorry...' Ben hesitated, hurriedly searching for a half reasonable explanation for his bizarre behaviour, while rubbing the dirt and dust from his clothes. 'It....it was just a reaction...I was so close to the edge...when I heard your footsteps...they distracted me.... and for a moment I thought I was going to overbalance...I tried to throw myself backwards, but I seem to have gone sideways...at least I'm still here to tell the tale.' The laugh he finished the sentence with felt as weak as his explanation.

'You've scratched your face,' the man said, ushering Ben by the elbow away from the edge. 'Come over here and I'll take a look at it.'

They moved to a large boulder where Ben leaned back as the man examined him. He had the air of someone used to helping people. 'Nothing too drastic old chap,' he said comfortingly. 'Just a graze...I'll put a sterile dressing on it, and if you give it a good wash when you get home I'm sure it will be fine.'

As he spoke, and started to take off his backpack, Ben noticed a plastic identity tag on the man's anorak. The name 'P. Dawson' was typed underneath the green logo of the Lake District National Park Authority, and underneath that were the words 'Volunteer Warden'.

Ben relaxed when he saw the name tag, and slowly recovered his composure. He had once written a short article about these solid citizens who volunteer to watch over and protect their beloved fells and anyone on them. They each watch over a specific area, reporting on damaged paths or walls, picking up rubbish, giving advice to tourists, and generally being good Samaritans. A mixture of retired locals wanting to feel useful, and visitors who regularly travel long distances to get there, they do sterling work without pay.

Peter Dawson, retired army officer, introduced himself as he took a dressing from his small first aid kit, and applied it to Ben's cheek.

'Thanks...thanks a lot,' Ben said sincerely. 'You must think I'm a complete idiot?'

Peter Dawson didn't reply. Slowly and methodically, he packed away his first aid kit. Then he straightened up, and leisurely put his backpack on. Eventually, he glanced up at the blue sky, then smiled at Ben. 'Nice day for staying alive,' he quipped, as he turned and walked away.

*

The dramatic views down Honister Pass and the soreness of his bruises occupied Ben's mind as he shuffled back down the mountain to his waiting car. In the comfort of his car the soreness dissipated, and he hadn't driven far down Borrowdale valley, when 'summer sniffs' insinuated its way back into his consciousness.

Eventually, after mentally going down another dozen blind alleys, he came up with 'what if, in spite of the way the words appear to go together in one meaning, they didn't. What if they were looked at as separate, unlinked words?'

Further mental gymnastics, at one point interrupted by a flock of sheep crossing the road, eventually brought him to 'what if 'summer' was someone's name, and they had the habit of sniffing? There would still be a linkage there, but the emphasis would have switched from the second word to the first.

Could Professor Metternich actually be naming the killer: a man called Summer? Someone who has a sniffing habit? But how could he possibly know the name of a stranger who appeared to pick his victims randomly? Surely the killer didn't introduce himself before committing the murders? Or, maybe he did. It could be part of his 'signature'.

He remembered reading that serial killers usually have a pattern of killing called their unique 'signature'. They kill to satisfy an inner personal need, usually triggered by hatred or revenge at some perceived wrong. They strike when the heat of their rage is at its peak, and kill in a repetitive manner as if trying to stamp their personality on the victims. It is the nature of this repetition that marks them out as serial killers, and reveals their unique 'signature'.

Ben continued his pondering as he drove along the shoreline of Derwentwater, approaching Keswick. Maybe the killer had introduced himself to all his victims before killing them, knowing that they would never survive to tell anyone: the professor being the one, unexpected, exception. Maybe that was his method of putting them at their ease, so that he could get close enough to attack. It made a lot of sense - there are few places to hide on the open fell tops - it would be difficult to approach someone without being seen first.

And yet, hadn't he just been approached on Dale Head summit, from behind, without knowing it. And....his mind suddenly shot into overdrive...I came away knowing the name of the man who was behind me - Peter Dawson. Ben's knuckles whitened on the steering wheel as his senses went into first gear. Had he found the answer? Was the killer putting his victims at ease by wearing the trusted name tag of the National Park Authority? Was he posing as a voluntary warden or even a full time National Park Ranger who also wore name tags? Could the killer actually be a warden or a ranger? They spend more time on the fells than anyone else, and know the fells better than anyone else.

It was the first rational scenario he had come up with since starting on the 'summer sniffs' trail. Buoyed up by his discovery, and convinced that his 'vibration' theory was starting to work again, he put his foot down along the A591 Keswick to Carlisle Road that took him most of the way to his lakeside cottage. He couldn't wait to get home to use the phone.

*

'What have you done to your face?' Helen asked, concernedly.

Ben hadn't expected to find her home at four o'clock in the afternoon.

'Hello dear...been sacked?' he joked, as he moved to kiss her.

'I asked first,' Helen insisted, as she withdrew from their cuddle.

'It was them darned Apaches again,' Ben explained in his best western drawl. 'They dry-gulched me at Honister

Pass. Just a glancin' blow from a tomahawk, you understand. Nuthin' to worry your perty little head about.'

He mentioned Honister Pass in case somebody might have seen him there, and innocently mention the fact in some future conversation with Helen.

'I take it you won again,' Helen went along, knowing he would never grow up, and that she would eventually get a proper explanation.

'Sure did, honey. Picked 'em off one at a time with my trusty Smith and Weston. They bit that dust as offen as a whore's drawers on a Friday night in Tombstone.'

'Oh shush!' Helen said, slapping him lightly on the shoulder. She then gave him one of her 'looks', and he knew it was time to be serious.

'I was walking up near Honister Pass and I slipped and fell on some rocky ground. I think I'm going to have a few bruises. One of those volunteer wardens came by and put this plaster on. Nice chap...used to be a major... says me cheek's just grazed and should soon heal up. Okay?'

'No, it's not okay,' Helen countered. 'You know you shouldn't go walking up there on your own. One of these days...' She abandoned her lecture. She knew he wouldn't take any notice. 'Be *careful,* you daft bat,' she emphasised. 'Now go and get in the bath, it will help ease the bruising.'

Ben was dying to get to the phone, but now knew it would have to wait until tomorrow when Helen was back at work. And the mention of the word 'bruises' seemed to have made them throb again. Helen was right, as always. An early bath was called for.

'If I'm not down in an hour, send for the cavalry,' he winced, as he took his leave, forgetting to ask Helen why she was home so early.

*

'Lake District National Park Authority, Jane speaking; how may I help you?'

Ben tried to find a comfortable position in his swivelling chair. The bruises seemed to be touching everything. He wanted to reply: 'By not making me listen to your ridiculously long, insincere greeting that you learned ad nauseam at some customer care course run by a sycophantic, money grabbing, suit clad prat who called himself a 'marketing consultant'.

Instead, he tried to find comfort in the fact that he hadn't been answered by an automatic answering system giving him five options, none of which he could be bothered to memorise, since on the few occasions that he had bothered, it had resulted in him listening to Mozart for 25 minutes, occasionally interrupted by yet another recorded voice telling him that he would soon be connected to one of 'our customer service consultants', who eventually turned out to be a 16-year-old girl called Sharon who knew damn all. He had nothing against Mozart, but preferred to listen to him for free on the radio.

'My name's Ben Foxley. I'm a journalist with the Keswick Tribune. I'm looking for some information about your voluntary wardens. I wonder if....'

'Putting you through.'

'Lake District National Park Authority, Public Liaison Department, Sarah speaking; how may I help you?'

Ben gritted his teeth. One more greeting like that and he would bark down the line like a rabid dog.

'Hello, Sarah,' he managed, calmly. 'My name is Ben Foxley of the Keswick Tribune...'

'Is that a newspaper?'

'Yes it is, Sarah.'

'How may I help you, Mr Foxley?'

'I'm looking for some information about your voluntary wardens. I assume you keep a list of all their names and addresses....'

'Yes, we do, Mr Foxley. But we can't give them out over the phone...'

'No....I know that.' His fuse was getting shorter. 'I just wanted to know if Mr Summer was still with you. He helped me a lot with an article I did about the wardens a couple of years ago. I'm planning a follow up and wondered if he could help me again. I just need to know if he is still working for you, and then I'll drop him a line care of your office asking for an appointment to meet him.'

There was a short pause, followed by a whispered conversation, then: 'I'll see what I can do Mr Foxley. Apparently we have over 60 volunteer wardens so it might take some time. I'll put you on hold.'

Now he was listening to 'Greensleeves', a tune once revered by nostalgic Englishmen, but now hated by millions as they see their phone bills rising with every note that passes.

Ben sighed, and started his habitual doodling. For no good reason he drew a man's face with a long pointed nose, and wearing a top hat. Then he wrote the word 'Greensleeves'. It looked strange. 'What the heck is a greensleeve?' He would look it up in his dictionary when he had time...

'Are you there Mr Foxley? It's Sarah again....'

'I guessed it might be you again,' Ben thought, unkindly.

'...I've checked all the names of the voluntary wardens on our staff data base and there doesn't appear to be a Mr Summer.'

'Are you sure?' Ben found himself using a demanding tone, so irritated was he with the reply. Then, remembering that Professor Metternich was a German, and may have pronounced the word differently. 'Maybe I've got his name slightly wrong,' he said. 'Have you got a Mr Sumner, with an 'n' or a Mr Semmer with an 'e' or even a Mr Zummer with a 'Z'?'

He leaned forward in his chair, phone hard against his ear, willing her to come back with an affirmative.

A short pause was followed by: 'I'm sorry Mr Foxley. The only S's we have are a Mr Simpson and a Mr Sugden, and we have nobody starting with Z.'

'I'm sorry to be a nuisance,' Ben said, in his best grovelling tone, 'but would you mind looking up your staff list of full time Rangers. Maybe Mr Summer was a Ranger. I sometimes get confused between the two.'

In the pause that followed he thought she was going to refuse, but then she said, with a hint of irritation in her voice: 'Just a moment.'

This time he was on the edge of his seat. 'Greensleeves' started up again, but didn't register. He was too busy willing her to come back with the right answer. There just had to be a Mr Summer or equivalent working for the NPA or it was back to the proverbial drawing board.

'Hello, Mr Foxley...'

'Yes!'

'We don't appear to have a Mr Summer among our Rangers either I'm afraid....'

'What about....'

'The only S is a Mr Spalding and there are no Z's... sorry.'

'Don't apologise, Sarah. You've been very helpful. I must have got his name wrong. I was going from memory, and it's not so good these days. I'll have to go back through my papers to see if I can find the right name. Sorry to have troubled you.'

He replaced the phone.

'Damn,' he swore out loud. 'Where to now?'

*

An hour later he was in Keswick library, thumbing through a German/English dictionary. After the phone call, and half an hour staring out of the bedroom window, vaguely watching a pair of red squirrels playing tag on his conservatory roof, it had occurred to him that Professor Metternich may have spoken in his own language just before he died. Maybe 'summer sniffs' were German words.

Eagerly, his fingers flicked the pages until he reached the S's. 'Sum'...'summ' ...yes...*yes...yes*...there was a 'summer'. He had finally cracked it. Was he clever or what? His eyes darted to the English meaning. It read: 'buzzer'. It was not what he was expecting. He let it bounce around his brain for a while, but nothing relevant came forward.

Baffled, but still excited, he flicked back through the S's to look for 'sniffs'. It wasn't there. Nor was there anything that looked like 'sniffs'.

'Blast', Ben bellowed, as he slammed the book shut.

A chorus of shushes flew at him from the other library users, sounding like a steam train starting up.

He raised his left hand in a contrite gesture without taking his eyes off the dictionary. With a sigh of submission he opened it again. Just for the record, he would check whether 'summer sniffs' translated into German, had any relevant meaning. As he expected, the translation into 'sommer schnuffeln' meant nothing to him.

He left the library in a state of distraction, and walked slowly down the narrow alley that led back to the car park. He wasn't aware that he was holding up a woman pushing a pram behind him, eager to get her crying baby back to her car where nourishment and, hopefully, peace awaited.

Head down, he concentrated hard on dealing with his disappointment. It had knocked him to his knees, but he must not let it put him on the floor. He had to toughen up; be ready for more set backs ahead. He must stay positive. For the time being he would put 'summer sniffs' on the back burner, and concentrate on gathering more background information on the victims, in the hope of finding a connection somewhere. 'Hope', he mused, as he reached his car, 'is all the fuel I have at the moment. I must keep it alight.'

Chapter 28

She shuffled to the edge of the stinking mattress, and took hold of the chain that lay coiled around her left foot. She eased it out of the way while she adjusted the manacle to a more comfortable place on her ankle. Not that there was much comfort. Years of wearing it had taken its toll, leaving her lower leg alternatively swollen, bruised, or covered in sores. It was never completely free of pain.

He had made the manacle from a bracket and bolt taken from a car exhaust system, so there were plenty of rough edges to contend with. He had used the same system to attach the other end of the chain to the steel ring that protruded from the ceiling above her head, well out of reach, even when she stood up and lifted her arms.

She presumed that the steel ceiling ring had been there for many years as there was an identical, unemployed, one a few feet away. She guessed that they were leftovers from an age when carcasses were left to hang, or cooking pots were suspended over fires.

At least, in recent months, he had been occasionally supplying her with a piece of cloth to protect her ankle when the damage became severe. But he was always careful to take it away when it had healed again. He refused to let her keep anything that might be used as a means of killing herself. The strange thing was that he didn't seem to have noticed that the plastic bucket he provided as a toilet had a steel wire handle. And one day soon, she hoped she would be making use of it to make her escape.

The sound of the door opening made her lie down. She could only hear the sound, above the constant blare of the love duet from Madame Butterfly, because it was a low frequency hiss, as though air had been released from a vacuum. Somehow, she managed to cope with the continuous din. The noise was no worse than the cacophony of Manila's traffic she had told herself, and slowly the sound's impact had receded into the background of her awareness.

She lay, tense, making sure her back would be facing him when he came in. He usually left her alone in the morning, when his throbbing hangover left him sullen and silent. But she could never be sure. She heard him place the plastic plate on the floor beside the mattress, and replace the soiled plastic bucket with a clean one. Then she sensed that he was standing over her, looking down. Then she heard him walk away and close the door.

She turned over and pulled the plate towards her. It was breakfast time. This was the only way she knew the time of day, because there were no windows in the blank walls and he left the lights on permanently. Over the years she had tried to keep track of the days, the weeks, the months, but she had eventually given up, and now time had become an irrelevance.

She was also having problems with her eyesight, as they never saw the peace of darkness. Sometimes she wished she would go blind, then she wouldn't be able to see the hideous photographs hanging on the walls. She knew that she would have to escape soon or risk going blind or mad, or both.

The breakfast plate contained a plastic bottle full of orange juice, two bananas, four slices of cold ham, four slices of buttered brown bread, and a tub of natural yoghurt. This would have to last her until evening, when he brought her dinner.

He did try to feed her well, but it was always with food that didn't require knives, forks or spoons. She always had to use her fingers, then lick them clean. At night, after dinner, if he hadn't fallen asleep in a drunken stupor, he would bring her a dish of warm water, soap and towel and stand and watch as she did her best to keep clean.

She ate three quarters of a banana and placed the remaining quarter on the floor beside the plate. Then she ate two slices of ham wrapped in one slice of bread. Finally, she drank some yoghurt from the tub and some orange juice from the plastic bottle. Then she took up a yoga position on the mattress and turned her attention to a corner of the room that was in shadow.

She didn't have to wait long. The rat appeared on cue. It shuffled towards her, nose twitching, eyes darting, and stopped when it reached the banana. It quickly devoured the banana with fast, purposeful, nibbles, then looked around for more, circling and sniffing the floor. When it came back towards the mattress, attracted by the smell of the food she still had left, she waved it away, and it dutifully scurried back towards the hole and disappeared.

She had been totally unperturbed by the rat. She had seen thousands in Manila; they were part of everyday life. On the contrary, she had been pleased to see it when it first appeared a few days ago. It had indicated to her that the timber-panelled walls of the strangely shaped room were not as solid as they appeared.

By taking up all the slack in the chain and then lying on the floor, she had managed to reach the corner and examine the hole the rat had made. Pushing her small hand through the hole, she had found, to her surprise, what felt like a gap between a wooden door and a stone wall. She surmised that the wall panelling had been placed over an old doorway, and that the rat, attracted by the food smells, had squeezed through the gap and then chewed its way through the wooden panelling that lined the room. Where the rat came in, she was determined to go out.

It was this that had renewed her efforts to dislodge the steel ring from the ceiling. Initially, she had climbed up the chain, and swung around on it, simply for exercise; determined to keep her muscles in good shape. But, a few days ago, as she was climbing and swinging, a few grains of grit fell on to her arm, and as she shinned up the chain for a closer look, a puff of cement dust dropped on to her face.

She grabbed the ring with her right hand, holding on with three fingers, and inspected the ceiling around the ring. Where the steel rod holding the ring disappeared into the concrete, a fine semi-circular crack had appeared. After a few more days of climbing and swinging, the crack had formed a complete circle and widened. It was now obvious to her that the rod had been welded to a circular steel plate, which had been embedded in the concrete during construction.

Recalling her working days in Manila, when she had attended talks and demonstrations given by German and British concrete repair companies, she remembered that unless steel is protected by a coating before being placed in concrete it is open to attack from water vapour; concrete being a porous material. The water then slowly corrodes the steel, causing it to expand, and the expansion then puts pressure on the surrounding concrete, causing it to crack at its weakest point. She had forgotten the technical term for the sequence, but she remembered the media had dubbed it 'concrete cancer' when badly constructed tower blocks and bridges started to break up.

She guessed that this might have happened to the steel plate in the ceiling, causing the initial crack, and her constant swinging had been enlarging it. The truth was that she didn't care what had caused it. She just hoped that she had sufficient energy and time to totally dislodge it before he noticed the ever-increasing crack in the ceiling, or the rat hole in the wooden panelling.

In an attempt to hide them from him, she had been carefully gathering the displaced cement dust and mixing it with bread and spit into a dough, which she trowelled into the crack with her thumb. She had then made the rest of the bread into a dough, without the cement dust, and used that to fill the hole in the panelling; the rat eating his way through it every morning before entering the room. She had also hidden the larger bits of grit and debris inside a hole in the mattress.

*

It had been about half an hour since he brought breakfast, she guessed. She always allowed this length of time before starting to work on the chain, in case he returned before he went to work. She assumed he must be out at work all day since he normally didn't come to see her again until evening.

Her attack on the chain began in earnest. Alternatively, swinging backwards and forwards, and then in circles, and using her full body weight to pull down on it with sudden jerks, she continued to dislodge small pieces of aggregate and debris from the crack.

She had been working at it for what seemed to be hours, occasionally stopping for a sip of orange juice when, during one of her downward jerks, she felt a slight give in the ring. Breathlessly, she shinned up the chain and found that the plug of concrete containing the ring's steel support had indeed dropped down, about four millimetres. It meant that the crack was now completely through the full depth of concrete. She dropped to the floor and began a frantic session of pulling and jerking the chain, expecting the concrete plug and its contents to fall to the ground. It slipped another few millimetres, but it didn't fall.

Desperation and fear took over. Now it was too late to turn back. There was no way she would be able to hide this amount of damage. If she didn't escape today, then she never would.

She shinned up the chain again, and pressed her tired eyes to the crack. She saw nothing but shadow. She dropped down again, and frantically searched for something reflective. She grabbed the white plastic top off the orange juice bottle, and shinned up again. It worked. It reflected enough light for her to see that, although all the crack was now completely free of small debris, the larger pieces of aggregate, still embedded in both surfaces, were randomly interconnecting with each other as the plug moved out of the hole. Her only hope was to apply a series of twisting actions to the plug in the hope that the aggregates would eventually find a place to pass each other when a pull was applied.

She took hold of the steel ring and tried to turn it clockwise. It didn't move. She tried anti-clockwise. It moved very slightly, but not enough. She didn't have the strength or the leverage to turn it. She dropped to the floor, gasping, and wanting to cry.

Then she remembered the bucket. Pulling some padding from a hole in the mattress, she wrapped it around the bucket's wire handle, and with a strength she didn't know she possessed, succeeded in pulling the flattened ends of the handle through and free from their locating lugs. Next, she doubled the wire handle over and stamped and pressed it into a single, strong, tool, about 30 centimetres long.

Back up the chain, she passed the tool through the ring and applied leverage. It worked. She was able to twist the plug in both directions. She worked at it for a few minutes, at one point releasing the plug slightly, but then she couldn't hold on to the chain any longer and fell to the mattress below. Exhausted, she lay still, knowing that she would have to rest and regain her strength for a final effort. Eventually, she leaned over and ate the remaining banana and bread, and drank the rest of the yoghurt and some orange juice. Then she lay back to rest.

She found herself waking up. Panic. Sleep had been the last thing on her mind. How long had she slept? She couldn't tell; it might have been ten minutes or two hours. She leapt to her feet, cursing her own stupidity. Grabbing the tool, she shinned back up the chain. Her strength had returned. Gritting her teeth she twisted the ring in both directions. With each twist, bits of aggregate broke away, and the plug started to slip. Suddenly, it fell out completely, catching her by surprise, sending her crashing to the mattress, the plug and the attached chain landing in a heap beside her.

Hurriedly, she picked up the concrete plug and the tool, and, gathering the chain into her arms, walked to the corner where the rat hole was. For the first time in years she was free to move. She felt very strange, almost guilty.

Kneeling down, and resting the plug and chain on the ground, she put her hand through the small hole in the panelling, and felt around. The panelling felt quite thin and insubstantial, more decorative than structural. It appeared to be held in place with steel panel pins. She gripped it and pulled. It flexed, but didn't budge. However, she had felt its weakness, and continued to pull in sudden jerks. She started to feel it ease off the panel pins.

Where it had eased, she inserted the wire tool and levered. Using a ratchetting action, she gradually freed a portion of the panelling big enough to allow her to get a grip with both hands. Now able to apply her full body weight behind the pulls, she soon had the complete panel removed. Only now did she notice that it was backed with thick insulation material, which had fitted neatly into the doorway she had exposed.

Pausing for a sip of orange juice, she surveyed the substantial old door in front of her. Her heart was pounding. She blessed herself with the sign of the cross and whispered: 'Please God - help me.'

Looking to the left, she couldn't see any hinges, which thankfully meant that the door opened outwards. Otherwise, she would have had to break out more panelling. On the right, where she expected to find a handle or a keyhole, she found a hole where a handle had been taken out. Looking into it, she saw that it was blanked off at the other side. There seemed to be no way of opening the door other than by brute force.

She charged it with her shoulder and bounced off it like a ball. But she thought she heard bits of something falling down the gap between the door and the wall. She charged again; again the sound of bits falling. She picked up the tool and pushed one end into the narrow gap between the door and the wall, and then using the concrete plug as a hammer, knocked the tool inwards. It travelled the width of the door, then met some resistance. She continued hammering against the resistance, and suddenly the tool shot through and almost disappeared. Carefully, she retrieved it and inserted it into a different area, and hammered. Again it went through, relatively easily.

Now she realised that the gap on the other side of the door had only been filled with a thin filler or plaster. If there was no locking mechanism in place, all she had to do was knock out sufficient filler to allow her to charge the door open.

She went at it with renewed vigour, hammering the tool through at intervals around the gap. Occasionally she stopped, to test it with a shoulder charge. It was taking too long. She didn't know what time it was; he might return at any moment. Her throat was dry with fear.

She stepped back for a moment, and gulped the last of the orange juice. Once again, she flung herself at the door. At last it gave way. Not much at first. But a few more charges, and she had opened it enough to allow her to pass through.

She flicked her long hair forward so that it protected her bare breasts, and gathering up the chain and plug, squeezed through the gap. The light coming through the gap allowed her to see that she was standing, in what appeared to be, an old wash-house. In the dark shadowed room she could just make out an old ceramic sink, taps, and tiles. She wasn't free yet.

She stood still and waited for her eyes to adjust to a darkness she had forgotten. In the absolute silence, she could hear her heart thumping in her ears.

She was desperate to move, to run and run and run, away from him, away from the nightmare. She couldn't be caught now - not after she'd come so far. It would be unbearable. If she was, she imagined, she would lose the will to live, and… She could see a doorway…ahead to the left and up one stone step. She almost ran to it.

It was a typical old tongued and grooved exterior door, with a simple iron latch. Barely able to breath, she lifted the latch and pushed. It didn't move. Then she pulled, and the door swung easily inwards. And she climbed the step to freedom.

It was dark and very cold. There was no light from the house. If he hadn't returned from work yet, it meant it was probably early evening in winter. Just for a moment, she hesitated, wondering whether her naked body would be able to cope with the cold. But she knew she had no choice. She would rather die quickly in the cold free air than return to the slow death of captivity.

She wanted to run, to feel the air again against her face, to escape as quickly as possible, but she knew she couldn't. The weight of the chain and plug, and the state of her left leg made it impossible. There was also the darkness.

Her first step was on to sharp, loose, gravel. She hopped, in pain, as the stones bit into her bare feet. But she didn't stop. She walked about 20 paces, feet screaming, before the gravel stopped. Now she was on, what seemed to be, a rough dirt track. In the distance she thought she could see a source of light. As she moved down the track towards it, the light grew brighter, and quickly, brighter still. Then she heard a sound. It was a car. It was probably him, returning from work.

She rushed to the side of the track and felt grass and foliage about her. She threw herself to the ground, face down, in the hope that her long hair would hide most of her naked back She didn't breath.

The car approached quickly, then slowed down when it reached her vicinity. Perhaps he had seen her in the distance. She heard the wheels turning, agonisingly slowly, as it came to within a few feet of her. If he stopped, she decided, she would go down fighting. She would use the chain and plug like a sling and swing it at him. She started to tense, in preparation.

The car moved slowly on, and on, and gradually she knew she was safe. As the tension of the moment left her body, it opened the door for the rest of the day to follow. She sobbed where she lay - huge, gasping, heaving sobs. She was utterly drained, utterly exhausted, and utterly free.

When at last she asked her body to move again, it refused. And to give her some peace, it took her into unconsciousness.

From the deep darkness of that state, came a memory of waking up, lying still, too exhausted to rise, shivering violently, before drifting back into the welcome peace of sleep.

Only a passing fox, doing its nightly rounds, saved her from sleeping to a hypothermic death. It sniffed around her naked feet, and licked the blood off them. Then it took an exploratory bite at the softest part. Suddenly, her senses switched on again, as her foot took instinctive evasive action. Her eyes opened and her body twitched. The fox ran off.

Dreamily, she forced herself to a sitting position and reached for her right foot. A harsh stinging pain pulsed through it, and brought her to full alertness. She could feel torn flesh and sticky blood, and now she could also remember where she was.

She struggled to her feet, hugging herself against the cold, and set off down the track. Now she was glad of the night; it was unlikely he would come looking for her in that cloud covered, jet black darkness.

The track soon merged on to a narrow tarmaced lane, which she began to hobble along. During the next half hour, as she forced herself forward, only the pain in her foot kept her from drifting back into a hypothermic haze.

Now, ahead, she could see lights from occasional traffic travelling at right angles to her. She must be approaching a main road. Her spirits lifted. She was going to make it.

As she arrived at the main road, a car swept pass, its headlights highlighting that she was at a T-junction, and that the road was bordered by a narrow grass verge.

She decided to turn right and, gingerly, stepped on to the verge, hoping it contained no hidden hazards. She had only travelled about 30 paces when she placed her torn right foot on to a sharp object. She tried to stop her weight going on to it by lunging to the left, but it was too late. The object penetrated her skin, and she screamed as she fell to the ground on her left side.

Recovering from the shock, she sat on the verge with her back to the road, and nursed her strident foot. The object had dislodged itself, but she could feel more leaking blood. Gradually, she began to feel dizzy, and then nauseous. This would have to do, she decided. She would sit and wait, and wave down the next car that came along.

*

Like most dairy farmers, Willie McNeil is a man of habit. He hadn't missed his Friday night drink and game of dominoes at the pub on the edge of town for 35 years.

And he had no intention of changing his drinking habits just because they had brought that no drinking and driving law in. That was to stop the young tearaways - not people like him who knew how to handle their vehicle after a few pints and had never had an accident, except for hitting the odd deer or badger.

That was when he was glad he had the bull-bar fitted to his Land Rover. It absorbed the impact and protected his vehicle from damage.

He was driving along the familiar winding road, back to his farm five miles away, when suddenly, on a bend, oncoming headlights were dazzling him. He hit his dip-switch as fast as he could, but the on-comer didn't hit his. Dazzled by the lights, and not knowing how wide the other vehicle was, Willie slowed, and swerved to the left to make more space. As the vehicle flashed past him, Willie felt his wheels mount the grass verge. A second later his vehicle registered a dull thud and he knew he had hit something fairly big. 'Probably another deer', he thought, as he brought the wheels back on to the road, and accelerated, and once again thanked the day he had fitted the bull-bar.

*

She lay in a dank ditch, beneath a barbed wire fence. She had disturbed the spiders and the cobwebs and the insects and a field mouse. Her left arm hung, crazily, over her face. Her eyes, and head, were wide open. She would not be disturbing them again. She had made the ultimate escape.

Chapter 29

'Don't tell me, Margaret,' Ben said to the woman behind the counter in Keswick Police Station. 'You've had four missing dogs, three thefts from cars, two drunken yobs and a partridge up a pear tree.'

'Bit more than that,' Margaret said, plainly, pushing slips of paper towards him.

Ben didn't feel very jocular, but his routine with Margaret had been going so long he felt that she expected it. He hadn't experienced a Monday morning gloom since his work days, but today it lay on him like a drab cloud. His mood was caused by his lack of success during a weekend of contacting relatives of the victims, to try to pick up background information on them and create some linkages. Most had been unavailable and hadn't returned his call yet. Of the three he spoke to, one refused to co-operate, and he gained only snippets from the other two. His information database continued to look disappointingly sparse.

He glanced at the first slip of paper. 'Mountain rescue seems to have had a quiet week,' he muttered, his casual observation hiding a great sense of relief.

'Aye...' Margaret's tone was quizzical, as though she was waiting for him to say something else.

He looked at the next slip. 'What's this?' he exclaimed in surprise.

'Didn't you know?' Margaret queried in a rising voice, as she leaned on the counter, ready for further discussion. 'I thought you might have heard about it. It happened not far from where you live.'

'I can see that,' Ben said, in disbelief, as he continued reading the slip of paper. 'I saw a couple of police cars and lots of barrier tape when I drove in this morning, but I just assumed there had been an accident. When did it happen?'

'We got it yesterday afternoon,' Margaret replied. 'Couldn't tell you when it happened. We are just about to release it to the media now. And we all know what that means,' she sighed. 'A town full of tabloid journalists and television crews again. Won't that be fun!'

Ben carried on reading the notes, then asked: 'Is Bill in this morning?'

Margaret's eyes rose in surprise, and Ben knew he had asked a stupid question. '*Everybody* is in,' she announced.

Ben knew it would be a waste of time asking to see Bill who, no doubt, would be tied up with his superiors. He would have to work with the brief information the slip of paper provided. He thanked Margaret, and headed for the offices of the Keswick Tribune.

After a short discussion about the incident, with Sue Burrows, he drove home and wrote the following report:

MYSTERY BODY ON A591

The naked body of a woman, believed to be of Asian origin, was found beside the A591 trunk road,

four miles north of Keswick, on Sunday afternoon.
She had suffered severe injuries to the head and body.
A heavy steel chain was found attached to her ankle,
with the other end being attached to a chunk of
concrete. It was evident that the woman had been
held captive for some considerable time.
The body was discovered at 3.30 PM by
a group of walkers returning to Keswick after a day
on Ullock Pike.
Keswick police are asking anyone who has
driven on the A591 between Bassenthwaite and
Keswick during the past week, and may have
witnessed anything unusual, to contact them on
Keswick 79003. They are also keen to hear from
anyone who may be able to help them with the
identification of the 5 ft tall woman, who appeared
to be in her 30s.

That was all he had at the moment, and as the paper didn't go to print for another couple of days, he put it to one side, hoping to be able to pad it out with more information from Bill, when he was free from his superiors.

It appeared to be an amazing and tragic affair, with which, no doubt, the tabloids would have a field day. Already, he could see the headlines: 'Sex Bondage Slave Slaughtered', or 'Slaughter Of Asian Sex Slave'. They would definitely all have the word 'sex' in them; he could guarantee it.

There was no getting away from the fact that it was a big story. But the fact that she had been found less than a mile from his cottage was, he believed, irrelevant to his investigations. The A591 was the main artery running from Carlisle on the Scottish border, right through the heart of the Lakes, to join up with the M6 motorway in Lancashire. The poor woman could have been murdered in Glasgow or Manchester and dumped on any roadside during the quiet of the night.

He had agreed with Sue Burrows that it needed plenty of attention, and normally he would have been glad to run down every last detail. But right now, he was convinced he had even bigger fish to fry.

Having had little success when contacting victim's relatives in the UK, he decided to try his luck with Professor Metternich's son, who, according to the police records, had come over to accompany his parents' bodies back to Munich. He found the phone number in the records and dialled, hoping the hour time difference would enable him to finish the call before Helen returned from work.

'Hallo...Peter Metternich.' A friendly voice greeted him.

'Guten Abend, Herr Metternich. Mein Namen Ben Foxley. Ich am Apparat von England. Sprechen Sie Englisch?' Ben hoped his very basic German was understandable.

'Yes, I speak English. Go ahead Ben.'

'Thank you Peter. I'm calling from the police records department, regarding your parents' deaths. I am very sorry to bother you, but I wonder if you could help me to fill in some personal details about your parents, so that we can close the file.'

'You should have been asked these questions when you were here, but I'm sure my colleagues didn't want to burden you at such a terrible time.' His ability to lie convincingly had been learned in the world of private industry, where it had become an art form.

There was a slight hesitation before Peter replied: 'There is nothing wrong is there?'

'No...no,' Ben assured him. 'It is just routine. We have a very comprehensive check system we have to go through when sudden death occurs. It is all to do with recording as much information as possible at the time of death. Firstly, it is to ensure that we have identified the person correctly; secondly, it is to have the information available for any investigations that may arise in the future, and thirdly, it helps with all the statistical analysis that goes on these days. It might all seem unnecessary to you Peter, and if you don't feel up to it, I'll understand. But we believe these records are important. It will take about ten minutes to answer all the questions on my list. I would be very grateful if you could spare me that time.'
He crossed his fingers, and took a deep breath.

'Okay, go ahead,' came the reply.

It actually took Ben about 15 minutes to run through all the questions on his database. Peter seemed to answer them as best he could, but frequently appeared to be on the point of querying why a particular question was necessary. When that happened, Ben rushed on to the next question, and somehow managed to conclude the interview without serious interruption.

'Vielen Dank, Peter,' Ben said when it was all over. 'Gefallen hinnehmen unser Beileid.' He read out his condolences from his pre-prepared notes.

After putting the phone down, Ben breathed a sigh of relief, and satisfaction. Now that he had three comprehensive sets of background information - the Frasers, Tessa, and the Metternichs, plus some other snippets - he might, at last, be able to find a common link.

Before he had a chance to enter the Metternich information into his database, the phone rang.

'Hello...Ben Foxley.'

A formal sounding, middle aged, voice said: 'Mr Foxley, my name is Austin...David Austin. I'm calling from the National Parks Authority office at Windermere. I was on holiday last week when you telephoned my assistant, Sarah, and asked about our voluntary wardens, particularly about a Mr Summer....'

'That's right,' Ben interjected, hoping he hadn't got the young girl into strife for giving out information on the phone.

'...Well, Sarah has only been with us for a few weeks. That's why I was checking with her what had happened while I was away. She was quite right to tell you that Mr Summer is not on our current list of voluntary wardens, but I thought you might want to know that Mr Summer left us about two years ago. Presumably, he was the man who helped you with your article?'

'Yes...that would be him.' The sentence came out mundanely, but inside, Ben was flying. He sat bolt upright, tense with energy and exultation. He'd been right...he'd been bloody right. He'd found the evil..........

He had to stay calm. 'It's very good of you to let me know, David. I appreciate it,' he said, as casually as possible. If I was to pop into your office, do you think you would be able to let me have his home address? I'm sure he can still help me with my follow up article, even if he's no longer with you....'

'Let me stop you there,' Austin intervened. 'When I said Mr Summer had left us, I meant he had died....'

'Died?' Ben shouted, unable to control his disbelief and frustration. This was unbelievable. Just when he thought he had found the answer, it had vanished again.

Through a self-pitying fog of frustration, he heard David Austin continue: 'It was very tragic. They found him at the foot of Eel Crag. He had obviously fallen while out walking. A nice man apparently...such a pity...we all went to his funeral....'

'Hallelujah!' Ben celebrated inside, not out loud. He was back in business. Sorry as he was to hear of the demise of Mr Summer, he realised that the way Summer had died carried all the hallmarks of the killer's work. It pointed to the probability that the killer had taken Summer's identity tag, and was using it to pose as a volunteer warden when approaching potential victims. Surely, he was right this time, he had to be.

'I'm so sorry to hear that,' Ben said, genuinely, when Austin had finished. 'He was a nice man. He helped me a lot with my article.' The lies were in a good cause.

Ben wanted to ask him if he knew the whereabouts of Mr Summer's identity tag, but couldn't think of a wording that wouldn't arouse Austin's curiosity. It was unlikely, anyway, that such a trivial item had been noticed or recorded during the shock and confusion surrounding such an incident. Which reminded him - why had he not seen Mr Summer's incident in the mountain rescue and police reports he had gone through. He needed to check on that.

'Sorry to bring you the bad news,' Austin was saying.

'Not at all,' Ben said. 'I'm grateful to you for letting me know. I know one or two of the local wardens. They'll probably be able to help me on my next piece. Thanks again for the call.'

'I'm sure they will, Mr Foxley. Good-bye.'

Ben sat back, and tried to temper his excitement. He had suffered so many false dawns that he was now very wary of apparent success. Yet surely, this time, he must be on the right track.

He sent it through his mind's computer again, to double check. A man called Summer existed. He had walked on the fells regularly. He is killed on the fells by someone who takes his identity tag and assumes his identity. Another man is found on the fells, dying. His last words are 'summer sniffs'. There had to be a connection. Surely, it couldn't be a cruel coincidence? If it was, then he was in for another massive disappointment.

He had to obliterate thoughts of disappointment, and concentrate on believing that he was right. That would be how the police would handle it; every possibility had to be followed through to a conclusion, satisfactory or otherwise.

He picked up his CLUES file and flicked through the notes he had accumulated. He found the sheet of paper on which he had recorded an earlier conversation with his friendly GP - Dr Philip Grearson, when he had been concentrating on the 'sniffs' element of the conundrum.

Ben had assumed that, if Professor Metternich was indeed saying that the man who killed him was called Summer and that he sniffed, then it had to be more than just a normal cold sniff, for it to be worthy of such important recollection.

He had, therefore, asked Dr Grearson what might be the cause of an habitual or noticeable sniffing habit. Dr Grearson had suggested that it might be caused by a condition called rhinitis - an inflammation of the nose's lining membrane. It was usually suffered by people who had been constantly exposed to irritants such as airborne chemical powders. Or it could be hay fever. Ben had discounted the hay fever possibility, since the Metternichs had been killed long after the hay fever season had passed.

So, as things stood at that moment, he was looking for a man who lived locally, who used someone else's identity when perpetrating his crimes, and who might have worked in a chemical environment. 'Piece of cake,' Ben said, sardonically to himself, as he realised that he might have won an initial skirmish, but the war was far from over.

As a last act, before going down to prepare the evening meal for Helen's arrival, he checked to see why he had not seen an account of Mr Summer's death in his pile of mountain rescue and police reports. Thumbing back through the reports, in datal order, he suddenly stopped. Spread before him were both sets of reports on Mr Summer. He couldn't believe it. He had either overlooked them, or they hadn't registered as relevant - he hadn't entered him on his victim list - or he simply couldn't remember the name because he had read so many.

Whatever the reason, it taught him a salutary lesson. From now on, he would have to be even more diligent, and check back on everything recorded, at all stages. Now, he knew how the police must feel when the media inform the public, in retrospect, that the police could have found their target sooner, had it not been for a clerical cock-up.

As he hid the files away, and prepared to go downstairs to Helen and normality, he tried to leave behind the most unwelcome discovery of the day - the horrific fact that the victim list was now longer.

*

The next morning, with Helen already off to work, and before he imprisoned himself in his office to continue the search for victim commonality, Ben strolled outside the cottage to receive nature's healing balm. A walk around the lawn, feeding the pheasants and squirrels and mallards, a survey of the lake and the sky above to see where the geese and ospreys and buzzards flew, a listen to the breeze in the huge surrounding trees, a worshipful gaze at the heavenly fells, eternally watching over them in an arena of incomparable beauty, and his soul was calmed and ready to take on the world again.

As he turned to go back in, he heard a vehicle splattering along the dirt track that leads to the cottage. He waited to see who it was. A police car, travelling quickly, appeared from out of the trees, and pulled up beside him with unnecessary abruptness, scarring the gravel. Bill Unwin, and a constable he didn't recognise, wasted no time in getting out of the car.

"Morning Ben,' Bill said. 'Sorry about that.' He indicated the scarred gravel, then looked with disdain at the constable. 'He thinks he's bloody Schumacher. Otherwise, he's not a bad bloke. Constable Murphy meet Ben Foxley, our local scribe.'

Ben shook hands with the constable, while he addressed Bill: 'So you **have** got a uniform,' he scoffed, and winked at the constable. 'I've only ever seen him in golf gear, you know. He told me he had a job, but I never believed him.'

The constable smiled, and Bill Unwin let the nonsense go. 'A coffee would go down well,' he said. 'Early start this morning.'

'Of course, come on in,' Ben offered, and led them inside. 'Busy on that A591 thing I suppose?' he said, as they sat down in the kitchen and he topped up the percolator.

'Hole in one,' Bill said. 'Feet haven't touched the ground since it happened. The smart boys from headquarters are investigating it, but they've got us running around doing all the donkey work as usual. Still, it's better than being stuck in the office dealing with that flaming media crowd - there's dozens of the bastards - God knows who pays them all!'

Ben was puzzled. This was the first time that Bill Unwin had ever visited him at home. Up to now, their socialising had been restricted to the 19th hole. And this at a time he claimed to be very busy.

Even though Bill seemed relaxed and friendly, Ben was on guard; something that would not have occurred to him had it not been for Sophie Lund. Even so, it still took an effort of will not to take Bill upstairs to show him all the reports, and what he had discovered, and invite him and his colleagues to take over from him. It would be such a relief to let it all go.

'Helen at work?' Bill asked, conversationally, as he took the proffered cup from Ben. 'Thanks.'

'Yes...early starter,' Ben replied, as he sat down with his own cup. 'So what brings you out here so early? Come for a bit of four-wood coaching?'

'If only,' Bill grumbled. 'No...it's an official call, mate....'

Ben held his breath.

'We have to check every household within a couple of miles of the incident. It's routine stuff - ask if anybody saw or heard anything unusual - check if they've got a chunk of concrete missing from one of their walls. Chances are it's not a local thing...she could have come from anywhere. But we have to go through the motions.'

'We've done Linden House at the top of your lane. I'm right in thinking there's only you and the Manor and Tony Williams' farm down this end of the lane?'

'That's right, Ben said, brightly, disguising his relief. 'Oh, and there's Tony's dad's house just behind the farm. Old Bill's retired...have you met him...quite a character.'

'Here's another old Bill who wishes he was retired,' Bill joked, as he gulped his coffee.

'I don't suppose you have any leads on the woman's identity yet?' Ben asked, looking to pad out his piece for the Tribune.

'We do, actually...' Constable Murphy blurted out, only to be stopped in mid sentence by a frowning Sergeant.

Shaking his head at the constable's stupidity, Bill said: 'It's not ready for official release yet, Ben, so you can't use it. But, yes, we do have the name of the woman. She's a Filipino. She's been on the missing persons list for the last four years. Apparently it's not unusual for Filipinos, and lots of others, to go missing in this country every year, but only a few make their way on to the missing person's list. That's because they've disappeared deliberately, and their relatives don't report them as missing, they are in on the act. They arrive on temporary visas and just disappear into the crowds. This one's different. Apparently, her parents have been pestering us to find her ever since they reported her missing about four years ago.'

Ben shook his head, as he thought of the torment of those poor people. 'Have they been told yet?' he asked, quietly.

Bill nodded. 'I believe so,' he said, sadly. 'It's a terrible job...I've done a few of those myself.'

The room went quiet for a while, as each pondered the awfulness of it all, staring blankly at the floor, or into their coffees.

'Poor soul,' Ben mumbled, and rose to pick up the pen and note pad they kept beside the kitchen telephone. 'I won't use it until it's officially released, but could you give me the woman's name while you're here. I want to make sure I get the spelling right.'

Bill looked at Constable Murphy. 'You've got it in your notebook, haven't you?'

Constable Murphy nodded, and hurriedly withdrew his notebook from his pocket. He thumbed through the pages, then stopped. 'The name I've got here is Vilma Tapales...V.I.L.M.A, T.A.P.A.L.E.S,' he spelled out.

Ben noted the name on the phone pad, and drained the last of his coffee. The others followed suit shortly afterwards.

Bill Unwin stood up. 'Right, let's get this over with.' He looked at Constable Murphy. 'Got yer notebook ready?' The constable waved it.

'Right, Mr Foxley, Bill said, earnestly. 'Have you seen or heard anything unusual or suspicious in this vicinity in the past week? And no wisecracks please.'

Ben studied for a moment, then said, seriously: 'No, I haven't.'

'Do you mind if we take a look around your property?'

'Really?'

''Fraid so.'

'Go ahead, but don't mind the mess.'

As they started on a tour of the house, Ben hoped he hadn't left anything on his desk upstairs. He was pretty sure he had hidden all the reports away, but he remained on edge until they came downstairs a few minutes later.

Next they went outside to look in the garage, and finally came back to the front door, where Ben joined them.

'Sorry we had to do that, mate,' Bill said, genuinely. 'But we can't make exceptions.'

'That's okay, Ben agreed. 'I understand. Where to now?'

'The farmhouse and then the Manor, and then up to Bassenthwaite village. Thanks again for the coffee.'

'You're very welcome.'

As they moved off to the car, Bill turned and said: 'By the way, I like your paintings.'

Ben breathed a sigh of relief as they drove away. Then he stepped outside his front door and took in his wondrous surroundings again. He needed an extra helping that morning.

Chapter 30

Scarness Manor is a rarity. Nestling in woodland, over-looking Bassenthwaite Lake, it is one of very few large houses allowed to be erected close to the shores of a lake; all Lake District villages and towns being built away from the shores, in order to leave the lakes in their natural, pristine, settings; the one exception being Lake Windermere, where early lake-side development was allowed, much to the consternation of local poet, William Wordsworth.

The 12-bedroomed manor was built in 1880 by a wealthy, land owning, Baronet from the east coast. It was his holiday home, built for the purposes of hunting, hawking, fowling and fishing.

He had it built in a gothic style, with steep roofs, tall chimneys, timber balconies, basement wine, coal, and laundry cellars, and surrounded it with formal gardens containing imported Canadian Redwood trees.

From its elevated position and grand, spacious rooms, there is a grandstand view of the lake and its surroundings. Yet, because of the surrounding woodland, and high hedges, nobody can observe its occupants.

It was this guaranteed privacy, together with its location and cellars, which had persuaded ex-bricklayer, and rising Scottish pop star, Jed Samson (alias Andrew McFeeters) to buy it. With the help of some trusted building site mates from Glasgow, he turned the wine cellar into a recording studio, hiding the previous doorways, from the hall and from outside, with panelling, and installing a new trap door entrance in the wooden floor of the lounge, hidden by an ostentatious Persian rug. This was where he churned out his songs, took his alcohol and drugs, and entertained his mates and female fans.

Inexplicably, when his husky voice degenerated into an impersonation of a rusty chainsaw, the public seemed to like it even more, and millions gave him their hard earned money in exchange for a small disc containing this sound. As his fame spread, so did the houses.

Now a superstar, with houses in London, Los Angeles, New York and Bermuda, he rarely visits Scarness Manor. He keeps promising his third wife, and scattered children, that they will all spend a cosy Christmas there, but it never happens; something else always crops up.

However, coming from the tenements of Glasgow, he has no intention of selling the Manor, or any of his other properties. He keeps them as an investment for his old age. He does not intend to live his last years like his aged parents did. Now, all his houses are looked after by local agents and caretakers, as he tours the world, bringing happiness to the masses, his accountant, his bodyguard, his hairdresser, his bank manager, and through him - his ex-wives and mistresses.

Some of this historical information was imparted to awe struck new boy, Constable Murphy, by Sergeant Unwin, as they drove through the cast iron entrance gates

- the scene of many hysterical gatherings in the past - up the dual carriageway drive, a beautifully trimmed high hedge separating the two roads, to the imposing front door.

As they pulled up, they spotted a man in cap and overalls, standing on a ladder, trimming the high yew hedge that bordered the formal gardens.

Having seen them arrive, the man climbed down the ladder, switched off his hedge trimmer, and came over to greet them. "Morning...can I help you,' he said.

'Are you the caretaker?' Bill Unwin asked.

'Aye.'

'Is there anybody else living here at the moment?'

'No.'

'Your name is?'

'Baxter.'

Constable Murphy had started making notes.

'Well, Mr Baxter, we're making some routine enquiries about the death of a woman found on the A591 not far from here. Have you heard about it?'

'Aye.'

'Have you seen or heard anything unusual or suspicious in this vicinity in the past week or so?'

'No.'

'Do you mind if we take a look around the house and the stables?'

Baxter hesitated. 'I'm not sure...it's not my property... maybe you should talk to the agent...he's in Glasgow.'

'This is serious police business, Mr Baxter,' Bill said with authority. We can come back with a search warrant in a couple of hours, and you'll have to let us in, so why waste our time?' He was bluffing; he didn't fancy the extra hassle of contacting the Agent.

'Aye...alright...I suppose it'll be okay,' Baxter said, timidly. 'I'll fetch the keys'.

He walked about 20 paces, disappeared through a door in a section of the building that jutted out from the rest, and soon reappeared, carrying a bunch of keys.

'Is that separate from the rest of the building?' Bill asked, indicating where Baxter had come from.

'Aye...that's my place,' Baxter said. 'It used to be part of the servants' quarters, when it was connected through, but they bricked it up inside and made it into a separate place for the caretaker to live.'

'Right, let's go,' Bill said. 'I'll have a look in there later.'

They climbed the stone steps to the large oak front door, and Baxter let them in; the noise from the heavy cast-iron door lever and handle echoing down the empty hall.

They spent about half an hour wandering around the elegant rooms, Bill occasionally expressing his disgust at the tasteless modern furniture he found under the dustcovers, and constantly having to drag Constable Murphy away from the plethora of show-biz photographs scarring the walls.

Next, they visited the stables, which had been converted into garages, then the old coal and laundry cellars, now full of gardening equipment, canoes and old bikes, and finally the caretaker's cottage.

There was nothing suspicious to see in any of the locations. The only things that caught Bill's attention were signs of recent activity in the laundry, which, Baxter explained, had been caused by him moving the ladder and hedge trimmer that very morning, and a small tub of baby's nappy cream on the mantelpiece in the cottage. The baby's smiling face on the colourful container had caught his eye in the austere room. But it had raised no questions in his mind; it, obviously, having other uses apart from nappy rash relief.

'Thanks for that, Mr Baxter,' Bill said when they gathered again outside the front door. 'Sorry to disturb you. We'll let you get back to your hedges.' He turned his head, looking in all directions. 'You've got a lot to take care of here, haven't you. It must keep you busy?'

'Aye...that it does,' Baxter replied.

'Do you ever get a visit from its illustrious owner?' Bill asked, conversationally.

'No...I've never seen him all the time I've been here.'

'And how long is that?'

'About a year and a half.'

'He probably prefers the sun of Bermuda these days,' Bill scoffed. 'It's alright for some, eh? He moved towards the car. 'Come on Murphy,' he said, sarcastically. 'Let's go and make *our* fortunes by talking to the good folk of Bassenthwaite.'

They got into the car and roared off, leaving the caretaker staring at two small piles of displaced gravel. Absent-mindedly, he levelled them back into place with his foot, then turned and walked up the steps into the manor.

Inside the manor, he walked to the far end of the hall and entered the large lounge. He crossed the polished wooden floor and removed a dust cover from a high backed rocking chair, and slumped into it. He started the chair rocking gently, and closed his eyes. Slowly, his thin lips parted in a half-smile, though, such was his emaciation, it looked like a skeletal sneer.

Chapter 31

Ben was back at his desk and ready to go, a period of frustration over. For two days he had been unable to get on with any of his 'own work' because of Sue Burrows' demand for copy on the A591 incident.

Much to her consternation, he had missed the press conference in Keswick's new 'Theatre by the Lake' - the only place in town big enough to hold such a plethora of media - when the chief inspector handling the case had officially released the woman's name, and other fresh data.

But, at Sue's insistence, he had visited the site where her body was found, and tried to paint a word picture, and he had interviewed a few people in and around Keswick to get an opinion picture. He had rattled off a quick 500 words for her, feeling slightly guilty that he hadn't given it his best attention. He wasn't too keen on this type of journalism, preferring facts to opinions, but Sue had every right to ask it of him occasionally.

At night, he had managed to input the information from Peter Metternich into the Metternichs' database, and now he was ready to look for victim commonalities again.

Against the 20 heading categories on his database,

he cross-referenced the information he had gathered on the Frasers, the Metternichs, Tessa, and the two others on whom he had only snippets.

At times, as he slowly went through the data, he would think he was on to something, when three people would match in a category, only to find a fourth or fifth not matching.

After about half an hour he selected the category - 'Member Of' - being his shorthand for 'member of a recognised organisation, be it professional, business, union, or similar.'

At first, he saw no commonality, as various organisations appeared on the screen against each victim's name. But then he spotted something. Among the disparate organisations they belonged to, he saw Greenpeace, Friends of the Earth, Green Party, and others.

Although they were all different, they were all environmental organisations. The Metternichs were members of the German Green Party, Tessa was a member of Friends of the Lake District, Mrs Fraser was a member of Friends of the Earth and the two 'snippets' were members of Greenpeace and Ecobridge. The only exception was Jack Fraser, who was a member of nothing but the Labour Party.

Ben was not too disturbed by this omission. It could be that Jack had been made to cancel any such memberships when he was appointed minister, particularly when he was dealing with the nuclear industry. More likely was the theory that his background was insignificant once the killer had learned that his wife was an environmentalist. He had then become nothing more than a witness to be silenced.

Ben started to get excited again. At last he had found a link, however tenuous. What was it the book said: 'Gain as much information as possible, study the minutiae of events, home in on the slightest clues, and chase them down.'

He came back to earth again. How the hell was he going to chase this down? And, if his environmentalist theory was true, how the hell did the killer know his victims were environmentalists if he hadn't met them before?

A strong coffee, and a stroll around the garden, brought an idea. Back upstairs, he picked up the phone and dialled.

'National Park...David Austin speaking.'

'It's Ben Foxley, David,' Ben said, momentarily grateful that he'd been spared the whole 'how may I help you' routine. 'Sorry to bother you again. We spoke recently about your warden, Mr Summer.'

'Yes, I remember?'

'Would you happen to know if Mr Summer was a member of Friends of the Lake District or any other environmental organisation?'

'I...believe he was...yes...I'm certain he was. I remember all the members came to the funeral and donated a joint wreath. What's this for - your article?'

'Yes,' Ben lied. 'I'm just pointing out the obvious - that a lot of wardens are attracted to the job because they are environmentalists. I just need a couple of names and a couple of facts and then I can usually pad it out.'

'I see,' Austin said, uncertainly.

'By the way,' Ben hurried on. 'I'm wanting to show the lighter side of a warden's job as well as the serious side.

I don't suppose you can recall any reports of funny or odd behaviour by a warden in recent times?'

Ben heard Austin sigh the sigh of a man who didn't want to be bothered with frivolous questions. 'I don't think so,' he droned. 'There's been one or two wrong directions been given, and the odd fracas with litter droppers, but nothing very reportable in my opinion. We've had a couple of complaints in the last few months about a warden pestering walkers with a market survey questionnaire. Apparently, he says he's doing it on behalf of the National Park Authority, but we haven't authorised one. He could be one of our over-zealous types gathering a load of statistics to present us with, to show how useful and efficient he is. It happens sometimes with retired managerial people who miss being in charge. But, anyway, it's not exactly stuff to excite a reader...is it?'

'Did they mention his name?' Ben asked, quietly.

'No. It's typical isn't it....'

Ben had stopped listening. Inside, he was shouting BINGO!. In one simple phone call he had confirmed the WHY, and found the HOW. What was it the book said: 'there was always a connection between the victims, usually simple in retrospect, because the killer is simple minded.'

He dragged himself back to David Austin. 'You're right, David,' he said. 'It's not really what I'm looking for. Never mind, I'll keep asking around. If I don't find anything I'll just have to leave the light side out of the article. Thanks anyway...you've been a great help again.'

'Glad to help,' Austin said, and put the phone down.

Once again, Ben tried to control his excitement, in case he might be jumping to the wrong conclusions, and suffer disappointment again. But, surely not this time. Seven out of eight victims had been members of an environmental organisation - that just had to be the WHY.

And the HOW had also turned out to be simple, in retrospect. The killer, posing as a warden, simply walked up to people and asked them questions about themselves, using the guise of an official looking questionnaire. Few fell walkers would refuse - they are a polite lot, generally. If they answered 'no' to the question: 'are you a member of an environmental organisation?' they were free to go. If they answered 'yes', then they, and anybody with them, was murdered.

Ben shuddered at the thought. What kind of person could have a face-to-face conversation with a stranger, suddenly attack them, disfigure them while still alive, then throw them to their deaths over the edge?

It had to be a person utterly consumed with hatred. A person who, according to the book: '...murders when the heat of his rage is at its peak. A person who takes revenge for some wrong done to them, usually perceived.' In this case the wrongdoers being some sort of environmentalists.

Ben's train of thought was momentarily stopped by this. Environmental organisations were not usually perceived as enemies of the public - just the opposite. They usually claimed to be acting on behalf of the public against the might of big business or governments. Maybe *that* was the connection? Maybe the killer had his business or career ruined by the actions of one of these organisations?

Again, the problem looked insurmountable: how to find one man amongst millions who may have worked in business or government.

Having decided that it was indeed an impossible task, he then made a second decision - to keep plodding on, in the hope that his vibration theory might bring something to him. After all, hadn't his persistent probing already brought him much further than he expected. He had answered the 'Why, When, Where, and How' questions. He had identified the victims as environmentalists. Now all he had to do was find the link between the victims and the killer, and finally - identify the killer.

'Should keep me busy for the next half hour,' he thought, ironically.

As far as Ben was aware, he had only one piece of information with which to kick start his search for the link - that given to him by Dr Grearson - that a man who constantly sniffs might have Rhinitis, possibly caused by working in a chemical environment.

So for the time being, that meant concentrating on business rather than government. Also, it was unlikely that a business owner or manager would be directly involved in handling chemical materials, so that meant that he was probably a process worker or similar. So, it could be a lost job rather than a lost business, or a lost job because of a lost business.

But why would someone become a killer just because they had lost their job? It didn't make sense; there had to be more to it than that. Then again, maybe sense didn't come into it. Maybe the killer had always been irrational or living on the edge of psychosis.

To try to find one individual lost job in the chemical industry was definitely impossible, so the next step had to be to search for a chemical business that had been closed due to the actions of an environmental organisation. And the closure must have taken place before the killings started - in Scotland, about four years ago.

Regrettably, it looked like the Internet, the library and the newspaper offices were going to dominate his life for the foreseeable future.

Chapter 32

He rocks in his chair, eyes still closed. The smile has gone. It made its brief appearance because he had outwitted the police. He guessed they would do a house-to-house; he knew how they worked, having had plenty of contact with them in his early years.

He had repaired the old doorway between the laundry and recording studio through which Vilma had escaped, taping over the joints on the laundry side, and piling canoes against the wall to hide the repair. He had put the ladder and hedge trimmer against the hedge, and dressed in overalls, the day after Vilma had escaped, and always been ready to present an aura of routine normality when the police appeared.

He had seen them coming on the monitor screen in his cottage: one of many throughout the house. They were linked to a camera concealed in the eye of an ornamental lion standing close to the main entrance gate. Jed Samson had not wanted to be disturbed by unannounced visitors.

He was grateful to Jed Samson for a lot of things. Only a Glaswegian would insist that his caretaker had to come from a dole queue in Scotland, a place he had often stood before his success. And only a man who had known hard times would have provided such a generous wage as well as free accommodation.

The Manor had proved to be far better for Hector's purposes than the remote cottages he had rented as he made his way south from Strathy Point. The hidden recording studio had been a bonus - the perfect place to keep Vilma.

Shortly after arriving, he had scoured the area and found a deserted gamekeeper's cottage in a remote valley beneath Grizedale Pike. Had Jed Samson wanted to use the Manor at any time, Hector had planned to use the cottage as temporary accommodation for Vilma until Jed left. Now, of course, that possibility would not arise.

Hector opened his eyes and rose from the chair. He pushed it to one side, kicked the Persian rug away, and lifted the trapdoor.

He moved down the stairs with a strange caution. Ever since Vilma had gone, a painful loneliness had gripped him. He paused at the control room and sat at a low desk in front of the window looking into the recording studio. From the myriad of switches and dials among the equipment surrounding him, he selected two.

This time, instead of the love duet from Madame Butterfly, the slow movement of Barber's violin concerto started up, as he moved towards the studio door.

The violin took over from the introduction, building up to a harsh crescendo of troubled chaos. It searched for somewhere to go. Suddenly it found a way out, through a tune so sublime, yet so painful, it tore his heart out. It told of the mystery and joy of life, yet warned of the inevitability of death. It tried to fight death off, but it couldn't, and it disappeared into a chasm of dreadful drums. It emerged briefly for a final effort, but fluttered helplessly, like a moth in a flame, before it faded away.

An emotion close to fear shivered through him as he entered the studio through the thick double-doors. Its emptiness hit him physically, made him sway unsteadily, almost made him sick. He knew he wouldn't be able to tolerate being alone for very long. He would have to find another companion soon.

Breathing deeply to combat the nausea, he moved across the room, glancing up at the repair he had done to the hole in the concrete ceiling. He had placed a new steel ring in a fast setting mortar, and now the whole thing was hidden by the suspended sound baffle he had initially removed to make way for Vilma's chain. Jed would never spot it if ever he returned.

In a far corner of the room, he stopped, knelt down on the carpeted floor, and gazed up at a large, framed, photograph of Leni; one of ten identical photographs he had hung, equally spaced, around the walls. His daily homage to Leni had been inspired by seeing her perform the 'stations of the cross' in church. But instead of praying, as he shuffled on his knees from one identical photograph to the other, he reminisced.

If he concentrated on the right side of her face, which was still perfect, her beautiful brown eye staring forever into his soul, he thought of the blissful times, when she had brought him untold joy.

But, if he glanced to the left side, to the blood-filled eye socket, the shattered bones, the ripped flesh, the dangling ear, the blood soaked hair, he relived the horror.

Then there was the smile...God ...she had tried to smile. He had asked her to smile while she died, and she had tried. It was there, caught forever, forced through the terrible pain - a tiny smile - a massive effort of a smile.

'Smile Leni smile,' he had shouted, as she lay, contorted, in the wreckage. She couldn't die if he photographed her, could she. She couldn't leave him if he was keeping her alive with his camera, could she. She would have to stay to smile. You can't die if you are smiling, can you.

'Smile Leni smile....Smile Leni smile....Smile Leni smile' he had screamed through a drunken haze as he saw her eye fill with blood, heard her gurgle and gasp, saw her quivering, tiny hand move to touch him.

Then it had come. A glowing glint of love in her right eye. A tiny smile on her beautiful lips. Then stillness.

He pressed the shutter release button again and again. He had to bring her back...he had to keep her alive... she had to live...she had to live..... He clicked and clicked and clicked....

Two passing motorists had found him sitting in the stream where the car had finished after hitting the bridge parapet. He was trembling and incoherent. They put it down to the alcohol they smelt on him. They had not yet looked inside the wreckage. Nor were they to know that he had just found his daughter's head beneath the water's peat brown surface.

*

His next recollection had been the funeral. A bitter wind had blown across the graveyard, prominent on the bleak headland, overlooking the grey sea. He had found Vilma standing beside him at the graveside, shivering, crying. She told him later that he had phoned her with the terrible news, and sent her the money to fly over for the funeral. He could vaguely remember doing it, although most of what he had done in that period after the crash was obliterated by a cocktail of alcohol and sedatives.

Leni and Grace were buried side-by-side, looking west towards Ben Loyal, in the best coffins, with the best headstone he could afford. On Leni's side of the glinting white marble headstone, he had engraved in gold an extract from Robert Burns' 'Ae Fond Kiss':

> *Had we never lov'd sae kindly*
> *Had we never lov'd sae blindly*
> *Never met...or never parted,*
> *We had ne'er been broken-hearted!*

On Grace's side he had engraved the words of WB Yeats:

> *'The innocent and the beautiful*
> *have no enemies but time.'*

Even the old priest, who had buried hundreds, cried.

*

If Vilma hadn't been there, he would have committed suicide that same day. It wasn't that she comforted him particularly. It was just that her return flight was not due for a few days and he felt obliged to look after her until then. For two days and nights they sat together in the croft house: she in Leni's chair at the other side of the fireplace. Little was said. Little was eaten. Plenty was drunk.

On the third day, no longer able to bear the pain, and without saying a word to Vilma, he went out to commit suicide. He cycled to the cemetery and kissed their headstone, then on to the farm at Ribigill, where he left the bike. He reached the cold summit of Ben Loyal, wearing only a short-sleeved shirt.

He walked to the edge of An Caisteal crag, and took one last look at the mighty scene. For a moment, Leni and Grace were at his side, holding his hands, sharing again their immortal feelings. Closing his eyes, he could see Leni's smile, hear Grace's tinkling laugh. He held on tight to their tiny hands as he summoned the courage to jump.

'Fantastic view isn't it.' The bellowing voice shocked his eyes open, made him teeter on the edge. Instinctively, he stepped back and turned. A bearded, weather-beaten, man stood a few paces away. The dreadlocks, bandanna, and baggy trousers all announced that he was still a hippie.

Hector wasn't capable of speech. He could do no more than dazedly stare at the man.

'You're a bit close to the edge, pal,' the man shouted, pointedly, in a lowland Scottish accent. 'Better watch your step, or you'll be eagle meat.'

Hector shuffled away from the edge, obediently, like a boy instructed by a teacher. Still he didn't speak.

'You alright, pal?' the man asked, routinely, without concern in his voice. 'You look a bit...funny... if you don't mind me saying. Why don't you have a sit down.' He gestured to a platform of smooth rock a few paces from the edge.

Hector did as he was told and trudged to the rock, where he sat and stared.

The man paced back and forth along the edge, like an actor on stage, head held high, taking in the vast panorama. 'What a county,' he shouted. 'The only wilderness left in Britain. Just look at the emptiness. Isn't it bloody wonderful?'

Hector stared, blankly.

Feeling that he had a captive audience, the man strode his stage, expounding his opinions and philosophies. Pollution, global warming, de-forestation, capitalism, were all denounced to Hector's un-listening ears.

Hector was suspended between two worlds. He should have been dead by now. He wanted to be dead by now. But this man was blathering non-stop, holding him up. He didn't want to listen to him, to be brought back into the living world; that was too painful. But then he heard the word 'nuclear' and his mind automatically clicked back to reality.

'Just look at that monstrosity over there,' the man shouted, pointing out Dounreay Nuclear Plant a few miles away. 'One of these days we'll get the whole bloody thing closed, not just part of it. Then we'll get the bulldozers in and wipe it out, and give the land back to the heather and the birds.'

Hector was alert now, anger rising. 'Who is 'we'?' he asked, plainly.

'The Greens of course,' the man boasted. 'I'm a member of the Scottish Green Party. We're on the march, pal. Mark my word, by the time this decade is over, there won't be a nuclear installation left in Scotland.

No submarine bases, no power stations, and no bloody Dounreay.'

Hector's anger suddenly boiled up inside him like magma in a volcano. This was the man who had lost him his job - him and his like.

The resurgent Green Party had struck some deals with the Labour majority in the new Scottish Parliament, and succeeded in having closed all nuclear facilities that came under the direct control of Scotland. This had included the part of Dounreay that dealt with export orders, a part that included Hector's Cementation Plant, which processed and stored the raffinate from Europe's reactors.

The rest of the plant, still under the control of a Green-less Westminster Parliament, had stayed open. Hector had been made redundant, and even his mentor, Callum McDonald, had been unable to find him another job at the plant.

If it hadn't been for them, Hector knew, he wouldn't have lost his job, and with it, his proud status as provider for Leni, Grace and Mama. Leni would not have had to go out to work, and he wouldn't have become consumed with jealousy and self-doubt, and tried to blank it all out with alcohol.

He wouldn't have been driving to pick them up from work and school every day. He wouldn't have been drunk at that time of the afternoon. He wouldn't have misjudged the bend before the narrow stone bridge over the stream. *He would have been at work.*

It had all happened because of these arrogant, self-righteous, interfering bastards. Leni and Grace were dead because of them. He was one of them. And he was boasting about it.

The man was still striding about, delivering his lecture, impassioned by the certainty of his virtue.

Inside Hector, the magma boiled to bursting point. The pent up self-hatred erupted. The lava exploded.

He ran the few paces between them like an agile ape, and charged his shoulder into the startled man. The man staggered backwards and fell, silently, over the edge of An Caisteal.

Hector paused at the edge, breathless, exhilarated. He looked down. It was a steep drop from the summit, but not as sheer as it was further down. Something had stopped the man's fall about 50 feet below him. He lay quite still on the steep slope.

Adrenalin pumping, Hector looked all around to see if anyone was about. He then lowered himself over the edge, and carefully scrambled down to where the man lay.

His face was covered in black marks and red abrasions and loose dirt. His clothes were spattered with some of the stones he had loosened during the fall. He lay on his back, moaning. His eyes were open.

Hector placed one foot on either side of his body, and looked down on him. A feeling of great power surged through him. He lowered himself until he sat on the man's abdomen. The man gasped and tried to protest. Hector punched him on the side of his face.

'Shut up...little man,' he snarled.

Then he just sat there for a while, enjoying the feeling of power, wondering what to do next. His initial uncontrollable rage had cooled down. Now he was in control. Now he had time to think how he could really make this man's punishment fit the crime. The man could see the coldness in his eyes. He looked terrified. Hector loved that.

Just for a moment, Hector closed his eyes and deliberately recalled the horror of Leni's death. He wanted to know again the agony she had suffered, he had suffered. He was looking for inspiration.

In that quiet moment, he found it. He saw again the shattered eye, the ripped flesh; the dangling ear. Close by, disturbed by the man's fall, lay a jagged, pointed stone. He picked it up and showed it to the man. The man's eyes widened with terror, and made a bigger target as Hector stabbed it into his left eye. The man screamed. Hector put his hand over his mouth, and thrust the stone in again...and again, harder. And again, harder still, feeling the bones crunching, watching the sinuous blood ebbing the 'greenie's' life away, taking his own pain away.

He turned the stone to find the sharpest edge, and attacked the man's left ear. With cold anger he hacked repeatedly at the joint to the head, until the ear lay flapping, held only by a thin, raw sinew of flesh.

Hector stopped, heart pounding. The deed was done. Leni had been avenged. He removed himself from the man's abdomen, and sat above him on the steep slope. He rummaged through the man's jacket, found his wallet, and pocketed it. Then he placed his feet against the man's side and thrust with his legs until the man started to roll over. Two more thrusts and the body had impetus. It continued to roll until it arrived at the sheer drop, where it disappeared over the edge to certain death.

Hector scrambled back to the summit of An Caisteal and looked all around. Nothing stirred in the vast emptiness. Slowly, his pounding heart slowed down, and he started to relax. Then he realised that, for the first time in months, he felt good. He felt renewed, and refreshed, as though some great burden had been lifted from him. He also felt strangely hollow inside, as if his stomach had been removed. Something basic had left him, he knew.

Finding the bloody stone still in his hand, he looked around and found a marshy piece of ground. There, he threw the stone in, and watched it sink beneath the boggy surface. In the peaty water, he started to wash the blood from his hands. Now he was aware that his desire for suicide had gone. Somebody else had died for Leni: the right person, the one who had caused Leni's death. It had never really been his fault.

*

Three days later, with the new power still coursing through him, he had stopped Vilma from leaving to catch her plane. He couldn't bear the thought of living on his own again, of having no one to care for. Even ugly little Vilma was better than nothing, better than an empty house, a lonely life. She would have to be Leni's substitute.

At first he had asked her, then pleaded with her, to stay with him. When she had refused and tried to leave, he had grabbed her, and tied her up with rope, and put tape across her mouth to stop her screaming.

Days later, when the police came looking for her, at the request of her mother, he told them she had left to catch her scheduled flight, using public transport to get to Thurso, and then to Inverness airport, and that he hadn't seen her since that day.

The police had taken his word for it, one of them commenting that she had probably taken the opportunity to stay in Britain, probably in London, and that she would probably become just another illegal immigrant statistic.

If the police had asked to search the house, Hector had taken the precaution of hiding her, bound and gagged, down a drainage sump in the old sheep shed. Weeks later, when things had settled down, he brought her into the house and chained her to an old iron bed in the second bedroom.

In the meantime, he had been called out by the mountain rescue team to look for a missing walker called Ian Baxter, a name he had found on the driving licence in the greenie's wallet. The team had offered to let him stand down because of his recent loss, but he told them it would do him good to get out and take his mind off things. In fact, he found it incredibly exciting to think that he would get a second look at the man he had killed.

When they eventually found Baxter at the foot of An Caisteal crag, Hector, as the team's photographer, discovered a new pleasure when taking a close-up of the man's facial injuries.

Now, kneeling in the studio, he looked at it again. It was the first of nine framed photographs, each one placed directly below one of Leni's photographs. It was the only male face to be seen in the line up, Hector having later switched to females to get a better match.

Hector's eyes scanned around the walls of the studio. He stopped at the empty frame below the tenth photograph of Leni. Only one more to go! Would it stop then? Would the killing be over? In the quiet sanity of that moment, he hoped so. But then, he always hoped so after the event; after the irresistible need had been met; after the rage had calmed. Realistically, he doubted if he had the strength to stop it. It was, after all, the thing that kept him alive.

He left those questions to time, as he rose from his knees, having finished his daily homage to Leni. With one last look at photograph ten, and with tears in his eyes, he left the studio. He stopped at the control room to turn off the violin concerto, and returned upstairs to the main lounge.

In that large, high-ceilinged, echoing room, surrounded by furniture covered with dust covers, Hector poured some whisky, sat in the rocking chair, and put on his headphones.

The music that started probably sounded normal to most people, but Hector had noticed, and liked its strangeness immediately. Only later, when reading about it, did he learn that Schumann had written his piano concerto in A-minor when out of his mind. Today, however, Schumann didn't fit his mood. He had things to do, plans to make.

He switched the music off, removed his headphones, and started to plan in his mind. But gradually, in the stillness of that ghostly room, his thoughts were drowned by a palpable silence. Ever since Vilma had gone, the silence had grown louder. Even though he hadn't been able to hear her moving in the sound proof studio below, the thought of her being there had been sufficient to create a sound in his mind, to keep him company, to dissipate the loneliness. He must get a replacement for Vilma soon, before the silence got too loud.

He had already selected a favourite candidate for the position, and done some initial interviewing. From the shelter of the trees surrounding Scarness Manor, he had watched her walking down the lane, to the village and back. Although she wasn't young, she was better than Vilma to look at, with a nice, kind face, and a lovely smile. He was sure she was right for the job. All he had to do now was to invite her for a final interview, and make her an offer she couldn't refuse.

Chapter 33

The search for a chemical industry closure, caused by the actions of an environmental organisation was still on. Ben had been at it for over a week, and was becoming increasingly anxious. It wasn't that the information was hard to find; the environmentalists were good at publicising their victories. He was anxious because each day that passed was another day of freedom for the killer, another day in which he might strike again.

He had painstakingly searched through old newspapers and library records without finding anything significant. More recently, he had concentrated on surfing the environmentalist's web sites. He had been amazed at how many green organisations existed, apart from the big boys such as Greenpeace. Many of them included the word 'earth' in their names.

So far, he had ploughed through the 'success stories' of The Earth Charter, Earth Force, Lovearth Network, Earth Action Network, Dept. of the Planet Earth, United Earth Alliance. He had also covered many others where the word 'earth' was replaced by 'eco' or 'conservation' or 'green'. Most of their 'successes' had been minor, such as a re-writing of local legislation, or the improvement of local waterways by diverting pollution. None had shown any 'victories' in chemical plants in Scotland about four years ago.

Now, he was returning to the web sites of the big boys - Greenpeace and Friends of the Earth, to make sure he hadn't missed anything on his first visit to their sites, which had proved fruitless.

Greenpeace was still attacking Dow Chemicals, claiming they had not yet cleaned up the mess at Bhopal where 2,000 people died from lethal gas at their pesticide plant. They claimed quite a few successes against chemical companies, but again, none had resulted in the closure of a plant in the right time period. They were currently fighting nine world wide campaigns, mostly to do with global warming, genetically modified crops, the nuclear industry, and forest preservation.

Friends of the Earth, who claimed over a million activists in 62 countries, started their web site with the headline 'Stop Esso', and featured a recent success in halting the construction of a new incinerator at La Hague in France.

However, a second search through their previous 'successes' did not come up with a chemical plant closure four years ago. They were currently involved with 12 worldwide campaigns, mostly to do with their anti-nuclear stance. Ben noticed that they shared the same jargon as Greenpeace, their 'Mission Statement' being 'Bringing an end to Nuclear Power.' Under this heading, the word 'Sellafield' caught Ben's eye, so he read on.

It was nothing more than a paragraph about Greenpeace divers collecting sediment in the Irish Sea in 1998. Tests had shown it to be radioactive, proving, they claimed, that Sellafield was pumping radioactive effluent into the sea.

Although this wasn't relevant to Ben's search, it reminded him of his trip to the Sellafield Visitor Centre, where he had learned that most of the processes at the plant involved the use of chemicals. He should, therefore, have included the nuclear industry in his search for chemical plant closures.

Sighing resignedly at the prospect of even more screen gazing, he took hold of the mouse, which by now felt like an organic part of his hand, and started to look for the 'successes' of Friends of the Earth and Greenpeace in the nuclear industry. And, just in case the successes were lost in the text of lengthy articles, he decided to read everything written under a promising heading.

After a long, two strong coffees, reading spell, he finally realised that their 'successes' in the nuclear industry had been confined to little more than breaking through security barriers, and attaching their names to the tops of buildings, thus gaining publicity for their cause 'Greenpeace evades pathetic security at Nuclear Port' was a heading that summed it all up.

Ben's disappointment was tangible; it had been a long slog without results. But, at least, he was now hardened to it, he had been there before. He knew that he had no alternative but to keep plodding on.

With a resoluteness inherited from his mother, as well as being born of necessity, he returned to his long list of smaller environmental organisations and started to put them through the nuclear industry search.

After another long spell, interrupted by a coffee and a walk around the garden, he had covered half of the list, but found nothing. Now he moved on to the many

'Greens', a group which, interestingly, included Green Cross International, founded by Mikhail Gorbachev in 1993.

Again, he found nothing, and was about to move on, when he realised he had not seen any Green *political* parties on his list. Presumably their web sites came under 'political parties' rather than 'environmental organisations'. He would check on them later, after finishing all the smaller organisations left on his list.

Later turned out to be almost 24-hours later, as Tribune work and domestic essentials took priority for a while. Helen had mentioned in passing - she would never nag - that the lawns were getting long, and the dust was getting thick, and the windows needed cleaning. He had to take care of them to prevent her asking why they were being neglected.

Back on the Internet, he brought up the Green political party on the screen. He glanced at the various international addresses, then clicked on Great Britain. The site was dominated by Scottish addresses, five in all. At the same time as he started his search for their 'success' stories, something began to stir at the back of his mind.

Then, suddenly, it was there in front of him, something he should have remembered. A whole page was given over to the Scottish Green Party's success in persuading the Scottish parliament to close part of the Dounreay Plant, and to adopt a policy of lobbying the British parliament in Westminster to close the Faslane nuclear submarine base, and all nuclear power stations in Scotland.

It had created quite a stir at the time, Ben remembered. It had caused many English MPs to renew their call for Scottish MPs not to have the right to vote on English as well as Scottish legislation.

He should have remembered; it wasn't all that long ago. Maybe, if he hadn't been looking for chemical plants all the time, he would have remembered sooner. No - that didn't do it - he still wanted to kick himself. He checked the date. Almost exactly four years ago. Right on the button - just before the killings had started in Scotland. He tried to ignore the now-familiar inflation of excitement, knowing how quickly it could revert to deflation.

A quick visit to Dounreay's web site told him that Dounreay had close links with Sellafield, and had been in the same business as Sellafield at that time, both coming under the auspices of the UK Atomic Energy Authority. In other words it was also involved in chemical processing.

It was all there - the right time, the right kind of closed plant, the right location, close to where the first killings took place, the Assynt region. He must not get too excited. All he had done was find support for one theory. The theory might be wrong. All this could be meaningless coincidence.

The telephone rang - Sue Burrows. 'Are you going to have that feature in tomorrow, Ben?'

Her tone was unusually abrupt and cold. It was the first time she had ever rang to remind him of his commitments. He couldn't blame her. With so much on his mind, he had been very lax in recent weeks.

It took only a micro-second to switch his brain to the meaning of her question, but she must have sensed the hesitancy. 'You're not going to let me down Ben, are you?'

'No…of course not,' Ben rushed, now fully in tune with the situation. 'I'm well on with it…I'll finish it in the morning, and I'll bring it in just after lunch...okay?'

'Glad to hear it...see you tomorrow.' There were none of the usual pleasantries.

Ben banged the phone down. 'Damn...damn... damn!' Not only was he responsible for a nice person like Sue becoming strident, but he was also having to abandon his trail again, just when it might be warming up.

He had, of course, lied to her. He hadn't written a single word of the feature she was chasing. It was quite unusual for a small weekly paper like the Tribune to incorporate centre-page feature articles. But when something big came up, which attracted national attention, like the recent discovery of the naked Filipino woman, Sue Burrows' policy was to try to keep her readers as well informed of developments as the readers of the nationals.

Normally, this involved Ben in a certain amount of 'legal plagiarism', extracting facts from the pages of the national papers, combining them with local interviews of interested parties, and mixing the whole thing up into a centre page feature.

He now had only 11 waking hours in which to do this. There was no time in which to obtain interviews, but he would phone the police press officer in the morning for the latest developments, and incorporate them.

In the meantime, he would work his way through the pile of national newspapers he had collected since the incident, and try to concoct a half decent article, based on facts rather than opinions.

The sooner this thing was over the better as far as he was concerned. And he knew Helen wouldn't be sorry to see the tottering pile of newspapers removed from the corner of what had once been their 'pretty' guest's bedroom.

Reluctantly, he switched off the computer, grabbed his notebook and the pile of newspapers, and went downstairs to work in the conservatory. When there was no computer work to be done, he preferred working in the conservatory where the light was better and the garden and the wildlife were in close proximity.

As he entered the conservatory, and laid the pile of newspapers on the floor beside an armchair, he heard a familiar pecking at the window. Freddy, the dominant pheasant, was begging food as usual. Ben took a scoop of pheasant food from a sack in the corner of the conservatory and, opening the double glass doors, threw it out on to the lawn. He allowed himself a few minute's break as he watched Freddy run to it, and start his robotic pecking action, all the while making his satisfied chortling sound, like a cat purring.

Then it was back to work. He settled in the armchair with his notebook, and turned the pile of newspapers upside down, wanting to start with the oldest issue and work his way forward.

As usual, he had bought two tabloids and two broadsheets each day, never failing to be staggered at the diversity of their reporting of the same story. Normally, he had no time for the tabloids, but in a case like this, which was their bread and butter, they sometimes stuck with it longer than the broadsheets, and could, therefore, be a source of more up to date information.

The first few issues contained nothing that he didn't already know. Then he came to the issues that had clearly resulted from the press conference he had missed. He started to make notes:

'Confirmation of woman's name/nationality – Vilma Tapales/Filipino.

Age - 32. Single (according to parents).

Found with steel chain attached to ankle by vehicle exhaust bracket/bolt. Other end of chain - same bracket/bolt arrangement attached to steel ring embedded in chunk of concrete.

Forensic report states - length of hair, condition of skin, nails, eyes and other organic factors indicate that she had been confined indoors for a period of at least three years.

Cause of death - Trauma to head and body probably caused by impact from passing vehicle. Vehicle may contain evidence of impact and is subject of police hunt.

Background - Sales Representative in Manila. Came to Britain four years ago to attend funeral of friend Leni Gonzalez who lived at Strathy Point, near Thurso, in Sutherland.'

'Know it well,' Ben thought, as he wrote it down, allowing himself a moment's fond recollection of unforgettable holidays. There was nothing else worth extracting from that day's 'press conference' editions, so he moved on.

He went through three more day's issues without finding any more facts worth noting. The broadsheets appeared to have dropped it altogether, while the tabloids carried the usual tasteless articles, featuring photographs of chained nubile women, under headings such as: *'How Common Is Bondage Today'*; none of which contained any facts pertinent to the case.

In the next day's issues, Ben was surprised to see that one of the broadsheets had picked it up again. Inside the front-page a headline announced: *'Filipino 'Slave' Case - Search for best friend's husband'*. Beside the headline was a photograph of a typical Sutherland croft house, and underneath it the caption: *'Last known location of Vilma Tapales'*. Clearly, the reporter had spent a few days in Sutherland gathering information.

Ben started to read:

Investigations into the Filipino 'slave' case have moved to the tiny community of Strathy Point in Sutherland where Vilma Tapales was last seen, four years ago, at the funerals of her best friend, Mrs Leni Snodd, and Mrs Snodd's five year old daughter, Grace.

After the funerals, she is known to have stayed for a few days with Mrs Snodd's husband, Hector, in his isolated croft house. When questioned by police, four years ago, about her non-arrival back in the Philippines, Mr Snodd is reported to have said that she left his house to catch her return flight, and that was the last he saw of her.

In response to continued pressure from Ms Tapales's parents since that time, police had carried out further investigations throughout the country without success, and she had remained on their 'missing persons' list, until the recent discovery of her chained body on the A591 in Cumbria.

Police are now anxious to trace the whereabouts of Mr Snodd, who subsequently left the area a few months after his wife and child's death. Snodd, 33, who worked as a concrete laboratory technician at the nearby Dounreay nuclear plant, is reported to be 5' 5' tall, of slim build, with thinning, sandy coloured hair. Local police said he was known to have suffered depressive episodes after being made redundant, and he was charged with causing the death of his wife and child due to dangerous driving while under the influence of alcohol. For that offence, he was given a two years suspended jail sentence, and banned from driving for five years, the judge in the case stating that the sentence was lenient because Snodd had 'already suffered irreparable loss.'

Ben was so busy methodically extracting the facts to his notebook, that he almost missed the significance of what he was reading. Then it suddenly hit him. 'JESUS CHRIST!' he whispered. 'IT COULD BE HIM'

He stared, unbelievingly, at the paper. 'What were the chances of that? None! It had to be the vibrations. *Thank God for the vibrations.'*

He held his breath as he re-read the paragraph. It was all there - the unstable character, the right location, the right industry, the job loss, the move from the area, the Tapales link to the Lake District. Even his job was definitive - a concrete laboratory technician; there had to be chemicals involved - the source of the sniff.

He paused, waiting for the inevitable doubts to appear. They had shown up so many times in the past, like unwelcome relatives, he awaited them with certainty, and foreboding. And sure enough, with the adrenalin flash calming, they pushed their way in.

He still had nothing to link the A591 Tapales incident to the rest of the killings. If it was murder, and had been committed by Snodd, then it was totally different from all the others, and therefore didn't fit the usual 'signature' pattern of a serial killer. If it wasn't murder, and just an accident, then her link to him and the Lake District could be pure coincidence. The whole 'bondage' aspect of it didn't seem to fit anything at all.

That was it - no more doubts emerged. He felt enormous relief. They were all just doubts after all; doubts that, he hoped, could eventually be explained away. They weren't the usual hard facts coming to knock his house of evidence down again. This time the evidence was compelling. This time he felt he had won.

He sat back in his armchair, and drew a deep, trembling, breath. His long journey was almost over. He had probably named his man. 'Hector Snodd,' he said out loud. It felt strange to have a name to deal with. Somehow it brought the terrifying reality closer. He was no longer looking for an anonymous killer, someone who existed in the distance. Now he had a name, he could see him, hiding in the forest, looming on the fell, standing outside his window.

And now he had to find him before he drenched the fells with blood again. Where was he...? Instinctively, he looked out of the conservatory window and searched the distant fells for an answer. A dark evening sky had started to blur them. Helen was late.

Chapter 34

The multi-coloured ball arched through the air and landed at his feet. 'Throw the ball back, skinny,' the podgy, shaven-headed boy shouted, while treading water.

Hector slowly bent down to pick it up. He needed to move slowly to control the anger, couldn't stand being called names. He wanted to hold that shaven head under the water, feel the struggle, watch the eyes bulge.

He threw the ball back hard and hit the boy on the head before he had time to get his hands into a catching position. That would have to do. The boy was about to protest, but caught the look in Hector's eyes, and quietly swam away.

Hector turned and caught sight of himself in the reflecting windows that surrounded the pool. He did look skinny in the baggy uniform. The red shorts and bright yellow shirt of the Royal Life Saving Society were too big for him, even though they were the smallest the supervisor could find. It didn't matter - the bigger they were, the better his chance of success.

The plan had gone well so far. Three days ago he had followed his target from home to work, arriving at 8.30 a.m. Inside the leisure centre, he had watched her pass through a door marked 'manager', and saw her sitting at a desk, through the window overlooking the swimming pool.

He had spotted the advertisement on the notice board seeking to recruit part-time pool attendants and, over a coffee in the cafeteria, eyes taking in the exits, his plan had formed.

Outside the building, he found the nearest bus stop, and noted that he could walk from it to the leisure centre without being seen from the centre, by taking the path around the car park, which was protected by a high privet hedge. He had watched her leave at 6.15 p.m.

Two days ago he had returned to the pool with towel and swimming shorts. He had taken a swim, and noted again that he could see her at her desk through the window overlooking the pool. He had also noted the position of the staff changing room, close to the emergency exit, at the end of the pool opposite the manager's office. He had surreptitiously opened the emergency exit door and been pleased to find that it led directly to the path outside of the building.

While still in the pool, he had spoken to the pool supervisor about applying for a part-time attendant's job. He had passed the basic swimming test given to him there and then, and agreed to attend a course to become a fully qualified lifeguard. The supervisor had given him a form to fill in, stating his name, address, telephone number, and national insurance number, and asked him to start the next day. He had negotiated hours from 5.00 p.m to 8.00 p.m.

Yesterday, he had handed in the completed form, and gone through the staff induction procedures, during which he had been given his bright red and yellow uniform, and copies of the 'Normal Operating Procedures' and 'Emergency Action Plans' to study at home.

The supervisor had taken him through some health and safety drills, fire drills, drowning incident drills, gas escape drills, and some admin procedures. He was then taken through the rules of the pool, in which he learned about zoning, the area of surveillance, station rotation, and what to watch out for.

Finally, he was given a daily job list, which, as well as observing the pool, included cleaning the changing rooms, filling the vending machines, and testing the water for chlorine content and calcium hardness.

He hadn't anticipated these off-pool duties, and was concerned that he might not be in a position to see her when she left for home. At 6.30 p.m, the supervisor had taken him to meet her in her office. She had been as nice as he had expected. Her hand had been warm and soft against his, her smile had been even better close up; her voice had been gentle and welcoming.

When he watched his new companion leave at 7.04 p.m, still smiling, he knew he had made the right choice.

*

Now he was on poolside duty, patrolling near the emergency exit, watching her through the office window. His clothes were in his sports bag in the nearby staff changing room, tracksuit bottom on top, ready.

At 6.46 p.m, she stood up from her desk and moved away from it. He tensed ready. She came out of the office without her briefcase, and disappeared down a corridor leading to the sports hall and squash courts. He relaxed.

At 7.00 p.m, the supervisor asked him to hose out the men's changing room while there was nobody in it. She hadn't returned; he might miss her. He dashed to the changing room, turned the water on full pressure and blasted the seating and floor, as instructed. It took him 14 minutes.

Back on the poolside, her office was still empty. Was she still in the building, or had she gone home? His stomach leaked acid. It had to be tonight; the information on the forms was all false; he couldn't come back tomorrow.

He marched up and down, grinding his teeth, ignoring his job, the screams of delighted children. She was back. Slow down, stay calm.

The supervisor was watching him. He looked at the children, walked slowly up and down, looked at her, looked at the supervisor, time was getting on.

At 7.30 p.m, she was still at her desk. He was off duty at 8.00; if she left later than 8.30 she might not see him in the dark. He willed her to move, the acid returned.

At 7.40 p.m, she stood up, lifted her briefcase on to the desk, and started to load it. Hector walked quickly to the staff changing room. He pulled his tracksuit bottom on over his shorts, grabbed his bag, and poked his head out of the room. When the supervisor wasn't looking his way, he walked straight to the emergency exit, opened the door, left the building, closed the door.

He ran along the path, beside the privet hedge. At a pedestrian gap in the hedge he stopped and looked into the car park. His heart pounded in his ears as he watched and waited. Here she came, out of the building, walking to her car. He ran the short distance to the bus stop, and stood on the edge of the kerb. Now the bright yellow shirt had to do its job.

He saw her distinctive old Saab come out of the car park and turn towards him. He turned his back and looked the other way. She had to see the shirt. And if she was as nice as she seemed, she had to stop.

He heard the car approach. He stopped breathing. The engine was building up power; she was going to pass him. The car was level with him when it screeched to a halt. She was waving at him.

He approached the car. She leaned over and opened the passenger door. 'It's Ian isn't it?' she smiled through tired eyes.

'Yes'.

'Can I give you a lift?'

'Yes...please.' He lowered himself into the seat, noticed her jacket hanging in the back, handbag and briefcase on the back seat, mobile phone in the centre console. He put his bag on the floor, between his legs. 'Thanks, Mrs Foxley.'

'Call me Helen, please. How's your first day been?' she asked, as she pulled away.

'Fine...yes...good.'

'You'll soon get into the swing of things...you've got a good bunch to work with.'

'Yes.'

'I'm going as far as Bassenthwaite. Where can I drop you?'

'Same place.'

'Pardon?'

'I live near Bassenthwaite as well.'

'Really...whereabouts?'

'Do you know the big house overlooking the lake... Scarness Manor?'

'Yes...Jed Samson's place.'

'I'm the caretaker there.' He was glad she had heard of Jed Samson.

'Good heavens! We're neighbours, and we've never met. I live at Scarness Cottage, just outside the Manor grounds. Did you know?'

'No.'

'Have you been at the Manor long? It's a wonder we haven't bumped into each other along the lane or in the village?'

'Just a few weeks.' He sniffed twice; he usually did when he lied.

'And is your wife with you? Maybe she...'

'She died.' *Better say more; act natural.* 'It's a bit lonely on your own in that big house. So that's why I've come to work at the pool...to be among people.'

'I'm sorry to hear that, Ian.' She left it at that; she didn't pry.

Later, as the car passed through Ambleside's narrow streets, she said: 'I take it you can you manage the two jobs. We need people we can rely on.'

'Its no problem…I do all my caretaker work during the day...it's mostly gardening. I was just watching television in the evening anyway...I was bored.'

'Good for you…I wish we could find more like you.'

He wanted to kiss her on the cheek for saying nice things; he hoped she would always say nice things when she was his companion. *Not long now, don't rush things, let her do all the leading, she'll ask the right questions, women are inquisitive, be patient.*

Silence followed as she drove slowly around the bounds of Grasmere lake, past Dove Cottage where Wordsworth lived, where sylvan beauty stopped conversations.

Then, out of the valley and up the hill, to bleak Dunmail Raise where Dunmail, the last king of Cumberland, was buried in 945 AD.

'Does Jed Samson ever use the Manor? We've lived at Scarness for nearly four years now, and we've never seen him.'

She was taking the bait. 'The agent told me he hasn't used it for years. I've never met him, or spoken to him. I just work for the agent.'

'Is it all still furnished? I mean, if he turned up tomorrow with his latest family, would everything be ready for them?'

'Just about...there's a typed list of things to do on the kitchen notice board...his wife would love the kitchen...I could have everything ready in a couple of hours.'

'The kitchen's a bit special is it?'

'Terrific. Everything's old except the kitchen and main bathroom. He must have had them rebuilt. They're like you see in them posh magazines...like film star's places.' *Don't overdo it!*

'It sounds lovely. But it's all just sitting there, unused. Doesn't seem right somehow. Tell him, if ever we win the lottery, we'll buy it off him. I could do with a bigger kitchen.'

'Will do.'

The seed was planted. Now he had to make sure she took him right up to the Manor, didn't just drop him off at the entrance gate.

He found the seat adjustment lever and pulled it. The seat's back went down and him with it. 'Didn't get much sleep last night,' he yawned, and closed his eyes.

Ten minutes seemed a long time, mind racing behind closed eyes, planning ahead, *her blouse smelt nice*, she must not take the phone in.

He felt the car turn sharp left, down a steep slope, into their lane, *not long now*. Another mile and she stopped the car. He knew they were at the Manor gates, where she would want to drop him. He didn't move.

A pause, and they were moving again. Into the Manor grounds, along the dual carriageway, then the unmade bit, then the gravel outside the front door. He didn't move.

'Ian.' She was shaking his shoulder; he wanted to touch her hand. He pretended to wake up, blinking, yawning.

'We're here.'

He pulled the seat upright, and looked around. 'Oh, sorry...you should have woken me at the gate...I could have walked the rest.'

He picked his bag off the floor.

'Big place,' she said, looking at the imposing entrance. 'Which part of it do you live in?'

He pointed. 'That bit sticking out over there...its a separate cottage.'

He opened the car door, and got out. *She wasn't biting, she wasn't asking, plan B.* 'Thanks again, Mrs Foxley...I'll see you tomorrow.'

He took one step away from the door, while she was saying 'you're welcome, and something else, which he interrupted: 'By the way, I'm just popping into the kitchen to turn the heating thermostat down for the night...would you like a look?' *Come on...come on...come...*

'Are you sure...you won't get into trouble?'

Got You! 'I'm not supposed to show anybody around, but...well...you won't tell anybody will you?'

'No, of course not.'

He had the front door key ready in his bag. He waited until she got out of the car, left her mobile phone, *good*, left her jacket, picked up her handbag, *didn't matter*. He climbed the stone steps, opened the door, turned to usher her inside.

He closed the front door, flicked two switches. Wall lights lit up the panelled hall. Behind the door, a monitor screen flickered on and displayed the entrance gates.

'What's that?'

'Security monitor...he's got them everywhere. That's the entrance gates you're looking at.'

He started to walk down the hall, Helen following. Past the dining room, the serving room, to the kitchen, once the gun room. He switched on the lights as he led her in.

'Wow!' she said, as she took it all in. The best of everything was on display - appliances, space, luxury. 'I could enjoy myself in here,' she said as she walked about, looking and touching.

Eventually: 'What a waste...just standing here... unused?'

'Would you like to see the main bathroom...it's even better?'

'Yes...I'd love to...if it's alright.'

'It's upstairs,' he said, and walked out of the kitchen.

She followed him along a corridor, and up a grand, wide staircase of carved oak. Along a narrow landing, past two doors, and through a third door. He switched on the light as he led her in.

This time she didn't say anything; she just stared, mouth open. The marble floors, walls and columns were in Greek style. A huge sunken bath in the shape of a heart, gold fittings, special lighting effects, ankle deep white rugs, space. It was completely over the top and she didn't like it.

'Impressive,' was all she could manage, eventually.

Hector moved across the bathroom to a second door. 'This leads to the master bedroom.' He didn't ask her if she wanted to see it; he just opened it and walked through. She followed.

He moved slowly around the large, high ceilinged room, *give her time to enjoy, don't rush, down to studio next, then....*

'Can we go out here?' She was standing at a large glass door that opened on to a balcony, which overlooked the lake and the surrounding fells.

He hesitated. 'Yes.' *Mustn't rush, keep calm.*

He found the key and opened the door for her. She stepped outside...he followed.

'What a wonderful view,' she said. 'You can almost see the whole lake from here. I thought we had a nice view, but this.... Yes...tell your Mr Samson we will definitely buy this when we win the lottery.'

There was a long silence as she slowly scanned up and down the lake and studied the fells opposite, now starting to dim in the evening light. 'I can see Catbells... Grizedale Pike... Dale Head...Barf, and Lords Seat, and Sale Fell,' she enthused. 'We can only see Lords Seat and Sale Fell from the cottage.'

A dramatic sunset was starting to outline the trees on Sale Fell. 'Are you a fell walker, Ian?'

'No...not really...I like to photograph them...but I'm not a walker.' Two sniffs.

'Photography, eh! That's an interesting hobby...'

'Would you like to see some photographs of my wife...she was beautiful.' *You rushed that, slow down; you were going to do the pity thing later.*

'...Yes...that would be nice...'

You've still got her, calm down. 'They're in the studio downstairs.'

He led her from the balcony, back through the bedroom, down the stairs, along the hallway, to the main lounge.

He moved the rocking chair, and kicked the rug aside, revealing the trapdoor. She started to say something, he interrupted: 'Promise not to tell anybody.'

'About what?'

He lifted the trapdoor. 'This is Jed Samson's recording studio...not many people know about it...he wanted to keep it secret...'

'Why?'

'I don't know...I was told not to ask questions...I have to make sure it stays at a warm temperature to protect all the equipment from condensation and damp.'

'And your photographs are down there?'

She looks unsure, is she suspicious, be convincing. 'Yes...I hang them around the studio walls...it's all wood panelling... it's ideal...I can remove them quickly if ever he came here...' *she's looking at her watch.*

'It's getting late, Ian. Maybe I could come back another day...'

She's backing out, she's worried, do something or you'll have to hurt her, you don't want to do that. 'It won't take a minute...I can show you my little girl as well...she died with her mother... she was beautiful as well...' *The pity thing again, good move, they can't resist the pity thing.*

'Alright, but I can't stay long. My husband will be wondering where I've got to.'

He led her down the steps, switching a light on as he went, along a passage, into a larger space, stopping at a large door. To the left, the paraphernalia of the control room, idle, beneath a window looking into the studio, dark.

With a key, he opened the first of the three-inch-thick insulated doors, pulling it towards him. He pushed the second of the three-inch-thick doors inwards and followed it in, into the dark room. He stood holding it and invited Helen to step forward into the avenue of light cast on the floor by the open door.

Helen stepped forward and he walked behind her and walked out, closing the door behind him. He closed the second door and turned the key in a hurry, just in case she screamed. He didn't want to hear her scream.

He switched on the studio lights, moved to the swivelling chair in the Control Room to watch her through the window.

There she was...goldfish in a bowl...looking at the

photographs...laughing or screaming...mouth opening... closing... eyes wide...arms swimming... his...forever... waving...banging on the window...hope she doesn't hurt herself...nice to look after...nice face... better than Vilma...I'm going to shit myself...the excitement.

He switched on the interconnecting microphone. 'Helen...excuse me, but I have to go to the toilet.'

Her hands went to her ears; he liked it loud.

'If you want to go...there's a bucket. Rest on the mattress, and put that clamp around your ankle...I'll tighten it up when I get back...put your car keys on the floor...be good...I don't want to hurt you...I want to love you...I'll bring you some food.'

He swivelled the chair to leave, then remembered something, and swivelled back. He pressed one of a multitude of switches to his left, and heard the love duet from Madame Butterfly start up. *That's better...everything back to normal now.*

He celebrated with a full swivel before he left the room.

Chapter 35

Helen's failure to return from work did not worry Ben. Occasionally, when she worked late, and needed an early start the next morning, she would stay overnight at a nearby hotel or guesthouse, to save time spent on the car journey. No doubt, she would phone after her evening meal and let him know where she was.

He spent the evening re-reading 'The Serial Killers'. He recalled having read something about bondage on the first reading, but hadn't made notes, because, at the time, it didn't seem relevant to the type of killings he was dealing with.

Now, he was looking for something to explain the connection between one chained body found on a road, and many unchained bodies found on the fells all having the regular 'signature' pattern of killing. Were there any precedents for this?

In the chapter 'The Power Syndrome', he read that some serial killers have a propensity for enslavement of women. Numerous cases were cited. All were carried out by shy, inadequate, unattractive men who had a craving for recognition. The enslavements were motivated by the desire for power rather than sex, to relieve their sense of inferiority and replace it with a sense of being **master.** The period of captivity ranged from a few days to seven years. The women were usually, but not always, abused during captivity, and then killed.

From all the evidence at Ben's disposal, it looked as though poor Vilma Tapales had been kept prisoner by Hector Snodd for close to four years. Why? He didn't sound inadequate; he had held down a reasonable job; he'd had a wife and child. But so had some of the killers in the book. It was how they perceived themselves that was crucial, not how others perceived them.

The question of *why* could be left for later. *Where*, was the important question. Vilma had been found about a mile from his cottage. After four years of confinement, she could not have been fit. She was carrying a heavy chain and a chunk of concrete. She was naked. She could not have walked far with bare feet. Therefore, her place of captivity had to be close to where she was found.

Ben glanced at his watch: 11.00 p.m, and no call from Helen. This wasn't like her; she always rang. As the evening progressed he grew increasingly anxious. At midnight he tried her mobile. It rang out, but she didn't answer.

He phoned the leisure centre, in case she was still there for some reason - maybe a boiler had blown up, or some other kind of accident. He got the routine answering machine message.

He didn't know which of the hundreds of hotels and guesthouses in Windermere she had gone to. There were too many to phone, particularly at that time of night. He thought of phoning other members of staff, but it was late, and they might think that Helen and him didn't communicate. It would be embarrassing for her when she turned up at work the next morning.

There had to be a simple explanation. She had probably had a really hard day, and fallen asleep after the evening meal and a couple of drinks. He shouldn't worry. She was nothing if not worldly wise. She knew how to look after herself

His head hit the pillow at 12.35 a.m. At 1.15, he was still awake, worrying. He finally got to sleep about 4.00, and woke up suddenly at 8.47. Helen would be at work by now.

He picked up the bedside phone and punched the Leisure Centre number. He recognised the receptionist's voice. 'Good morning, Maria, could you put me through to Helen please...it's Ben.'

'I'm not sure she's in yet, Ben. I'll just check.' A long, hope filled, pause. 'No....nobody has seen her yet, this morning.'

'Do you know what time she left last night?'

'No...I don't. She was still here when I left at 5. You'd need to ask one of the late shift supervisors...they'll be in at 2 this afternoon. Is anything wrong?'

'No....no... She stayed in Windermere last night. I was just checking to see if she'd had plenty of sleep...you know what she's like...'

'We know...we're always telling her she works too hard. She'll be putting a bed in her office one of these days. Maybe she's slept in for a change...do her good. As soon as she comes in, Ben, I'll get her to ring you, okay?'

'Yes...right...thanks, Maria.'

He tried her mobile again. No reply.

He showered, dressed and had breakfast in an expectant, but uninterrupted hour. He went outside and fed the wildlife, leaving the conservatory door open. He trundled the wheelie bin to its collection point, leaving the front door open. The phone didn't ring. He tidied up and washed the dishes. The phone didn't ring.

Using yellow pages, he rang the four hotels closest to the leisure centre. She hadn't stayed with any of them.

It was 11.30 a.m. Something was wrong. He rang Maria again.

'No…we haven't seen her yet. We were going to ring you to see if she had turned up at home. Apparently she's missed two appointments already…it's not like her....'

'Thanks, Maria.'

He rang Helen's sister who lived 30 miles away. They were close; maybe there was a family problem he knew nothing about; maybe Helen had a problem she could only discuss with her sister. She wasn't there. He made a lame excuse for the call.

He tried to stay calm, think logically, in spite of his churning stomach. Who had last spoken to her? How had she appeared to them? He needed to go to the leisure centre, talk to the afternoon shift.

He drove fast on the road to Windermere, tried to ignore the pervasive beauty.

At 1.30 p.m, he was reading the papers on her desk, looking for notes, messages, anything, finding nothing. By 1.55 p.m, he had spoken to the morning shift supervisors. Nothing unusual to report, she had seemed fine, been her usual, cheerful self.

At 2.00 p.m, he waited in the reception area as the afternoon shift supervisors took over from the morning supervisors, exchanging information, messages.

They came to see him, having got the message about Helen's non-appearance. He had met them once or twice before. Paul was the pool supervisor. Brian looked after the dry side.

'I saw her twice yesterday,' Brian said, in answer to Ben's question. 'We had a chat in her office at the start of my shift, about 2 o'clock. She seemed fine. Then she came to see me in the sports hall at about 7 o'clock last night. She seemed okay...maybe a bit tired...' He shrugged his shoulders.

'What about you, Paul? When did you last see her? Did she seem okay to you?'

'Yes, she was fine all day. I see her all the time through the pool window....'

'Did you see her leave?'

'Yes...she went about 8 o'clock...'

'Was she on her own?'

'Yes…she waved goodnight...'

'Did you see her get into her car?'

'I did actually. After she'd gone, I came out to the reception area, looking for a member of staff who'd disappeared. I looked outside the front door to see if he was sneaking a smoke in the car park. I didn't see him, but I saw Helen get in her car and drive away.'

'Was she definitely on her own?'

'Yes...as far as I could see. She passed pretty close to me, and waved again...I didn't see anybody else in the car.'

'Did she mention to either of you that she was staying overnight in Windermere?'

Both heads shook. 'No...no,' Paul added: 'I'm pretty sure she was going home. Whenever she stays in Windermere she lets us know, so we know where to contact her in an emergency...its routine.'

'God, this is hopeless!' Ben snapped. 'Where the hell is she?'

The two supervisors stared, uncomfortably, at the floor.

'Did anything at all unusual happen yesterday... *anything*? Even if it had nothing to do with Helen.'

'Paul paid for the...coffee.' Brian's joke died in his mouth.

Paul frowned fiercely at him.

'Sorry,' Brian sighed.

'Anything, other than that?' Ben said, cuttingly.

Brian shuffled his feet, and looked at the ceiling. 'No...I really don't think so. I had a routine sort of day.'

Ben turned to Paul.

Paul stood, concentrating, gently shaking his head, as he ran the day back through his mind.

'Anything,' Ben reminded him.

'The only thing...but I can't see any relevance...was we had a bloke walk off the job before his shift was over. That's who I was looking for when I saw Helen in the...car....'

They realised it together. 'Who is he?' Ben demanded.

'A new bloke,' Paul stuttered. 'A new casual; he's only been with us a couple of days.'

'Jesus Christ!' Ben's jaw tightened. He couldn't allow himself to believe anything yet - he wouldn't function. 'Name...address?' he asked, deliberately.

'Ian something,' Paul stammered. 'It's in the office.' He walked away quickly. Ben followed. Brian looked lost.

In the staff office, Paul opened a filing cabinet and produced a grey file. He lifted a form from it. 'Ian Thomson,' he announced. 12, Bank Street, Keswick. Telephone number 017687 76413. National Insurance number....'

Ben grabbed the form. 'I'll borrow that...'

'You can't,' Paul protested. 'I shouldn't even have read it to you...it's all protected information under the Data Protection Act.

'Fuck the Data Protection Act. What did this bloke look like? Was he tall, short, thin, fat...?'

'He was small, about 5 foot 6, very thin...gingerish... sandy hair...'

'Accent?'

'Hard to tell...a bit Scottish I think.'

'Did he sniff?'

'Pardon?'

'Did he sniff…you know...up his nose.' Ben gave a demonstration.

'Yes...he...'

Ben turned, knocked over a chair, sprinted through the office doorway, across the reception area, fought with the main door, fought with his mind, it can't be happening, there has to be another explanation.

He drove, dangerously fast, on the road back to Keswick. The beauty didn't exist. His mind was trapped in a surreal world, swimming between reality and unreality. Was this real? Was it happening to somebody else? Terrible things only happened to other people. Not to people like Helen, like him. Half of him wanted to let it go, pretend it wasn't happening. The other half shouted FOCUS - STAY FOCUSSED – IT'S REAL – IT'S UP TO YOU.

He wasn't sure who was winning when he jarred to a halt in Bank Street, Keswick. It was in the town centre, a right angle offshoot from the main shopping street, the shops in it suffering poor income in comparison.

Ben ran along the short street and soon found number 12. By the sound of the name above the shop window, it had once been a ladies dress shop. Now it was up for sale, boarded up, rusting nails, flapping notices, graffiti.

Ben felt equally empty and desolate. Up to this point, other scenarios had been possible. Not now.

He went through the motions of crossing the road to a telephone booth and trying the number on the form. It was, of course, not recognised.

He stood in a quiet street and stared into space. He didn't know what to do.

A few minutes later, he was approaching the cottage. The sight of the cottage, nestling in its beautiful surroundings, lifted him. It always did; it was home, and Helen, and contentment. He would walk in and she would be there, apologising for not contacting him, explaining her disappearance. He wouldn't listen. It didn't matter. He would hold her so tight they might fuse. He would hold her till the trembling stopped.

The emptiness of the house shocked him. It was absolute. Even when she wasn't at home, he had always sensed her presence in every room. Now he couldn't. There was nothing there but space and furniture. Her spirit had left. She wasn't coming home.

Chapter 36

For the first few seconds, after the door had closed behind her, leaving her standing in the dark, Helen thought it was a joke. The staff at the leisure centre frequently played practical jokes on her and each other. She encouraged it, within reason. It created a happy atmosphere, a good team spirit. They had put this new starter up to it, hadn't they?

Even when the lights went on, and her eyes adjusted to the brightness, and took in rows of photographs on the walls, she was not perturbed. It was what she expected to see - photographs of his wife and daughter.

It was when she stepped forward to look at them that the shock punched her backwards. Her feet left the ground as her instincts threw her away from the horror. An involuntary gasp left her lips.

Then her breath was held, as she focussed again. Sockets overflowing with dark red blood, gushing all over, into hair, into mouths; ears hanging, torn flesh, gashes, teeth bared in agony, one eye open, bright. They had been alive when the camera clicked.

She turned away, screaming, and saw him sitting, smiling through a window. Instinctively, she launched herself at it, pounding it with her fists. Suddenly, a loud voice: 'Helen...excuse me, but I have to go to the toilet.'

She clasped her hands to her ears. The voice boomed on. Something about a bucket and a clamp, car keys on the floor, hurt you, love you, food. Then the voice stopped, and she saw him move. She took her hands from her ears. Silence, then deafening music, suddenly. Her heart leaped. Her hands went back to her ears. He was swivelling on a chair. He was gone.

She stepped back from the window. She knew who he was. Ben had been right all along: silly, imaginative Ben. 'Time you got a proper job,' she had told him. Where was he? Where was Ben? She needed *his* arms around her...not the cold, tight, tentacles of dread that were beginning to envelop her, squeeze the breath from her.

The fear and noise took over her mind, paralysed her, made her a frightened child again. She backed herself to a wall and wrapped her arms around her trembling body.

Then she saw her reflection in the darkened control room window. Smartly dressed, business like. She wasn't a child. She was a strong, confident, woman. She'd brought up a family, travelled, climbed mountains, swam rivers, given lectures. She was a Manager. She managed people. She had to manage the fear, get rid of it, think proactively. Otherwise...she was just another lamb to the slaughter.

First things first, small things first, be practical. Shaking hands opened her bulging handbag, her mobile office. No makeup here, but pens, highlighters, paperclips, diary, dictating machine, calculator, credit cards, nail scissors, chocolate, travel wipes, handkerchief, cotton wool. No mobile phone. He must have noticed that she left it in the car; otherwise he would have searched her handbag.

She pulled two pieces of cotton wool, rolled them, and stuffed them into her ears to blunt the noise. Now she could think.

She stood very straight, shoulders back, and pulled deep breaths down into her stomach. She let the air out slowly. Gradually, the fear went with it, and she began to calm.

She looked around the strangely shaped room, trying to avoid the photographs. It was multi-sided, no two walls being parallel. Two opposite corners had been partitioned off, creating two small triangular rooms within the main room, a window looking into each of them. Thick, black, square shaped pieces of rigid foam hung from chains in the ceiling.

Had she been in the music business, she would have known that the room shape was designed to break up sound reflection, recognised the small rooms as accompanying musicians' isolation booths, and realised that the ceiling pieces were sound deadening baffles.

As it was, the strangeness of the room only served to increase the feeling of disorientation within her.

Now, her eyes settled on a mattress on the floor, a bucket beside it, and a chain suspended from one of the ceiling baffle rings. She guessed their significance. She had heard about the Filipino woman found with a chain attached to her ankle. What she didn't know was how long he kept his victims prisoner before he disposed of them. She clenched her teeth. How long could she bear this? How long could she stay strong?

She began to think about the instructions he had shouted through the microphone. Though blurred by having her hands over her ears, she had got the gist of them. He wanted her to put her ankle in the clamp attached to the chain, and to leave her car keys on the floor.

Her first instinct was to do exactly as he asked, in case he was volatile and violent when his instructions were ignored. That would buy time; give Ben or the police time to find her. But she didn't know how much time she had; he might be planning to kill her today, tomorrow. She had to assume the worst. It was no use waiting to be rescued. It was up to her to escape.

She needed to discover the kind of enemy she was dealing with. Clearly, he was insane or on the edge of insanity. But was he aggressive and vicious, or were there moments of sanity when he could be reasoned with, or even influenced?

She decided to take a calculated risk. She would test his reactions by obeying one of his instructions, and disobeying the other. She took her car keys from her handbag and laid them in the middle of the floor, as requested, but she didn't put her foot in the ankle clamp.

Thirty seconds later, the control room light went on. He was coming back. She moved close to the control room window and faced it, some instinct telling her not to show fear.

Suddenly, he was there, right in front of her, looking into her eyes. Her heart jumped into her throat, but she stood firm and stared back. She didn't see any obvious animosity in his eyes; if anything, he looked puzzled.

He moved away, pausing to press a switch. The music stopped. Soon the two thick studio doors opened. He came in slowly, warily, as though he was expecting her to make a break for the door. He closed the inner door behind him and locked it.

'Sit on the mattress please.'

Helen just managed to hear him. She took out one of the cotton wool earplugs. The 'please' surprised her. She did as she was told; the mattress stank.

He moved towards her, slowly, carrying a plastic bag and a steel wrench. He put the plastic bag down beside her, and stood over her, wrench in his right clenched fist. Helen tensed, ready to dodge the blow.

'You didn't put the ankle clamp on?' he said, simply.

'Did you ask me to?'

'Yes'

'I didn't hear. Your voice was too loud. I had my hands over my ears. All I heard was: 'Put the car keys on the floor. I've done that.' She pointed to them. He moved across and picked them up.

'I have to go now...get rid of your car. There's some food in the bag. It's not much...I'll try to do better tomorrow. Don't be frightened, I don't want to hurt you.' He lifted the wrench. 'This was to tighten your clamp. When I get back, could you have the clamp on please? I'd like to trust you...leave you free...but I trusted Vilma...she kept trying to escape. You would as well...wouldn't you?' He turned and left the room, not waiting for a reply.

Helen let out a trembling sigh, and felt something moving in her lap. She looked down. Her hands were shaking, violently. They didn't seem to belong to her.

Madame Butterfly started up again. The Control Room light went out. Helen put her earplug back in and flopped back on the mattress, exhausted. She closed her eyes. She wanted to fall asleep, let it all fade away, let her dreams take over. Maybe it **was** just a bad dream? She opened her eyes. The black baffles on the ceiling told her it wasn't.

She forced herself to sit up, registered the mattress smell again, and stood up, hastily, brushing down her blouse and skirt with her hands. Gingerly, she looked inside the plastic bag. It contained a ham sandwich, two bananas and a plastic bottle of orange juice.

Her normal appetite was missing, no doubt ousted by the tension. But she knew that she had to keep up her strength. The ham sandwich was out of the question - he had handled it. She took a drink of juice, first wiping the top of the bottle with one of her travel wipes. Then she peeled a banana and started to eat.

As she chewed, she tried to re-assess her situation. It didn't look as though he intended to kill her, at least - not immediately. But it would be dangerous to assume so. She didn't know what went on in his mind. It might be exactly what he wanted her to think. Put her off her guard to make the killing easier.

If, as he said, he didn't want to hurt her, but intended to keep her in chains...like a dog, like a plaything...then the thought of what that meant made death seem almost preferable. While it gave time for Ben and the police to find her, and she was confident they would, eventually, she dreaded to think of the state she would be in, mentally and physically, by the time they found her. She wouldn't want Ben to be lumbered with a broken, soiled woman to look after. She loved him too much for that.

Either way, it came down to the same thing. She had to make every effort to escape immediately.

Another glance around the room confirmed that the only way out was through the double doors. She had noticed that when he went out, he didn't bother to lock the door that opened inwards, into the studio. He only locked the outer door that opened outwards, into the control room.

She walked over and tried the inner door handle. The thick door opened, and she swung it back until it met the wall. While there, she tried the outer door, just in case. It was secure.

Maybe she could surprise him when he came back. He would probably look through the control room window first, to check on her position. If he saw her sitting on the mattress with the clamp apparently around her ankle, it would put him in a relaxed state of mind. While he moved from the window to open the outer door, she could jump up from the mattress, and be in the doorway, ready to attack him as soon as he opened the outer door.

He wasn't very big, and he wouldn't be expecting it. If she timed it right, and charged the door just as he opened it, she could knock him aside and run past him.

On the other hand, he would be carrying that steel wrench to tighten the clamp. If she didn't manage to knock him off balance, and he started to use that on her, then she had little defence; it would soon be over.

She looked around for something to defend herself with. There was nothing but the plastic bucket, the plastic bottle, and her handbag. The two brittle plastics would soon disintegrate when struck by metal, and the handbag was too soft to cushion a sustained attack.

Another look around and this time the photographs caught her eye. They were quite large, about two-feet square, and had solid looking wooden frames. If she held one up in front of her, it might prove strong enough to ward off a few blows. Alternatively, she could use it as a weapon to smash over his head if the opportunity arose.

She walked across and lifted one of the photographs off its wall hook. She couldn't help glancing at its hideous content again, as she balanced it in her hands to feel the weight. Behind the terribly damaged face, there was something familiar about that long, tangled, hair. It was someone she knew...it was Tessa Coleman.

She stifled her scream, but her hands shook so much she almost dropped the photograph. She was holding Ben's friend in her hands. She had met her once or twice at art exhibitions. Now, here she was, hanging as an exhibition in a madman's gallery, her familiarity adding to the terror. How long would it be before she joined Tessa on the wall?

She couldn't afford such negative thoughts, and fought them off with accompanying deep breathing. The photograph did feel heavy and substantial. She held it up like a shield in front of her face. She practiced using it as a weapon, bringing it down from over her head, thrusting it forwards, edge first.

As she manoeuvred it through different positions, she noticed a label stuck on the back. It read:

No. 8

T. Coleman

Dale Head

He was obviously keeping records. She remembered Ben's theory that the victims were random, unknown to him. He must, therefore, have added Tessa's name after getting it via the media. She couldn't read any significance into that, but soon she was asking herself why he had bothered to allocate numbers. She looked again along the two rows of photographs, and counted them. There were ten along the top row, all of the same disfigured, exotic, woman. She turned one round and read a single word on the label:

Butterfly

There were nine along the bottom row, of different women and one man. She turned the last one round. It read:

No. 9

J Metternich

Place Fell

Next to it, under the tenth top row photograph, a photograph frame hung, complete with mount and glass, but with no picture in it. Obviously, it was waiting for victim number 10. Since both rows ended there, did it mean that he intended to stop after number 10? Was **she** to be his final victim?

Maybe the back would tell her. With shaking hands, she turned it round. There was a label. She stopped breathing as she read:

No. 10

Barf

So there it was. He was counting them, and pre-arranging the place of their deaths, but no person's name had been pre-selected. There was a slight glimmer of hope here. Clearly, he had plotted and planned and pre-selected her, yet had not put her name on the label. Maybe he killed random victims only? Maybe he didn't kill people he knew, or was trying to get to know?

Or maybe, she was on some sort of probation, and her survival depended on how she behaved in captivity? She could yet be victim number 10?

He had chosen Barf as his next, possibly last, place of death. It was a small, steep, fell on the other side of Bassenthwaite lake. She knew it well, being almost opposite their cottage, just hidden from view by lakeside trees. It was also visible from the Manor. Maybe it *was* going to be the scene of his last killing. Maybe he had chosen it so that he could sit on that balcony and repeatedly relive the thrill.

Whatever the dreadful scenario, whoever the next victim, whether she escaped or not, she knew she had to try to get this knowledge out. If not her own, it could save someone else's life, and possibly lead to his capture.

She picked a spot as far away from the mattress as possible, and sat on the floor with her back against the wall. There was some serious thinking to do. She had to come up with a plan to get the information out, even if she didn't get out herself.

Twenty minutes later, she glanced at her watch. He had been gone almost an hour; she had to assume he would be back soon; she had come up with nothing. Her brain seemed to have a brake acting on it. She would start along a promising thought pattern, then find herself being side-tracked by the terror of her situation, at which point a blankness would set in, as if the brain was trying to protect itself from reality.

Repeatedly, she tried to fight her way out of the fog, but time and again she failed.

'Damn!' she shouted, as she hit the floor with her fists in frustration. The action seemed to release something. Maybe she needed to move or occupy herself with something, while trying to think. Maybe the clarity would come then.

She opened her handbag and tipped all the contents on to the floor beside her. She started to rummage around, randomly picking things up, putting them down, all the while trying to think of a way to get the information out.

It worked, up to a point. She was no longer being sidetracked; her brain was following through. But, she was still unable to come up with a feasible plan. The problem, it would seem, was simply too difficult for her.

Time was getting on. He could return at any minute. She had to do something, come up with something, however simple or unsubtle.

If only she could get the word BARF out to Ben or the police, they would understand its significance. The only way she could get it out was by taking it through the door when she tried to make an escape.

She would, therefore, write BARF on as many things as possible, and hope to scatter them, undetected, once outside the room.

She searched among her pens and found a dark blue fibre-tip. She tore a few blank pages from her pocket diary, wrote BARF on them, then carefully tucked them up the right hand sleeve of her blouse. Next, she wrote on her handkerchief, and tucked that up the left hand sleeve of her blouse.

The soles and insteps of both shoes were next to be inscribed. There was nowhere else. It didn't seem enough.

Among her bag contents, she spotted the bar of chocolate. She slid the wrapper off the chocolate and, using her nail scissors, cut the letters b, a, r, f, from the words Cadbury's Fruit & Nut. The crumpled wrapper was then tucked down the top of her bra.

For a while, she contemplated using the nail scissors as an attacking weapon, but came to the conclusion that they weren't large enough to stop him. It was better to try to get away from him than attack him.

While she was thinking of this, she quickly ate the chocolate, hoping its energy-giving properties would help her when the time came.

Slowly, she started putting her things back into the handbag, all the while checking whether she could find an alternative use for them.

She was putting the last item in - a felt tip pen - when the control room light went on. He was back.

*

His hair was dishevelled, his face slightly red, when he peered through the control room window. 'Probably a long walk back after hiding the car,' Helen surmised, as she sat breathlessly on the mattress, having sprinted across the room.

She had placed the clamp on top of her ankle so that he could see it. It seemed to reassure him. He glanced at it, then moved away to open the door, pausing to switch off the music.

Helen leapt to her feet, pulling both earplugs out at the same time. She ran to the wall, grabbed a photograph, opened the inner door, then stood two paces back, legs braced, ready to charge.

She heard the key turning in the outer door. It started to open, away from her. She lunged forward and threw her left shoulder against it.

She heard a gasp of surprise as it hit him on the right side of his head and body, spun him off balance, and sent him to the floor, wrench thudding loose from his grasp.

She leapt past him, avoiding his desperate hands, ran across the waiting area, along a passage, saw the stairs ahead, lit up by light shining down through the open trapdoor.

She was half way up the stairs, when a hand grabbed her ankle from behind. She stumbled and turned and saw mean eyes closing in. Without hesitation, she brought the photograph down on his head, heard the glass smash, heard him yell in pain, felt his grip on her ankle loosen. She started up the stairs again...gasping...shouting 'HEEE...LP!'...trying to go too quick...stumbling...banging her knee...'HEEE.. LP!'...scrambling on her knees...driving for the light above...nearly there...then hands again...on both ankles.... strong and pulling...her hand inside her blouse...finding the wrapper...throwing it up into the light...into the lounge... turning to fight...arms against arms...fists against hands...a thud to the temple... stopped...dizzy...sick...unable...

*

She woke up on the mattress, head throbbing, throat dry, feeling sick. She forced herself into a sitting position. Something heavy pulled her left ankle. Looking down, she saw the tightened clamp, the chain starting upwards, his feet.

He was leaning towards her, offering the bottle of orange juice, blood down his cheek, drying. She took the bottle, and gulped, while her panicking eyes told her that the inner door was still open, the wrench was on the ground.

'I want us to be friends,' he said, quietly.

She didn't respond.

'There's no need to escape. I'm not going to hurt you. I'm going to look after you...'

'Please let me go,' Helen said. 'I already have a husband who looks after me...'

'But I haven't got a wife...**they** killed her.' He pointed to the photographs, his voice rising.

Helen remained silent, disturbed by his show of anger.

'I *have* to have a wife...a companion.'
There was a long pause, followed by: 'How did you expect...?' He was holding the diary pages she had concealed in her right sleeve. He shook his head. 'Nobody would have seen them. Nobody ever comes here.'
While he was speaking, Helen surreptitiously moved her left arm against her body to feel if the handkerchief was still in her left sleeve.

His hand went to his trouser pocket, and out came the handkerchief. He showed it to her. He didn't need to say anything.

She looked down and saw that she still had her shoes on. But what did it matter now; she wasn't going anywhere! She felt her head and shoulders slump; she knew she was beaten.

He must have noticed - his tone was conciliatory. 'We'll be happy together...you'll see...'

He picked up her handbag and, using the wrench as a lever, tore the handle straps from it. Then he opened it, and started to transfer things from it into his pockets. 'I'll leave you what I can'.

She saw scissors, paperclips, pens, dictating machine, and calculator, transferred from the bag to his pockets. Travel wipes and cotton wool, he dropped back in. Out came the slim wallet in which she kept her credit cards.

He pulled the cards out, one at a time, studied them, then slipped them back. Suddenly, his face changed; a deep frown, a narrowing of the eyes. He was staring at a card in his hand. 'You're one of *them*,' he hissed.

Viciously, he threw the card at her. It struck her, harmlessly, on the shoulder and landed on her leg. He bent down and screamed in her ear: *'You've spoiled everything...I thought you were nice.'*

Helen recoiled from the blast, and shuddered at the absolute hatred in his voice. She picked up her 'Friends of the Lake District' membership card, and looked up at him, puzzled.

'You're the same as *them*,' he ranted, pointing at the photographs. 'Interfering know-alls...grouping together... wanting things your way...nothing better to do...killing jobs... killing people...'

'I've never killed anyone,' Helen shouted back, now beginning to understand the cause of his madness. ' And I create jobs...I gave you a job...'

His contorted face came within an inch of hers. 'I *had* a job...*bitch*.' He spat it out so venomously she felt a shower of saliva on her face. He stepped back, glared at her, and swung his open hand, viciously slapping her across her left cheek. '*You* took my job. **You** killed Leni.'

Tears came to Helen's eyes as she cradled her stinging cheek in her hand. Her ears were ringing, her head throbbing, her fear rampant. He seemed beyond reason. She cowered, waiting for the next assault.

He moved away and started pacing up and down, looking at the floor, looking at her. 'You spoiled it...you spoiled it. We could have been...'

He was pacing along the line of photographs now, looking at them, looking at her, stopping, thinking.

Suddenly, he grabbed the empty one from the end of the row, the one that said: 'Number 10, Barf' on the label. He brought it over to the mattress, and held it close to her face.

He seemed calmer, and spoke in a matter of fact tone. 'Why couldn't you be nice...you've upset everything... I'll have to find somebody else.' He touched the cold glass against her stinging cheek, and continued: 'You'll have to join your green friends.'

Chapter 37

'Do you believe me now for Christ's sake?' Ben pleaded, desperately. He was looking over the shoulders of Bill Unwin and Constable Murphy, who were sitting in the middle of his bedroom office, surrounded by piles of papers. The two of them had spent an excruciating 20 minutes going through all the evidence Ben had put in front of them.

He had shown them everything that backed up his fantastic claim - police records, mountain rescue records, post-mortem reports.

Nothing else mattered now. Not his own arrest for possessing them. Not exposure by Sophie Lund. All that mattered now was finding Helen.

Before phoning Bill for help, he had decided that Helen had not been a random target, unlike the mountain top victims. She had probably been selected as a replacement for Vilma Tapales, who Snodd had known before he enslaved her. This probably meant that Snodd knew Helen, or at least had seen her, before planning to abduct her.

Since Vilma Tapales had been found within a mile of their cottage, it was almost certain that Snodd lived in the local vicinity, and had, therefore, spotted Helen while out walking on the local fells, or around the lake, or up the lane to the village.

He concluded that Snodd was holding Helen captive in the same place he had held Vilma Tapales. That place was somewhere among the scattered houses, farmhouses, and village houses that lay within a few miles of where Vilma had been found.

Bill Unwin and Constable Murphy had recently searched those houses, and found nothing suspicious. But maybe they had met Snodd and not known it. He had to question them, involve them, seek their help to search, even though it meant exposing himself as a criminal, and possibly losing Helen's love. Her life was more important.

While waiting for them to arrive, he had found himself still hoping for a miracle. He wanted the phone to ring, to say she was in hospital after a road accident, a loss of memory, or even a mental breakdown. Anything, but in the hands of a psychopathic killer.

When Bill and Murphy arrived, he had immediately bombarded them with questions, sought quick answers. Bill had told him to slow down or they would get nowhere, and demanded to see proof of his claims.

Now, infuriatingly, they were poring over all his records, and wasting valuable time. All they had to do was believe him, answer his questions. He had prowled the floor for 20 minutes, and now he'd reached the end of his tether.

Suddenly, Bill was standing up. 'What's the number of Helen's car?' he shouted at Ben.

'Do you believe me?' Ben insisted.

'Yes...what's the number of Helen's car?'

'.... J656 EVN.'

'Murphy, make a note of that, then get on the car radio. Tell them we believe that the man wanted in the Tapales case is involved in a number of homicides, that he has abducted a woman from Scarness Cottage, Bassenthwaite, and that he is holding her hostage, somewhere in this area. Give them that car number, and ask them to set a perimeter and go house to house. Then get on the mobile to the duty officer. Give him the names - Hector Snodd and Mrs Helen Foxley. If they ask any questions you can't handle, tell them to hang on till I get there. Now hurry up, I'll be down in a minute.'

Murphy raced out of the room, notebook in hand.

Bill looked apologetically at Ben. 'I'm really sorry mate...I don't know what to say.' His head went down. 'If anything happens to Helen, I won't be able to live with myself. I should have listened to you...I should have pushed our lot more...'

'You did your best,' Ben said, coldly. He let the ambiguity lie there, too stupefied with worry to bother about it.

Bill shuffled, uncomfortably. 'You know I'm going to have to report all this,' he said, reluctantly, pointing to all the scattered documents. 'I just wanted to forewarn you....'

'Do you really think I give a fuck,' Ben yelled. 'For Christ's sake man...my wife's in the hands of a maniac, and all you're bothered about is paperwork.'

'Calm down, Ben. We have to do these things methodically...'

'I'll calm down when you forget about your bloody uniform, and your bloody procedures, and just answer my bloody questions.'

'...Fire away,' Bill sighed.

'But I've already asked them...can't you remember ...Jesus Christ...'

'Alright...alright...had we seen anybody matching Snodd's description. What was he again...small and thin?'

'Bloody hell...five feet, five inches, thin, sandy coloured hair...you're supposed to be looking for him anyway... for the Filipino case...'

'Go easy, Ben. Remember we're uniform, not plain clothes. We deal with a hundred little things a day, from car thefts to lost pets...we're not assigned to one case. We just do what we're asked to do, and then we move on to the next thing...we don't retain much.'

'Right...I understand all that...now can you answer the question.' Ben was about to explode.

Bill paused to think. Then he shook his head as he said: 'We covered a lot of ground, you know. From the outskirts of Keswick to Bassenthwaite village...from Dash Falls farm down to the lake....'

Ben gritted his teeth. 'I asked you to forget about Keswick and the village...remember. Vilma Tapales was running away...looking for help. If she'd been held captive anywhere near Keswick or the village, she would have knocked on the first door she found. Instead, she was found halfway between them, on the A591. It means she probably escaped from an isolated place, somewhere along this valley, between Skiddaw and the lake. What does that narrow it down to? About ten properties...mostly farmhouses?'

'There's a lot of small, wiry farmers about,' Bill blustered. 'And they all wear caps...you can't see their hair...'

'And they all have Scottish accents I suppose.'

'Ah!'

He was rescued by Constable Murphy, breathless in the doorway: 'They want to speak to you Sarge.'

Bill waved him into the room. 'Come in...leave that...I'll go down in a minute. We need to concentrate on Ben's questions. Can *you* remember seeing a small man, five feet five inches, thin, sandy hair, Scottish accent, when we did our house to house around the farms here...just in this valley...not the village or down towards Keswick?'

Constable Murphy concentrated, then: 'That farm near the village end of the lane...he had a Scottish accent... but he wasn't small. That farmer near St Bega's Church was pretty small, but he had a cap on...and I think he had a local accent....'

'You're doing well...keep going,' Ben encouraged.

Constable Murphy shook his head. 'The only other small bloke I can remember was that caretaker at the Manor. But he had a cap on as well, and I'm not sure about the accent...sounded a bit Irish to me.'

Ben grasped it, urgently. 'That could be the Sutherland lilt. Did he sniff...did he make a regular sniffing noise with his nose?'

Bill said 'I can't remember' at the same time as Constable Murphy said 'yes'.

'Are you sure?' Ben demanded.

'Yes...he was trailing around after me when I was looking at those pop star photos...Sarge was in front...I heard him sniff a few times...'

'Did you get his name?' Ben fought the urge to race out of the room. He had to make sure.

Murphy pulled out his notebook, thumbed through the pages, and read out, carefully: '...Scarness Manor...Mr Baxter, caretaker.'

Ben rushed to the scattered records, and started rummaging, frantically, cursing the mess they were now in. Finally, he picked one out and started to read.

'Yes,' he shouted, triumphantly. 'I knew I'd seen that name before.'

Bill and Murphy gathered round to look at the police record with him.

'He was the first Assynt victim,' Ben announced. 'The only man with the same injuries as the women.'

'And look,' Bill pointed further down the page. 'According to this he was found with no identification on him...yet his family say he always carried a wallet with his driving licence and credit cards in. Snodd must have stolen them, and then used them to create a new identity for himself. He's our man ...let's go...'

Ben had already gone - down the stairs, three at a time, along the hall, grabbing his anorak, out the front door, into the back seat of the police car, voices on the radio, Murphy into the driver's seat, Bill into the front passenger, 'move it Schumacher', the car punching forward, spraying gravel, Bill picking up the transmitter: 'K3 urgent'... 'Go ahead K3'... 'Suspect believed to be in Scarness Manor, Bassenthwaite...we're heading there now...request immediate assistance.'... 'Copy K3' ...messages going out to other cars... messages coming in....Ben trying to think...knuckles white on the door handle... ready to jump...only half a mile away... practically their neighbour...unbelievable.

*

Hector was nearly ready. His car was parked outside the main door, boot lid open. He had his anorak on, loaded camera in his left zipped inner pocket, plastic tape in the left outer, granite stone in the right outer. He'd used it on the last three, and it had stood up well. The hard tip hadn't broken off when it struck bone, like some of the others. It still had a good point and all the edges were still sharp. He had, of course, scrubbed off the last lot of blood. A cotton tea towel and two lengths of rope lay ready on the lounge table.

All he needed now was his Walkman and his 'Zadok the Priest' tape. He liked the first stab in the eye to coincide with the first mighty 'ZAAADOOK' introduction by the choir, and then keep the next thrusts in time with the pounding, repetitive, beat of Handel's great music. Oh, the ecstasy when he got the timing right! He *was* the priest dishing out the penance.

He was looking forward to getting rid of the bitch. She had upset all his plans, caused him a sleepless night; made his hangover worse then ever. And he'd had to spend most of the day tidying up the mess she'd made, developing a new photograph, mending the frame, cutting a new mount and glass, putting it all together, and hanging it back up again.

While in the studio, he had shown her the silly chocolate wrapper he'd found in the lounge, and made her eat it, her last meal. She'd looked older and paler, and he'd decided the next one would have to be younger. Now, everything was almost back to normal. He still had to find a replacement for Vilma, but at least he didn't have to go looking for number 10. She was downstairs, and it was time to go and get her, even though he felt tired, and his head throbbed.

He felt for his car keys, slipped the Walkman earphones around his neck, picked up the wrench, and almost forgot the tea towel and ropes. He wouldn't need the warden's name tag or questionnaire today.

He lifted the trapdoor, switched on the light, walked down the stairs. A glint on the passage floor caught his eye. He bent down and picked up a shard of glass. He'd obviously missed it with the brush and shovel. Need to bring the vacuum cleaner down later.

Into the waiting area, a look through the control room window. She was curled up just like Vilma used to be. Switch off the music.

Open both doors, enter. She sat up on the mattress, eyes red.

'Either you co-operate or I damage you with this,' he snarled, indicating the wrench in his right hand. It was a bluff. If he used it, the post-mortem would show injuries inflicted by a smooth object, and a gap in the timing of the injuries. The reality was: if she resisted, he would have to overcome her in a messy wrestling match, taking care not to damage her. He was counting on the bluff to save him all that trouble.

Helen had already decided not to resist in the house or anywhere near it. Her only hope was to appear resigned, and, if possible, put up a fight away from the house, out in the open where he had no retreat.

'I'll co-operate,' Helen said, resignedly.

Hector asked her to push her left leg out, and proceeded to release the bracket, using the wrench. Next, using a short piece of rope, he tied her hands together in front of her. He needed them in front, so that she could assist herself into the car boot.

Now he wrapped the tea towel around her neck, tucking it into the collar of her blouse. This, to avoid rope marks showing on her neck. He tied the long piece of rope around her neck, on top of the tea towel, making sure it was fairly tight so that she would respond to his pull on it. Like taking a dog for a walk, he thought. Finally, he tore off a piece of plastic tape and forced it over her mouth.

He picked up the long piece of rope in his left hand and jerked it upwards, making Helen rise to her feet. With his right hand, he picked up the wrench and showed it in a threatening manner. 'Keep pace with me,' he ordered.

He walked backwards, out of the studio, keeping the rope between them taught. Helen followed, carefully, trying to relieve the pressure on her neck. Her legs felt weak.

Through the waiting area, along the passage, up the stairs, they travelled, in slow, silent procession. At the top of the stairs, Hector caught the back of his heel on the final step, and stumbled backwards into the lounge, causing Helen's head to jerk forward as she followed him. She let out a nasal cry of protest.

'Shut up bitch,' Hector snapped, as he brought his stumble to a standstill. They stared at each other across a few paces - predator and prey, alive as never before, knowing it of each other, sharing it, each drifting momentarily to their better worlds where the nightmare wasn't happening.

Hector broke the reverie. He backed out of the lounge, and into the hall. Along the hall to the open front door, glancing at the monitor as he passed it - all clear. Reversing down the outside steps, warily; she might try a jump from the top. On to the gravel, so far so good.

A few paces and they arrived at the rear of his car, boot lid already open.

'Inside,' he ordered, backing away to the side, to give her room to climb in. She made a pleading look with her eyes. He ignored it and motioned her to get on with the job.

Helen placed her tied hands on the boot rim, and prepared to climb in. As she shuffled her feet into position, she placed the toe of her right shoe on the heel of her left shoe, and held it down while she slipped her left foot out. She kicked the shoe under the car, but didn't make very good contact.

She had to hitch her skirt up, using the inside of her elbows, to allow her to cock her leg up and over, into the boot. Taking the weight on her hands, on the rim, she then lunged forward and rolled into the boot, banging her trailing leg on the boot rim.

Hector moved closer, still holding the rope. He bent down, reached under the rear of the car, and re-appeared holding her discarded shoe. He didn't notice the word scrawled on it. He threw it into the boot.

'You'll need that,' he said. 'There's a bit of walking to do.'

He threw the rope in on top of Helen, and watched her cower down as he slammed the boot lid shut.

He walked back towards the house, and up the main

steps. He had all the doors to close - the studio doors, the trapdoor, the main door.

He stepped inside the main door, glanced at the monitor, and saw a police car coming through the main gates. The adrenalin knocked his hangover to one side, primed some fast thinking.

Choices - stay or run. If he stayed he could have the studio hidden before they arrive, hope she didn't attract their attention from the boot, answer their questions, might, or might not, get away with it. If he ran, they would find the studio, he could never go back, but he would be free.

He'd been thinking about moving on after number 10, it was getting riskier; the police don't come back without good reason. He would run.

He ran back outside, down the steps, into the car. A burst on the accelerator and, within a few seconds, he was on the left side of the drive's dual carriageway, leading out of the grounds. The separating yew hedge kept him out of sight of the incoming police car. He immediately slowed to a stop so they wouldn't hear his engine.

Two seconds later, he heard the police car race past on the other side of the hedge. He waited two more seconds, then drove off, quietly.

*

As they approached the Manor, Bill spotted the open main door. 'Right, Murphy, I'm going in the main door. You stay with the car. Tell them I've gone in. Watch the cottage... don't go in on your own. Hit the horn if you need me. You stay in the car, Ben, this is police work'

'Try and stop me,' Ben snapped, opening his door as they slithered to a halt on the gravel.

Ben was up the steps and through the main door before Bill, braking at the sight of the monitor.
Bill joined him. 'I'd forgotten about those things,' he hissed with annoyance. 'He must have seen us coming...'

'He's made a run for it...'

'If he left in a hurry, Helen might still be here. Search every room. You take the right.'

Ben raced to the first door, the dining room, head in, quick look around, behind the door, out. Next door, serving room, head in, quick look around, behind the door, out. Next door, kitchen, head in, quick look around, behind the door, out.

Bill was just ahead now, having done the cloakrooms and toilets on the left side. They entered the lounge together, saw the open trapdoor, Bill started to say something, Ben brushed past him and hurtled down the stairs into the darkness, a light went on, Bill had found it, along the passage, into an open space, through an open doorway, a mattress, a bucket, photographs...*my God*... Helen...not here, nothing here, behind the door...scrawled on the back of the door in big black letters B A R F... 'that's my girl', crashing into Bill as he enters the room, showing him the back of the door, nothing said, both back up to the lounge, along the hall, running, jumping the steps, into the car.

'Drive very fast, Schumacher. He's got about five minutes start on us. Head for Thornthwaite on the other side of the lake...go the Castle Inn way.'

'Right Sarge.'

'K3 urgent'...'Go ahead K3'... 'Leaving Scarness Manor...suspect with victim has decamped. Now believed to be in car, make and registration unknown, headed for Barf fell summit...Bravo, Alpha, Romeo, Foxtrot. It's on the west side of Bassenthwaite lake...we're heading there now...request urgent assistance...'...'Copy K3....'

In the back seat, Ben recalled his walks to Barf. He'd always gone around the flanks of the massif which contained Barf and other fells, and approached it from the north, via Wythop valley; the access from the east, alongside the lake, being too steep.

Bill interrupted his thoughts, shouting over his shoulder. 'We can't be sure he's going to Barf, can we. If he saw us coming, he knows we're on to him. He might be heading for the motorway, get as far away as he can.'

'I don't think so,' Ben shouted back, as he braced himself for a sharp corner. 'These people work to a pattern, they don't deviate much. He'll still feel safe, in control. Anyway, it's our only hope. If he goes anywhere else, we've had it....' He had to pause as they leaped a hump back bridge. His head hit the roof. '...How is he going to get to the top of Barf with Helen?' he continued. 'She isn't going to go willingly. And if she's unconscious' ...*don't dwell on it...* 'he won't be able to carry her far. He'll have to get the car close to the top. Is there any way he can do that?'

They held on as Murphy swerved to avoid an oncoming car on the narrow stretch to Dubwath. Mud and stones splattered underneath, tree branches scoured the windows.

Bill waited until they were back on the road, then turned his head. 'If he drives to the south end of the lake, and goes over Whinlatter Pass towards Lorton, he can cut back into Whinlatter Forest, and use the forestry commission dirt roads. One of them climbs to within a hundred yards of Barf's summit. I was up there a few months ago, looking for cars stolen from Workington ... joyriders sometimes dump them there.'

Ben suddenly remembered his Wainwright Guide in his anorak. It was always there, in the outside chest pocket, his constant companion on local walks. Hurriedly he undid the zip, and dragged out the small, well-worn, handbook.

A quick flick through told him there were ten pages on Barf, including Wainwright's superb hand-drawn maps and sketches. On the third map, headed 'Ascent from Thornthwaite' (1220 feet of ascent), he found the forest road Bill had mentioned. Wainwright had added small dashes from the end of the road to the summit of Barf, indicating a regular footpath. No doubt, this was where Snodd was headed.

Ben noticed that the dashes also continued, almost in a straight line, down the page, ending at the road they were approaching, near the Swan Hotel. This marked a footpath up the very steep eastern slope.

He turned back to the introduction, and read: 'Insignificant in height............ There are few fells, large or small, of such hostile and aggressive character, for unrelenting steepness is allied........ Passers by look up at Barf with no thought of climbing it.'

He skipped back through the pages, stopped at the sixth map headed: 'Ascent from Thornthwaite (1200 feet of ascent) Direct Route.' Here was another path, straight up the steep eastern slope, direct from the road to the summit.

A footnote at the bottom of the map read: 'Not a walk. A very stiff scramble, suitable only for people overflowing with animal strength and vigour.'

They were now on that road, hurtling south, alongside the lake, approaching Barf's abrupt eastern flank.

'Bill,' Ben shouted. 'How long will it take him to drive from here to the top...on the route you said...over Whinlatter Pass... back through the forest?'

Bill paused, adding the miles up in his head. 'About half an hour. It's not that far, but the forest roads will slow him down.'

'Drop me near the Swan Hotel,' Ben said, decisively. 'I'm going to climb up from there...try and beat him to it...'

'It's too steep, Ben...'

'Wainwright's marked a track...I'll follow it...'

'It's a young man's climb, Ben...'

'I have to try. You two keep after him...just let me out and get after him...catch the bastard...'

A few moments later, Murphy hit the brakes outside the Swan Hotel, depositing yards of rubber. Ben jumped out, and started to run, heard wheels spin in violent acceleration.

He ran across the road, up a short lane to Beckstones farm, over a stile, across a field, to the foot of Barf - a scree slope dotted with gorse and bracken. He started up, grabbing the vegetation to pull himself up, standing on it to aid his feet grip. Soon his hands were punctured, bleeding, painful. Where there was no vegetation, his feet slipped on the scree, sometimes two steps down for one step up. His heart knocked in his ears, his breath snorted like blacksmith's bellows. 'Ignore it, keep going.'

He veered to the left, towards The Bishop's platform, as directed by Wainwright's map.

Gasping, clawing, pushing, he finally reached the small platform of slate on which The Bishop stood. He leaned against the seven feet tall landmark, chest bursting; hands stinging. He looked at Wainwright's map and then his watch. He had covered the first 400 feet in nine minutes. He had to go faster.

The next 100 feet, which narrowed into a gully, was even slower, as the scree became steeper, with no vegetation to hang on to. He had to seek handholds in rotten rock. Sometimes it fell apart or pulled out, leaving him clinging on with one hand. His arms started to tremble as the exertion took its toll. He fought on, ignoring the fear in his heart, the sweat in his eyes.

With a mighty effort, he pulled himself out of the gully, on to a small arête. A few more paces, and he was on to an easier, heather-covered slope. He collapsed on its welcome cushion and lay gasping. Every part of his body told him to stay there, told him not to move until he had recovered. He had to ignore them.

He tottered to his feet, and climbed up the heathered slope. Passing a solitary rowan tree, he reached the base of a sheer faced crag.

He checked the map again and read Wainwright's instructions on how to negotiate Slape Crag. Angling to the left, he crossed another scree, then traversed across the rock face, above a small oak tree.

Exhausted again, he found relief on the heather slope above the crag. He checked his watch. 850 feet had been achieved in 19 minutes.

A sharp, burning, pain in the backs of both knees, hot heaving lungs, and a parched throat, told him to stop. He ignored them.

Diagonally left, across the heather, he found his way around the next escarpment, passing the base of a pinnacle, and joining a sheep track.

The slopes ahead looked easier now, but Wainwright's map warned of two false summits before the true summit was reached. Ben fixed his eyes on the first one, as he asked his body for a final effort. He started upwards, moving through barriers of pain and exhaustion.

*

Hector stopped his car at the end of the forest dirt road. Apart from having to swerve to avoid a fallen tree branch, the fast journey had been uneventful. He had driven quickly because he wanted to get it over with, and get out of the area as soon as possible.

After it was over, he had decided, he would head for the flat lands of East Anglia. With all ten photographs completed, he hoped the rage would subside. He could start a new peaceful life there, away from the mountains, away from temptation.

He opened the car boot, and stepped back - she might be planning a surprise attack. He needn't have worried. She looked dazed, tired, disorientated. The bumpy forest road must have taken its toll. He noticed that she had put her shoe back on.

He reached in, took hold of the rope and jerked it upwards. 'Out!' he ordered.

Slowly, Helen eased herself on to her knees, then twisted around until she sat on the boot rim. Then she swung her legs over, and dropped to the ground, stumbling to her knees as her legs gave way. Hector let the rope go slack until she recovered.

He pointed to a path that led upwards, through the forest. 'Go ahead,' he motioned.

She stood still, shivering, as the cold evening air pierced her thin blouse.

'Move,' he shouted, and tugged on the rope.

Helen jerked forward, and started up the slope.

After 50 metres they reached a fork in the path. 'Right,' he ordered.

A few more paces, and they arrived at a dry-stone wall. Stones had been piled up on either side, to assist in scaling it. Beyond it, 100 metres of gently sloping fell led to the top of Barf.

Hector motioned her to go first.

Helen climbed up the stones, leaning on them with her tied hands to keep her balance. Hector followed closely behind, holding the rope. At the top, Helen turned around, and reversed down the other side, again leaning on the stones for balance.

As she stood on the firm ground, watching Hector starting down from the top, concentrating on the stones below him, she lifted her hands, grabbed the rope and pulled hard. It was enough to pull Hector off balance, made him let go of the rope. She saw him grasping for air, trying to stop his fall, before she turned and started to run.

She ran along the path, towards the summit. She knew about the sheer drops on Barf's north and east faces, but, hopefully, she could escape to the west, down to Wythop valley.

Desperation put energy into her tired legs. They pumped like pistons under her skirt, dodging the boulders buried in the path, leaping bog holes, wash outs, heather clumps.

She was fit from all the swimming she did, but with tied hands, and a rope dragging in the heather, it was difficult to keep balanced, run at full speed.

Halfway to the summit, after leaping a boulder, her balance gave way and she felt herself falling. She flung herself sideways on to the heather and, on impact, rolled over on her shoulder. Within seconds, she was back on her feet, and running again. In those few seconds, she saw him - running fast, closing in.

Ten more metres, and she could hear his feet pounding the path behind her. Ten more, and she heard his panting breath. She begged her legs to go faster. Five more, and her head jerked back as he stood on the rope.

The sudden jolt shot pain down her neck, made her dizzy. She staggered, disorientated.

Hector's impetus, and step on the rope, threw him forward, off balance. He collided with Helen, and they crashed to the ground together. They lay in the heather, gasping, chests heaving, vaguely aware of pain, uncommonly aware of each other.

He wasn't moving, he hadn't moved since they fell. His body lay at a strange angle, legs askew. Maybe he'd hurt himself. She had to try again…dizziness…pain…as she pushed herself up.

She was on her knees. She started to crawl away. Her neck jolted to a stop again. She looked back and saw the rope trapped under his body, saw him smiling at her.

He got to his feet, wrapped the rope around his left wrist, and pulled her to her feet. 'You must be in a hurry to die,' he breathed.

Helen swayed on her feet, dizzy and nauseous. She could see the summit, 20 metres away. It was now or never…

She charged at him, tied fists flaying in front of her, feet kicking. He saw her coming, and jumped out of the way, a glancing kick to the right leg being the only contact.

Now they circled each other, he holding the rope, like a cowboy with a wild horse. He put his right hand in his anorak pocket. She charged again. He swayed out of the way, wrenched her back with the rope, brought his stone-filled hand out of his pocket, and hit her on the temple.

He caught her in his arms before she hit the ground, hugged her with his left arm until he had the stone back in his pocket, then used both arms to hoist her over his shoulder.

He staggered along the heathered path, knees bending under the weight. Gradually, the heather gave way to grass, and then to a platform of bare rock pavement at the summit. Large chunks of pavement were missing, leaving deep grass filled holes pockmarking the surface.

Hector carefully negotiated his way around the holes, and approached the summit's south eastern rim. Ignoring the magnificent views about him - the lake below, the towering fells across the lake - he walked around the summit's perimeter until he reached the north eastern edge. Here, facing Skiddaw, the edge broke away, down a sheer crag. He had been there before, at rehearsal.

Two metres from the edge, he found a flat section of pavement. He squatted, lowered Helen down, turned her on to her back, put her hands on her stomach, placed her feet together. She was ready to be rolled over the edge.

Hector knelt down beside her. From his inner, zipped, anorak pocket he pulled out his camera. He switched it on, checked it had film in, removed the lens cap, and laid it on the pavement, beside her.

He pushed back his anorak hood, lifted his Walkman earphones from around his neck, and placed them on his ears. His right hand went to his anorak's outer pocket, and emerged with the stone. He was ready.

His left hand went to the Walkman, strapped to his waist. He switched it on, pressed the 'play' button, and waited for Handel's music to inspire him. He raised his hand, ready to strike. She was coming round...her eyes were beginning to flicker. What excellent timing!

The music didn't start. He pressed the 'play' button again. Still nothing. He pressed the 'open' button and looked down. The cassette holder was empty. He had forgotten to put the tape in. 'SHIT!'

He slammed the cassette holder shut, and tore the earphones from his head. He was furious with himself...he had spoiled the ritual...a noise...footsteps...somebody was coming....

*

With the two, agonising, false summits behind him, Ben dragged his screaming knees up the final slope. Just a few more thrusts.

He stepped on to the top, gasping. With his hands on his knees, chest heaving, he raised his head to look around. There was nothing to be seen.

He'd beaten him to it. Or, he wasn't coming - he'd headed for the motorway. Or, worse still, he had been and gone. He looked at his watch. 33 minutes. It answered nothing.

He'd arrived on the top a few metres to the south of the highest point, a few feet below it. He would check the whole summit, then head down the path towards the forest. If he was still on his way, he could intercept him there.

He started up the gentle slope, walking northwards towards the highest point, his legs like quivering jelly. As he gained height, distant Scottish hills came into view.

Now, as his head cleared the summit's curve, he could see Sale Fell, then the lake's northern tip, then...a small man kneeling...a woman lying...rope... Helen's hair... legs...close to the edge.... HE WAS HERE!

The sight was unbearable. Instinct took over. He roared: 'NO.O.O.O...,' as he charged the short distance between them. His legs stuttered and wobbled on the flat, hard, pavement, slowing him down.

Everything seemed to slow down. In slow motion, he saw the man rise...turn to face him...put up no defence as he hit him with a rugby tackle...heard him yell as his head hit the ground...Ben landing on top of him...heard Helen shout 'BEN...'

Lying on top of him, Ben smashed a punch into the man's cheekbone.

Helen shouted something.

Ben hesitated...held the next punch back...found he was looking at Ian, the Controller of Keswick's mountain rescue team.

'Ben...it's me...Ian..' Ian shouted, still not defending himself.

'What's your fucking surname?' Ben hissed.

'Smith....' Ian shouted.

Its banality caused Ben to hesitate again.

'I heard the police radio messages on my scanner,' Ian hurried. 'I live in Wythop valley...I came up to see if I could help...I found your wife lying there....'

Helen was shouting again: 'BEN...it's not him...it's not him...*he* saved me'

Confused, but cautious, Ben held on to him, as he turned to look at Helen. She had propped herself up on one elbow. He saw the rope around her neck, blood on her temple, matted in her hair. Tears drenched her face. She held her hand out to him, her face twisted in a cry of pain and relief.

'He saved me, Ben,' she confirmed. 'Look...he cut my hands free.' She held up the rope.

Ben rolled off Ian Smith, and crawled across to Helen's side. He grasped her hand, and hugged her, gently. 'Are you alright...are you alright?'

Helen nodded between sobs of relief.

Ian Smith moved closer, holding his cheek. 'Where did he go?' Ben demanded.

'I didn't see him,' Ian said. 'He must have seen me coming...I stopped here to help your wife...'

Ben rose to his feet. He knew there were few places to hide on the top of Barf.

'Stay here,' he ordered Ian. 'Get that rope off her neck. Watch out for him...shout if you see him.' He would thank him later; worship him forever.

He moved away from them, away from the edge, alert, arms out, crouching, almost like an ape. He wished that he had a weapon.

Slowly, he edged forward, forcing his shaking legs around the pavement holes, looking down each one, looking to the distance, turning to check on Helen, head swivelling, eyes everywhere.

He hadn't gone far, when, directly in front of him, out of a hole in the pavement, Hector Snodd climbed into view.

Hector didn't run. He stood still and raised his hands, palms out, in a gesture of surrender.

Ben tensed, ready for anything. He wasn't going to trust a mass murderer, however small and pitiful he looked.

His instincts urged him to rush forward...to kill him...strangle him...feel his evil life ebb away in his hands... smash his head against the rocks...break all his bones...throw him, like a rag doll, to the buzzards. He had kidnapped his beloved Helen, imprisoned her, terrorised her, roped her like a dog. He would have killed her in the most hideous way. A hideous death is what he deserved.

Ben moved forward, face contorted by the thoughts within.

Hector moved to his left, towards the edge, hands still in the surrender position.

Ben circled to his right, closing in, careful about the holes.

Hector shouted: 'I'm glad you came.'

For a moment, Ben hesitated.

Hector kept on moving to his left.

Ben continued, closing.

Hector reached the eastern edge of the summit, stood right on it, his back to the sheer drop behind him. He waited for Ben to come near.

Ben approached, cautiously. He could see where Snodd stood, hands still up. He couldn't attack - it was too dangerous.

He stopped within two paces of Snodd, still alert, ready for anything.

'I'm glad you came,' Snodd repeated, quietly.

Now, Ben was in trouble. He was standing in front of the man he had imagined for months. He was listening to his lilting voice, hearing him breath, seeing his size, feeling his presence, hating him, fearing him. Was this happening? Was this reality? He felt himself floating above the scene....

Hector sniffed.

Ben came back, forced himself to focus.

He looked into Snodd's eyes. They were not alive. They were grey, blank. They had seen something terrible. They had retreated to another place, unreadable, un-contactable. This pathetic little man didn't need to be killed. He was already dead.

Something in Ben's eye's relaxed, and, for a moment, a glint of life came into Hector's. They looked deep into each other, and knew they were the same.

Hector said: 'I'm sorry,' and turned, and stepped off the edge.

Chapter 38

Ben swung his eight-iron in an uncertain arc. Again, the timing was bad. The hips went through before the hands, resulting in an ugly lunge. The dandelion, and most of its roots, flew into the air. It joined a swath of similarly exhumed dandelions on the unkempt lawn.

The backs of his knees still twinged. The specialist had told him to rest them for a few weeks. He had done irreparable damage to the knee linings, causing the joint's synovial fluid to leak out and swell existing cysts. Rest was the only cure, and would continue to be, if ever he over-stressed them again. Three weeks had passed since their scramble up Barf.

In the first week they had managed the daily drive to Carlisle hospital to visit Helen. She had been lucky. After a few days' treatment and observation of her head injuries, she had been given the all clear. Her whiplash neck injuries turned out to be no worse than that typically suffered in a minor car shunt. A neck collar and rest had been recommended, and she had been sent home to recuperate.

A few sleepless nights, and quiet, shaky, days had followed, but she was getting better by the day.

In that first week, Ben's knees had also carried him to a meeting in a Penrith hotel with two high ranking, plain clothes police officers, and a third man, who was not introduced.

They had a deal to offer. They wouldn't charge him with illegally being in possession of police and post mortem records, if (a) he gave them the name of the person or persons who had hacked into their computer systems, and (b) he accepted the story they were about to feed to the media - that the discovery of Hector Snodd's bad habit, and his subsequent demise, had been the result of police investigations over a long period. If questioned by the media, he had to play the part of an innocent bystander whose wife had been kidnapped by the killer.

It was, of course, a bluff. There was no possibility that they would bring a case against him, and have a court and the nation hear that **he** had been responsible for Snodd's discovery and demise, that the police had refused to listen or help, that it was possible for hackers to access police records.

When he had pointed this out to them, the third man had intervened and appealed to his sense of civic duty and, would you believe, patriotism.

After a lengthy diatribe covering the consequences of co-operating with them or being charged and going to court, he ended with: 'Don't you agree, Mr Foxley, it would be in nobody's interest if any of this went into the public domain. We would all lose wouldn't we.'

Behind the polished Oxford accent, Ben thought he heard a veiled threat. On the other hand, it might have been his overactive imagination.

It didn't matter. He had already decided that he didn't want to make headlines, get involved in a court case, or do anything that would drag Helen into a media circus. He had plans to take her away for a peaceful holiday, to the Mediterranean, lie on a beach, swim, read a book. They both needed the rest.

So, he had accepted their version of events, and in the following days marvelled at the ability of police spokesmen to lie so convincingly to the news cameras.

He had given them Sophie Lund's name reluctantly. He couldn't, of course, give them her address.

Strangely enough, the plea to his patriotism had worked. It couldn't be right, he felt, that someone like Sophie, and her 'boys', should have access to the nation's records.

He hadn't bothered contacting her to let her know that Trade and Industry Minister, Jack Fraser, had been the victim of a serial killer, not a political assassin. He had no desire to speak to her again, and he assumed she would pick it up from the media.

*

He knew that, as soon as the police arrested Sophie Lund, she would know who had betrayed her. She would exact her revenge.

For almost two weeks now, he had waited anxiously for the inevitable parcel, addressed to Helen, containing that tape, telling her of his adultery. How he was going to handle it, he didn't know. Why it hadn't arrived, he didn't know. Perhaps the police were having trouble finding her.

In the past two weeks, Ben's knees had also taken him to the Armathwaite Hall Hotel where he'd treat

Sergeant Bill Unwin and Constable Alan Murphy to a special meal, in appreciation of their efforts. To mark the occasion, he presented Bill with a silver tankard for his ale, and gave Alan a replica of a red Ferrari.

After dinner, sitting in the elegant lounge, where the great novelist, Sir Hugh Walpole, had waxed lyrically about the stunning view down the length of Bassenthwaite lake, they waxed lyrically about the local ale, got drunk, and had to be taxied home.

Ben had invited Ian Smith to the dinner. It was Ian he wanted to thank most of all. Ian had said it wasn't his kind of thing. Ben had asked him how else he might be able to show his appreciation. Ian had selflessly suggested he make a donation to the mountain rescue team.

Ben had taken the cheque to Ian at the team's headquarters, shared a coffee, apologised again for the thump, thanked him profusely, tried to get to know him better, failed.

For the remainder of the last two weeks, Ben's knees had been under his computer desk, where he had written an account of events, based on the police version, for Sue Burrows. He had also sweet-talked her into letting him disappear with Helen for a couple of weeks.

The rest of his time had been spent domestically, looking after Helen, reading brochures, arranging their holiday.

*

One more swing, and he'd call it a day. This time, the dandelion flew, but not so many leaves and roots. A bit better.

He walked off the lawn, through the conservatory, into the kitchen. Helen was standing, baking, humming in-tune to some light music on the radio. She had taken the neck collar off that morning, determined to get back into her routine.

Ben walked behind her, pausing to kiss her neck.

'Tea or coffee?' he whispered in her ear.

'Tea please.'

He walked to the adjoining worktop, listening to the hourly news bulletin, which had replaced the music on the radio. He checked for water in the kettle, then switched it on.

As he reached for cups, the radio newsreader said: 'The well known journalist and television personality, Sophie Lund, was found dead in her London flat last night. She had been shot a number of times. Her flat had been ransacked. Police believe she may have been the victim of burglars, but will not be issuing an official statement until further investigations take place....'

'Burglars my arse,' Ben thought.

He pondered for a while, then walked into the hall. He came back into the kitchen, wearing his anorak.

'Now, where are you off to?' Helen asked, as he walked past her.

Ben turned in the kitchen doorway. 'I'm going down to the lake to talk to my fishing friends. Then I'll probably go on to bring about the government's downfall, and possibly save the world from a nuclear disaster.'

'Very good dear,' Helen smiled, glad that he was being silly again, glad that things were getting back to normal.

Epilogue

The post-mortem on Hector Snodd revealed that he had suffered from Rhinitis. The pathologist's notes stated that the inflammation of his nasal membranes was consistent with continuous exposure to fine cement powders. (The cement powder reacts with moisture in the nose, forming a corrosive solution.) He had not worn the protective face masks supplied by his employer, finding them uncomfortable.

*

Hector Snodd was buried beside Leni and Grace. Callum McDonald, who arranged and paid for the burial, watched alone, as a butterfly landed on the lowered coffin, and stayed there while the grave was filled.

*

British authorities flew the body of Vilma Tapales back to her family in the Philippines, where she was laid to rest close to her recently deceased uncle.

*

On the island of Mindoro, Mrs Carla Gonzalez received a parcel containing photographs of her beautiful daughter. She looked at them with eyes too tired to cry.

Acknowledgements

I would like to thank the following people for their assistance in the research of this novel:

Andrea Caddy of British Nuclear Fuels and Nick Hance of the United Kingdom Atomic Energy Authority for their information on the nuclear industry.

Mick Guy, Chairman of Keswick Mountain Rescue Team, and Willie Marshall, Team Leader of Assynt Mountain Rescue Team for a detailed insight into their wonderful service.

Dr David Rivett and Mr Robert Thomson for their medical expertise.

Police Officers Ron Starkey and Ken Cropper for information on police procedures.

Phil Matthews of Soundmaster Recording Studios for studio layout.

Alan McKim, Tony Wilson, Nick Graham and Professor Manfred Judt also made significant contributions, and I thank them all.

Finally, a special thank you to Dorothy, my partner in crime, for her support and encouragement.

Note: The names of the mountains in the novel are all factual. However, for the purposes of the story, I took some liberties with their positions and configurations.

MW

About the Author

Michael Wood has combined a career in industry with that of a freelance writer, contributing feature articles and short stories to a variety of journals and magazines.

The Fell Walker is his first novel. He has also written a second novel called *Climate Change*.